Gorfen Letch

The Devil's Child

Helen Brunton

Gorfen Letch
The Devil's Child

Dedicated to:
Lillian Champion
'My Ayah, my friend and the kindest human-being I've ever met'

Special thanks to Nigel Bleazard for his role as editor and vicar, plus Marlene Brunton for being the best advocate ever.

Design, typesetting and publishing by Brunton Publishing

ISBN: 978-1-3999-0131-4

Chapter 1

"Out, out, brief candle!
Life's but a walking shadow, a poor player
that struts and frets his hour upon the stage
and then is heard no more: it is a tale
told by an idiot, full of sound and fury,
signifying nothing."
(Macbeth, Act V)

Martha Dickinson, God fearing resident of the small hamlet of Aspley and retired headmistress of the local infants' school, sat quite still, staring into the flames of her log burner. A famous quote of Shakespeare flooding her brain, she had a feeling of total and utter desperation. She was old but she wasn't ready to die, not yet, not like this. She thought of all she had been through in her life, her struggles and her plans - all snuffed out.

It didn't take long for her large living room to warm up but she couldn't feel the heat, she couldn't even remember lighting the burner. Once the fire was going, she sat staring at the flickering orange patterns dancing before her, watching her whole life play out in front of her eyes. She sat thinking about the bad things she'd done in her life but they were always things she needed to do to survive, she was sure people would understand she only did what was necessary.

Being a former English teacher she would always have a head full of quotes and one kept springing to mind. It was the first phrase she memorised at university and she would often use quotations as a means to impress. This quote now had a more poignant meaning - *'Life is but a*[i] *speck of dust falling through the hands of time.'* How right that was she thought, her life was over and she felt she had only just mastered how to live it. She struggled for more, wanting positivity to help her cope. There was another quote she tried to forget but it kept coming back into her head, even though she fought it, and that was from Richard III - *'What ugly sights of death within mine eyes!'* It was going over and over in her mind.

Her tragic and somber mood had been brought on by a visit to her local hospital in the town of Ashington, a depressing place at the best of times. She had known when the middle aged Oncology Doctor said to her: 'Do you have anyone with you today Mrs Dickinson?' that the news wasn't going to be good.

Her blue, water filled eyes spilled over, which really made her cross and she inwardly chastised herself for being so weak and stupid. Martha always hated any signs of weakness. All her life she had fought it and she especially hated self pity. Her philosophy in life was 'if things are bad you either make a plan to change them or forget about it and move on'. 'For God's sake, get a grip of yourself woman,' she repeated to herself, until the tears eventually dried up and she was back to being the real Martha Dickinson again.

Suddenly the whole cottage was filled with noise as the telephone rang out and she moved quickly to answer it, hoping to be able to share her bad news with another human being and not just her rather bored cats, who were now sitting oblivious in front of the fire. 'Hello', she picked it up, praying it wasn't someone selling something.

'Hi Martha, it's Rani, I'm just wondering how you got on at the hospital this morning'. *Thank God for her young friend Rani,* she thought to herself.

Rani had been her next door neighbour for years. Martha had watched her grow from a young child into a beautiful independent young woman. She was proud of how Rani had turned out, especially since the poor girl had faced more tragedy in her life than some people do in a whole lifetime; losing her entire family in a tragic car accident. One moment the girl's life was fine, the next everything turned upside down.

Over the last few years Rani had been so considerate to Martha, especially since she had been diagnosed with pancreatic cancer last year. Although Rani had a busy life running a charity, she had always made time for Martha and a couple of other residents in Aspley. 'It's not good news I'm afraid sweetheart, they say it's spread.'

'Oh Martha I'm so sad to hear that, I was praying for good news. Aspley has had too much illness and tragedy going on lately, I just wanted some good news, just for a change.'

'This isn't a tragedy Rani, this is just life. I've been lucky to get to my age I suppose... a lot of people don't get that luxury, remember that! A tragedy is when things fall out of order, like your beautiful brother dying in his teens. He had so much more life to live - now that is a tragedy. I've had my life, if you get your three score and ten, you've done well - anything after that is just a bonus.' Martha could hear herself saying the words but she wasn't sure she meant it. She wanted more, she always wanted more.

'Look I haven't got much time to spare but I'll pop over to see you, I'll come straight over.'

'OK love, that would be fantastic if you could.'

The small hamlet of Aspley consisted of eleven houses situated in the middle of a wood, deep in rural Northumberland. The wood itself was high up on the Rothbury Moors, where they were surrounded annually by the beautiful purple heather that coloured the local landscape. The nearest town was Rothbury, some six miles away, so it was quite a remote spot. The hamlet had no through road and no signpost, so not many people actually knew it even existed. It gave the place that 'cut off from the real world' feel to it. The location and isolation made the neighbours more resilient and more intertwined than most communities. Winters could be hard up on the moors, so they learnt to support each other. Summers however were beautiful in Aspley, with parties and barbecues frequently taking place. It wasn't unusual on a summer's evening for neighbours to be found altogether, drinking wine and gin in one of the enclosed walled gardens.

Martha's house was in a converted block of stables, with thick walls and a private, safe walled garden in the centre of a block of six conversions. It had doors out into the walled garden in every room in her house, all except the bathroom. Martha had specifically chosen the house so she could make a quick getaway if needed, it had been ideal for her needs at the time.

The drive from Warkworth to Aspley took Rani about thirty minutes. She pulled up in front of her old house and popped next door to Martha's.

'Thanks for coming pet,' she said, 'I don't want to be a burden mind, I know you're so busy at the moment.'

'You're not a burden Martha, come on tell me about today. What did the doctor say exactly?'

They both went into the living room and sat in front of the fire.

Known for her direct speaking, Martha didn't beat around the bush when she recounted the story. 'I'm just trying to digest the news pet and hoping for a miracle that they've perhaps got it wrong, as unfortunately they're saying at most... and the doctor repeated to me - at the very most, I have only three or so months to live.' She found herself laughing, trying to soften the blow for the young woman.

‘I don’t know what to say Martha, that’s shocking news.’

‘Well, it’s certainly not the best is it, but ‘hey’ what can I do?’

They spent about an hour talking all about Martha’s day and what had happened.

‘Look, I haven’t got a lot of time today, as I must stay at Warkworth tonight to help look after the kids, but how about I come back for the weekend? I’ll pop around, perhaps we could do something together?’ said Rani, feeling a little guilty that she would have to leave the old woman on her own with no one, no family, nothing.’

‘It’s fine pet, I understand you’re busy.’

‘Honestly Martha, I’m tied up with work at the moment, otherwise I’d have stayed with you tonight if you had wanted.’

‘Oh my God no, you don’t need to do that. Don’t worry pet, we’ll spend some time together at the weekend, that would be lovely.’

Rani drove away feeling incredibly bad about leaving the Martha with such bad news. She was thinking of ways she could help her, knowing that her dad would have found more time for their old family friend.

Martha had come to Aspley years ago, the remote hamlet being perfect for her. She needed to stay in Northumberland, specifically near Rothbury for work. It had been hard going becoming headmistress at the local infants’ school and she was determined to give it her all. Aspley was hidden away from the general public and being down a long private lane, she soon found that the neighbours seemed alert to strangers - this suited her too. The stable conversion itself was all on one level, all the doors leading into the central courtyard garden providing the quick and easy egress she needed. The central courtyard garden with its high walls was virtually impenetrable. She had needed to get out of her current house and disappear, so the barn conversion at Aspley had been a perfect choice.

Whilst working at the school she had felt protected by two of her male colleagues, who knew the score, but at home she had always been more vulnerable - he could always get to her at home. She had told him she wanted no contact with him at all, because she knew if she let him back into her life again she wouldn't survive this time - but stupidly she had always gone back. They were what young people called today, - in a toxic relationship.'

Chapter Two

It was Saturday morning, a few days after Martha had received her lamentable news, when she heard the noise of a car coming up the driveway towards the central square. As she got to the window she saw Rani parking up outside her old home - next door. She breathed a sigh of relief, the young girl had kept her promise.

Rani had discussed with Martha the idea of renting out her old family home after the tragic accident, but it was so full of memories of her family that it was too difficult a task for the young girl even to start. All she did was pay the bills and stay the odd weekend, her time just spent on the upkeep of the garden and the cleaning. Martha was glad that she held onto it, she didn't want strangers living next door.

Since six o'clock in the morning, Martha had been wide awake, not quite knowing what to do with herself. She would sit on the sofa but then would find herself bouncing straight back up again. She had tried dusting but found herself just standing staring into space, duster in hand.

It was a cool May morning but Martha decided to have her coffee outside on the patio, just so she could breath in the fresh air and listen to the chattering of birdsong. She had even switched on the large three tiered stone fountain that dominated the small courtyard garden, trying to grab a moment's 'peace of mind' from the sound of the running water. It didn't really work, her mind kept going back to her diagnosis, hearing the doctor's somber words over and over in her head, seeing his slightly tilting head and the rehearsed sympathetic look on his face.

These doctors must think us all so gullible, she thought to herself, *as if we wouldn't realise it was fake*!

She had noticed the trees surrounding Aspley were particularly beautiful this year. They were just too beautiful for her to contend with; she was going to miss those breathtaking, strong, protective trees. It troubled her how such beauty could cause her so much pain. She hadn't really felt pain like it. She needed desperately to pull herself out of this fog and do it fast, she had things to do, people to see and the garden needed to be sorted. 'My beautiful fountain,' she said quietly to herself, 'you've brought me so much pleasure for well over twenty-five years now, pleasure and contentment that no one will really understand.' She couldn't believe where the time had gone. Last week it seemed like she was just in the middle of her life but now she was having to come to terms with the fact that she was an old woman at the end of her life.

The fountain had played a massive part in Martha's life; it was an old friend who would calm her in times of trouble and a confidant holding all her secrets. Her memory took her back to the construction of her beautiful fountain; young Ronnie from the Old Coach House around the corner had helped her by laying the concrete base for the fountain, along with some of the other neighbours who had helped dig out the base. She'd bought it at the local garden centre and the staff who delivered it had to carry it through the shared courtyard. The bottom tier needing three of them to carry it. She vividly remembered Ronnie's face when the structure was in place; he had looked on, slightly worried, worried he had helped her put such a massive construction in such a small garden. But Ronnie was wrong, it was perfect - she would look at it everyday for the rest of her life with such unadulterated pleasure.

The knock on the door broke her from her thoughts and cascaded her straight back to the present. Through the glass in the door she could see

Rani, the little girl from next door, the girl she had watched blossom into a special and unusual type of young woman. 'Hi Rani, come in sweetheart,' she said, pulling the door open.

'I've been to the bakers in Rothbury to get us some breakfast.' Rani handed Martha a large white shopping bag, the smell of freshly baked bread immediately hitting her.

'There's croissants, fresh orange juice and I brought some Danish pastries too, as I know you're rather partial to a Danish pastry. I hope you've still got an appetite.' Rani rifled through the bag. She looked at Martha's sad face and grabbed the tiny framed woman into a hug. Martha wasn't used to being hugged and hadn't had another woman's arms around her for years. She tried to remember the last time and couldn't. Martha thought she must have looked like she needed it. She slightly stiffened in the grip of the arms of the young girl; it felt too emotional for her to be in such close proximity to another human being.

Rani Weiss' new life in Warkworth, a village on the Northumbrian coast, took up so much of her time but it was this work that Martha thought was making Rani grow into the new woman she saw before her. She had started a charity with her uncle, working with orphaned children from all around the world and giving them a holiday at the beautiful Moon Castle, her uncle's home. Perhaps, she thought, that was where the ease of hugging came from - the children probably demanded lots of cuddles.

'I know you'll be in a very black place at the moment Martha, but you need to quickly work through it so you can enjoy the time you have left.'

'Heavens above child! You freak me out sometimes at how like your dad you are, so direct. I can just hear Joe saying those exact same words.'

Rani smiled and continued,' we need a plan Martha. Is there anything you really want to do, something that I could perhaps help you with?' The answer came quicker than Rani had expected, 'I need to go to a special place on the north side of Rothbury Moors - where all the gorse bushes used to grow, do you think you could help me get there? It's on the far side of Rothbury, it's about three and a half miles north west. It's a bit of a climb but I think I can still do it - the doctor said there was no reason why not,' she lied.

'OK, but are you sure you're well enough? I think I should have someone else come with us just in case you get too tired.' Martha could feel Rani's eyes perusing her diminishing frame, concerned she wasn't fit enough for such a journey.

'Anyway,' said Rani, 'what's so special about this place?'

'It was always a family walk, we would all walk to the 'two boulders' nestled in amongst the purple heather and yellow gorse bushes. Most of the gorse bushes are gone now but it's so beautiful up there. One of the boulders is huge, about twice the height of me and the other is much smaller. They're like a mother and baby. Every year it was a family pilgrimage,' she lied, well aware that her family never went out together and hardly ever even left their farm. 'That place is very special to me.'

Rani reached for her handbag and brought out her diary, 'lets see when I'm free.'

'No, it has to be on May 11th, it's a special family day.'

Martha had desperation running through her, 'please Rani, please.'

The young woman was left with no other choice but to say yes. She'd have to cancel a meeting she had but there was nothing else she could do, she didn't feel she could say no. *Martha had always had a bit of a talent to get people to do exactly what she wanted*, she thought.

Martha now felt a little bit of that peace enter her body, the peace that had evaded her earlier. She was going to visit the boulders one last time, to say goodbye, then she could put everything to rest and to say sorry - sorry for not doing more.

'Do you have any family to help you, your sister perhaps, or maybe I could come and stay with you the odd night?'

Martha had to shake herself back into the present as her mind was on the 11th May, all those years ago. 'Erm... well, I do have a niece who's often sending me emails saying she'd love to come and visit and help out, you remember her don't you Rani? But I'm afraid she's a bit of a strange girl, a bit of a flaky fairy, if you know what I mean?'

Rani laughed, 'what's a flaky fairy?'

'Ah, she just does weird things sometimes. She once took a water pistol to a Tom Jones concert to shoot him with it, caused a massive storm, I mean Tom Jones of all people, who'd want to shoot poor old Tom Jones? The security thought it was a real gun, caused massive problems at the event. It couldn't have been a politician, journalist or banker she wanted to scare, no, she's not switched on enough for that. It had to be poor old Tom Jones, what's he ever done to anyone?'

'I've never met your niece, have I? Tell me about her.'

'Actually you have met her, way back when you were small, I thought you'd remember her. She's been here a few times when she was older too, but you mustn't have been around. Well, she now lives in Sheffield, so she's got that real South Yorkshire twang. My younger sister had her in her forties, way too late if you ask me, but that's Julia, just goes through life not thinking about anything. All they did was absolutely ruin her. She was a bit of a precocious child when she was young, but a big heart. They named her after a bloody continent, honestly my sister…and not even a continent they'd even visited, honestly, sometimes I would despair at Julia... or Dolly as we used to call her.'

'Ah, I think I remember now, is she called India?' asked Rani.

'Nope, guess again.'

Rani was puzzled 'ah got it, Europa... Asia, or something similar?'

'Nope, I'll tell you, it's Africa, her name is blooming Africa, poor little mite, fancy going through life being called Africa Wells! They sure gave that girl something to live up to.'

'Well Martha, I can't really say anything can I, being called Ourania. I'm named after a celestial muse of all things.' They both laughed. 'I'm plain old Martha,' she said, 'child of the Devil.'

'What, that's not what Martha means is it?' Rani said in surprise.

'Oh it's far too long a story to explain, another time perhaps,' said Martha.

Martha was starting to feel a little better, Joe's daughter was always a tonic to be around, as was her father before her. She thought of her old friend Joe, poor Joe, he'd been gone around six years now. Joe the psychologist, a rather brilliant psychologist at that, had helped her come to terms with all sorts of problems she'd had in her life. When Joe died in the car accident, along with his wife Heather and son Addie, it meant that the only man in Martha's life that she had any respect for was gone, gone in an instant. He had once laughingly described her as a 'misandrist'. She laughed too, and afterwards she'd looked it up in the dictionary just to confirm it was a man hater, and she knew he was absolutely right. But she was also acutely aware that this had been something forced upon her by others, right from the very moment she was born.

Chapter Three

The two women sat all morning in 'One Aspley Stables', talking about the dreaded cancer and making those special plans to ensure Martha had some quality to the end of her life. Rani told Martha she would help as much as her role at the charity would allow and that she hoped she didn't mind but she had phoned Arthur from 'Number One' to update him. He also said he'd help out as much as he could but had also pointed out that Ella, his wife, came first. Ella suffered with dementia, so his time would be limited. Martha really did need some form of extra help.

Martha and Rani chatted for a while, the tense situation becoming easier as Martha realised she wasn't now facing this totally alone.

'I guess you know that Ella very rarely recognises anyone these days, but she's still a happy soul and always pleased to see people,' said Martha.

'Yes, we had her over at Moon Castle a couple of weeks ago, we have to watch her like a hawk as she thinks she's lady of the manor and she bosses everyone around. She thinks all the charity staff are servants. It's hilarious watching her, she really is in her element. I think it stems from when she used to visit us in the early days. George would call her Lady Eleanor and he'd totally push the boat out for her. I don't think he realised at the time he was creating a monster,' she laughed.

They sat quietly for a while, thinking over the future.' So Rani, how is life at the castle? I still can't believe that you live in 'the' Moon Castle.'

'I know, it sounds very grand when people ask me about the castle, I still feel quite guilty that it's mine.'

'Well, you inherited it darling. It is definitely all yours.'

'I know, it's really hard work keeping everything going. People think it's easy but there's a lot to think about. I do love it though.'

'Tell me all about your uncle - George Percival... your mysterious benefactor, he sounds quite a character.'

'Oh there was nothing mysterious about George, he was loud, he was bolshy and rude, but underneath he had a heart of gold - but would only show you that side of him if he liked you. Except for my dad, he was the most influential man in my life, he taught me so much about life and about what makes a family. George never had a close family when he was growing up, he was actually brought up by a succession of nannies, bad ones at that. I don't think he saw that much of his parents, so I guess he wanted to make up for that.'

'He was your dad's cousin, wasn't he? - so there was bound to be similarities between him and your father.'

Martha watched Rani pause and look more deeply into her eyes. 'Actually Martha, they weren't really related at all. That isn't common knowledge mind Martha, not really to be repeated, it would only make things more difficult with George's distant cousins who thought they should have inherited the estate.'

'What, he left you all that and he wasn't even related to you?' she said, confused.

'George didn't believe in the concept of family, he wanted to choose his family and also to choose who inherited Moon Castle. We actually did think we were related when we first met but it turned out not to be - he said we were related through chance and that it was always how it was meant to be.'

Rani went on telling her the story. 'If George had gone down the blood line of the Percival's and you had met the distant relative who would have stood to inherit Moon Castle, you'd soon realise why he balked at the idea. He was called Hugo and was from London and in the first week I knew him he pushed me up against a wall and had his hands around my throat. He was a real nasty bastard Martha, if you pardon my french.'

'I know all about them darling,' she said, 'in fact I seem to have attracted them throughout my life. I hope he got what was coming to him.'

'Yes, I kneed him so hard he dropped to the floor like a stone, then George threw him out and said he was never to darken his doors again. When it came to the reading of George's will the idiot still thought he was in line to inherit Moon Castle but George just left him the family shotguns. I have a feeling he just invited him to the reading of the will to humiliate him further.'

Martha started to talk about her husband and reveal things Rani had only ever heard whispers about.

'Can you remember my husband James, Rani? No, I doubt you can, I'm not sure you were even born when he lived here. He took himself off to live abroad.'

'No, I can't remember him at all.'

'No, you're probably far too young.'

Martha wanted to get the story off her chest, she wanted Rani to know just what she had gone through. 'Arthur would remember him, your dad too and a few more of the neighbours, they all disliked him. Beat me to a pulp he would, I'd have to go into school wearing sun glasses. I've had broken ribs, a broken arm, burns and bruises all over my body. But the thing is Rani, I would go back for more. He wasn't even faithful, he had tarts all over the place and didn't care who saw him with them either. I moved to Aspley to get away from him. I managed a few years on my own and then allowed him back into my life after he said he had changed. I was a fool...it's amazing what I actually did put up with. One night I just 'saw red' and whilst he was asleep I hit him over the head with a frying pan. I screamed at him that he should watch his back. He might be much stronger than me but he needed to sleep and when he did, I'd pounce.'

'Did it stop him?'

'Oh, I stopped him alright, should have done it years earlier.'

'Bet he was frightened to go to sleep after that,' Rani laughed.

Martha just smiled and nodded.

Martha was starting to feel tired, she had talked more today than she had done for weeks, so she was slightly relieved when Rani said she should go to 'Number Three' and check up on Arthur and Ella as she hadn't seen them since their visit. Rani kissed her on both cheeks and gave her a long hug, which was easier this time around and she told her to call if she needed anything, anything at all. Martha felt for the first time that there was someone on her side, someone fighting her battle with her. She knew she would sleep much better tonight.

Chapter Four

Martha woke up finding herself freezing cold and lying on the bathroom floor, totally unaware of how she got there. Reality was here she thought, now knowing it was time to seek help. The choices open to her were limited - either pay for a complete stranger to come to the house in the mornings, lunchtime and night time or risk asking her niece 'Africa' to come and stay. She didn't have contact with any other relatives as most were dead now, all except her sister Julia who she didn't bother with and was probably totally incapable of looking after her anyway. The question was - could she cope with her niece if she went off the rails, plus could her flaky niece really cope with looking after a dying woman?

Like so many other things in Martha's life, she planned to leave it to fate. She'd set the wheels in motion and would just step back to watch the result.

She picked up the phone and dialled Africa's number. If she was in she'd ask her, if not she'd forget all about it and hire a home help through Social Services.

'Hello'... the now thick Yorkshire accent sung out.

'Hi darling, it's Aunt Martha, how are you doing?'

'Hey, great you've called, more importantly, how are you?
Mum mentioned you were really, really ill.' *Africa sure didn't hold back,* Martha thought, she really didn't have that filter most people had.

'I can come and look after you Aunt Martha, I've just been made redundant. I'll help you to transition to the other side.'

Oh my God! thought Martha, *is this really a good idea*? She was such an odd girl at times. What an odd thing to say… 'my transition to the other side'. Martha started to worry what side she would actually be going to, the hot side or the cool side. But she stuck with the original plan and asked the young woman to help her.

How would this strange niece of hers fit into a quiet place like Aspley? The neighbours would be quite shocked at some of her ways. Her clothes were weird enough but Africa would think nothing of meditating in public, sitting cross legged in the most bizarre of places. The girl had her good points, she would give you the shirt off her back if you said you liked it, literally take it off in front of you. Removing her clothes in public was another thing Africa had no problem with. Martha contemplated the life that had moulded Africa into the strange creature she had become. The child was a product of Martha's spoilt younger sister Julia, who spent her entire life wearing hippy garb and smelling of patchouli. She had flitted from one religion to another, living in a commune in Surrey for three years then totally pleasing her mother for a whole seven months by attempting to become a nun. But then she met 'Heath', a Buddhist monk who threw off his orange robes to be with Julia. Martha had always known that her younger sister took far too much interest in the TV series 'The Thorn Birds', thinking she probably had 'de-frocking' a priest on her actual bucket list.

Heath was what you'd describe as a gentle giant, born in America, spending most of his youth travelling and basically never returning home. Like Africa, he would give you the shirt off his back and often gave away all their money or food and once even gave away their sofa. He never left behind his Buddhist principles. Africa was brought up with an abundance of love but no structure or discipline in her life. The three of them moved around the world chasing one rainbow after another, usually doing some form of charity work. Strangely enough Martha thought, they had never worked or even been to Africa.

Martha had been horrified one year when they came to visit and she realised Africa could hardly read or write, she was ten years old. She read the riot act to Julia and Heath and the result was that Africa was left with her for the six weeks of the summer holidays to teach her as much as she could. Martha had never seen a child absorb information as quickly as Africa, in all her twenty years in teaching. She was an amazingly bright child. When Julia and Heath arrived to pick her up at the end of the six weeks, she was like a different girl. She had thrived in a structured environment.

Seeing how their daughter had learnt so quickly gave them the incentive and probably a good portion of guilt to put down some roots. They announced proudly they had bought a house in Sheffield and had enrolled Africa in the local school. At last the child would get some stability in her life.

Martha worried for Africa, that she might not fit into a school environment. She was exceptionally tall for her age and had the biggest mass of chocolate coloured curly hair that just couldn't be tamed - easy pickings for bullies. But she needn't have worried, as reports came back that she was fitting in fine and that she now had developed a rather cute Yorkshire accent and came top in History and English - her favourite subjects.

Africa's booming voice suddenly pulled her back to reality, 'I can come tomorrow if you want, although I did want to go to the library first to get some books on your condition, and also one on palliative care.'

'I'm not sure I'm quite ready for that yet Africa.'

'Yeah, I know but it's best to be prepared.'

Africa was a chocolate coloured whirlwind that was about to blow into her life. Martha prayed she was doing the right thing.

'How about next week, next Monday?'

'I'd prefer to come much sooner, you need help now Auntie M!'

'Right, come when you like but you'll have to sort out the spare room yourself.'

'Of course, of course, right…I'm going to pack for my new adventure. See you soon Auntie M,' she said, excitedly.

Oh God, this feels like it's one major mistake and how could she get rid of her if it all went 'pear shaped', especially if she wasn't well? She'd phone Rani and tell her her plans, see if she could make her feel any better about the mad decision she'd just made.

Whenever Martha phoned Rani, the sound of children enjoying themselves could be heard in the background. Martha had volunteered a few times to help out with the children and it was a real pleasure. The children were allowed freedom like they'd never experienced before and you could see their little faces light up when they were told to go outside and explore, the high walls surrounding the castle providing a perfect safety barrier. There were no rules but Rani had installed a few strategically placed CCTV cameras just to watch the woodland and make sure the children didn't get into any difficulties. The children always gravitated towards the vegetable garden and the pet Pygmy goats.

Rani agreed to help Martha out if her well intentioned nursing niece was totally unsuitable.

Chapter Five

It was May 11th - Martha's special day, her treat, the day of the visit to the boulders on the north-west side of the Rothbury moors.

Martha had been with Africa for three days now and so far she was enjoying the company of this tall, vibrant but slightly battered down and wacky young woman. She had arrived at Aspley the morning after talking to Martha on the phone, with bruising on her sunburnt and rather freckled face. When asked, she said she had been walking her neighbours' four dogs and they had pulled her over - hence the bruising. She also showed Martha one of her knees, which was all scuffed. Plausible, thought Martha but her own life experiences had made her suspicious, it looked like 'man marks' to her.

Early in the morning they sat having breakfast together, Africa telling her about a recent two month visit to Portugal and about her love for a fisherman called Rodrigo. She couldn't speak Portuguese, nor he English but she said they had spoken the language of love. Oh, how Martha would have loved another shot at finding love - she was always attracted to the strong and rugged types, not the educated men such as her male colleagues - but it had never ended well. Her psychologist friend Joe Weiss had told her it was to do with her relationship with her father, apparently she was always striving for attention and affirmation, something her father had never given her. Oh, how Martha missed Rani's dad Joe, he always helped her to come to terms with her life choices, making sense of the strange and somewhat cruel world around her.

The doorbell rang out and she knew it would be Rani - ready for their hike, their 'mini adventure' the girls were calling it. Africa was up in a shot racing towards the front door. 'Hi,' she said, opening the door, 'I'm Aaa....freak.....a!', using jazz hands whilst introducing herself. Martha could see Rani taking a step back, a little shocked and surprised at the greeting by this strange girl. Africa grabbed her hand and pulled her into the house. 'You must be Rani, I've heard so much about you, I practically know you already. Actually, we do know each other but you were probably too young to remember, I stayed here once for a full summer.'

'Jesus, Mary and Joseph - Africa! Let poor Rani speak, will you?'

'Sorry Rani, I get wrong for babbling on all the time, I'll shut up.'

Rani smiled, 'I do vaguely remember you coming to stay, all beautiful curls and freckles. You haven't changed at all,' she laughed.

'Ah heck, yes that's me. I've never been able to tame my curly mane.'

Rani had intended to tell Africa about their shared fortune in having an unusual name, but the girl just kept talking and talking. She glanced towards Martha who raised her eyebrows.

'Well' said Rani, clapping her hands together in the hope it would shut Martha's over-friendly niece up, 'how about we get going?'

'Can we stop on the Main Street in Rothbury, I'd like to buy some flowers to take - it's just a family tradition?' asked Martha.

'Yes, no bother, I've brought one of the charity cars. I thought you'd get in and out of it a lot better than mine. Plus, I've arranged for us to park at Foggo's farm - I phoned the farm yesterday, it's the nearest point you can get a car to the boulders, so you haven't too far to walk.'

'Oh my, you've thought of everything my darling, just like your daddy Joe.' Martha had been to West Moor Farm many times and wondered if she'd bump into her old friend, Burt Foggo. She hoped not, it would probably be for the best if she didn't, due to the circumstances.

Martha got into the car without a problem. She knew getting there shouldn't be hard, it would be getting back that would be difficult. She knew she'd probably fade towards the end. She had found over the last few weeks that she was now easily running out of energy, the illness starting to take its toll.

Rothbury Main Street wasn't too busy and Rani managed to get parked near the little tourist shop with buckets of flowers outside. 'Africa, would you pop in and buy me a bunch of white flowers? A white rose would be lovely but any white ones if there are no roses.'

Martha handed over twenty pounds and sat back in her seat whilst Africa went inside. She came out with a bunch of white roses and a huge smile on her face - she had succeeded in pleasing her aunt.

'She's a good girl really,' said Martha.

They turned off the main road just west of Rothbury and headed towards Foggo's Farm. The road was full of pot holes and they bounced around in the four wheel drive with Africa giggling like it was the first time she'd ever sat in a car, Martha finding it very painful.

The old farmer was in the yard when they arrived. Martha felt uptight seeing Burt Foggo again, it had been such a long time since the friends had seen each other. He stared towards Martha for some time. 'Hello Martha, how are you, it's been a long time pet, hasn't it?' He looked at the white roses in her hand and a moment of recognition passed between them and he smiled sweetly, but then he turned to go back towards the house. 'Well, I'll leave you girls to it, if you need anything just give me a knock. Your car is fine parked there,' said Foggo, as he disappeared into the old farmhouse.

Martha felt fine on the start of the journey, breathing in the cool Northumbrian air felt like a tonic. She had forgotten the beauty of this part of the moors and the smell, that earthy, mossy smell she had missed so much. 'Not far now,' said Martha, who was now linking arms with Rani. Africa was up ahead like an excited child.

'There they are Auntie, there look, is that the place up ahead?'

Martha could see and feel the relief coming from Rani, as they both were starting to realise she'd possibly bitten off more than she could chew.

The girls sat Martha down on a raincoat, near the large rock and Rani commenced feeding her salmon sandwiches, cookies and a rather lovely homemade trifle in a small jar, all made by Eileen, the housekeeper at Moon Castle. Martha had just been so pleased to get there she hadn't yet fully taken in her surroundings. After they all had lunch she asked to be stood up. Both girls got her up quite easily - she was as light as a feather. She looked at the two young women; Rani was quite small in frame but Africa was more robust - in Northumberland she would be referred to as 'built like a brick shit-house'. She was tall, had strong arms and legs with rounded hips and bust - *someone you'd want around you in a fight,* thought Martha.

Martha asked for the flowers and picked her way to the smaller boulder. The girls watched as she placed the flowers at the base of the rock and put her two palms on it. She couldn't stop tears rolling down her face, 'if only things had been different', she said, thinking her life would have taken a very different path.

'What's she saying?' Africa mouthed at Rani.

'I think it's a poem, listen.'

The two girls watched transfixed as Martha continued…

'My only love sprung from my only hate, too early seen unknown, and known too late! Prodigious birth of love it is to me, that I must love a loathed enemy.'

They stayed at the boulders for about an hour, then Rani said it was best they leave now as there were some black clouds building up in the distance. They set off down the hill. About halfway back, Martha's legs went from under her, the old woman obviously exhausted - it had been too much for her after all. The two girls discussed what was the best way to get her off the moors. They held onto each others' wrists and made a seat for Martha to sit on between them, then Martha put her arms around each girl's shoulder. There were a few stumbles along the way, the heather difficult to negotiate but relief settled over Martha's face when they could see Foggo's farm getting closer.

Old Burt Foggo saw them coming from some distance away and walked quickly to greet them. For his age he was unusually spritely, 'here girls, I'll take her.'

'Are you sure? I'm sure we'll manage the last bit,' said Rani.

Martha was embarrassed and didn't really want to be carried by her old childhood friend Burt, but her back was sore and when the old man lifted her into his arms she felt so much more comfortable.

'I may look old girls but I'm still as strong as an ox, she'll be fine with me, aye Martha?'

Martha thanked Burt and stared into his eyes in a moment of connection from their past. She was concerned Rani had picked up on it. She knew Africa wouldn't notice but Rani was a little different, she was a bit of a master in reading non verbal communication. She was like her dad for picking up on other people's moments, you couldn't get many lies past Rani's dad, he was an absolute pro.

When they eventually arrived home, Africa put her aunt straight to bed with a hot water bottle and a hot drink. It was just what Martha needed and she drifted off to play on her purple moors and laugh with the ghosts that dwelt there. She could die more contented, knowing she had said goodbye.

Chapter Six

Two days after the visit to the moors, Rani received a phone call, 'Hi Rani, it's Africa, I've just been told by Auntie's GP that she doesn't have long left.'

'What?' Rani was shocked. 'She seemed OK the other day. She told me that the doctor said she had months left - she managed to walk all that way on the moors.'

'Apparently she's known for a while it was very close. I think she lied to us to get us to take her up to the stones. The GP couldn't believe we took her up there, let alone she had walked anywhere near a mile - he said she had the 'heart of a lion'. She duped us both Rani, she's a clever old bird my aunt Martha, isn't she?'

'I just can't believe it,' said a shocked Rani.

'To be honest Rani, she's kind of freaking me out with some of the weird things she's saying. She's rambling on and on about some very strange things,' confessed Africa.

'Would you like me to come over?'

'I'd love that, I've read all the palliative care books but to be honest I'm a little scared. Arthur has been popping in to make sure everything's OK and he's brought us wood for the log burner, so I don't have to leave her but I'm no expert in dealing with the dying. To be honest I'm frightened in case I do anything wrong and make the situation worse.'

'I'll come straight over. We don't have any children at the castle today, so it's really not a problem.'

Africa sat on the sofa with her head in her hands and wept, thankful that Rani was coming. She had just admitted to her poor aunt Martha that she was completely out of her depth - she knew this was going to be much harder than she had anticipated.

Martha could hear the phone call going on and was also thankful Rani was coming. Africa had done an amazing job but Rani had a calmness about her that made her someone you wanted to be around, especially at a time like this. Africa had a big heart but she talked far too much and she was too unpredictable for Martha. Rani was that one person she wanted with her at the end of her life. She still couldn't believe it was going to be the end.

When Rani arrived at the cottage she could smell a heavy perfume scent before the front door was even open. Africa had put scented candles throughout the house. It seemed like every room had a lit candle - throwing out rather pungent scents.

'Jeez Africa, the smell in here is overpowering, it's making my eyes water.'

'I just thought I was making it pleasant but please feel free to change anything you want, I won't take offence. I'm just trying my best and to be honest I don't really have a clue what I should be doing, everything in the books I've read doesn't seem appropriate.' Her chocolate eyes filled with tears, 'I'm out of my depth here Rani, totally and utterly out of my depth. I just don't know what to do for the best.'

'I'm going to open a window or two, it's lovely but we don't want to overdose on vanilla and cinnamon, do we?'

Martha could hear the discussion and muttered under her breath, 'praise be' - no more scented bloody candles to remind her of her gormless hippy sister - Africa's mother, who as expected had not shown face, not even a phone call. She'd be too busy looking after orphans in a war zone, or puffins in danger, or something else much more important than her older sister. Julia was a flake too, more so even than her daughter.

She felt Rani's presence in the room, put out her hand and felt a cool hand meeting hers. 'I'm here Martha, it's Rani.'

'I know pet,' she said very quietly, 'I'm so pleased you've come.'

'Can I do anything for you Martha, anything at all?'

'I just want you to listen to something.'

'OK, I'll just move a little closer so I can hear you.' Rani pulled her chair nearer the bed and put her head forward towards the tiny frame in the bed.

'I'm afraid I've done bad things in my life Rani, real bad. You see, I'm quite easy to get on with but sometimes I just have to sort out situations and I guess I made some bad decisions. You would see life in yellow but I think I see life in red. I've tried all my life to contain it but sometimes it got the better of me.'

'We've all done things we regret Martha, we wouldn't be human if we didn't. Just concentrate on all the good things you've done, think of 'yellow' Martha, flood your brain with 'yellow'.'

'No pet, you don't understand, these were real bad, these are really black things. Your dad knew some of it, he helped me to come to terms with my problems and showed me how to control myself.'

Martha started to cough and Rani gently sat her up, giving her a drink from a jug at the side of the bed.

After the drink, Martha shockingly announced 'I've killed people Rani.' Martha had to get it out, she wanted to explain.

'Martha, it's just the morphine talking.' Rani looked into the confused looking woman's eyes.

'I grabbed my mother's skillet Rani and I bashed heads in, bang - they were gone. Took a knife to one, easy as buttering bread. I've used mushrooms, ah the beautiful heather, the yellow gorse bushes, the nettles too, always water, lots of blue and green water.'

Rani sat confused, watching the old woman drifting in and out of consciousness. The nurse had set up a drip to make her more comfortable but why was she talking about killing people and the nettles and mushrooms? Was she perhaps talking about a place when she was a child or perhaps cooking something?

Martha knew she had to tell her more, but she was running out of time and cognition. The last morphine drip was now pouring through her body.

'Are you still there Rani?... do you know what ugly sights... of death within mine eyes, within my eyes! Seven Rani, remember that I have 'seven' within mine eyes!'

'I'm holding your hand Martha, I'm staying right here. You just relax, don't talk.'

'It was always their fault, well I suppose not always. I tried, oh how I tried Rani. The moors changed me. Like a different girl after the moors. I have death within my eyes Rani. The yellow moors helped me too, they helped me, they gave me comfort when I needed it. They gave me everything, they gave me life, then they took it away. My hand took away the little breath, I need to go to the moors.'

Martha was now drifting over the purple heather and the yellow gorse bushes near her childhood home. The nightmare memories over, she was at peace.

'On the moors Rani,... don't forget... the beautiful moors.'

With that Martha relaxed back onto the pillow and became silent, so silent Rani could no longer hear her breathing.'

'She's gone Rani, hasn't she?' said Africa, watching on whilst hanging on to the door frame.

'I think she has Africa, I think she has.'

Africa had been standing watching the full proceedings. She slowly began to sob and tears filled Rani's eyes too. She had never seen anyone die before. When George, her friend and benefactor had died, only Eileen the housekeeper was allowed to tend him. He didn't want everyone to remember him on his deathbed, he wanted to be remembered alive and cussing.

Rani started to feel for a pulse but there was nothing. 'Could you phone for the doctor to come back Africa? Tell the receptionist that Martha has died. I think we'll need to phone the undertakers too but we'll wait until the doctor comes back eh, get some advice about what we do next.'

Africa walked towards Rani and threw her arms around her, 'I'm so pleased you were here at the end. I was so scared but it was peaceful, wasn't it Rani, well, except for that bit about the frying pan, what the hell was that all about? Could you make sense of any of that Rani?'

'It was just the strong medication talking, she was taking morphine Africa. She did tell me once that she had hit her husband with a frying pan, perhaps that's where it came from. She's at peace now - on her beloved moors.'

Chapter Seven

Ronnie sat quietly in his living room, book on his knee and his feet up on a pouffe. The peace was interrupted by a gentle tapping on the front door. He rose up, seeing the outline of a woman through the glass in the door. He opened the door to see Rani, the young girl from next door standing there, 'Some bad news I'm afraid Ronnie,' she said, 'I just thought I'd better let you know that Martha died this morning. It was really peaceful at the end, she fought like a Trojan... which I guess we all knew she would.'

Ronnie felt a sense of shock moving from his brain right down to his toes and he could feel his stomach tightening into a knot, 'I thought she had much longer to live, she was only diagnosed a couple of weeks ago.'

'I'm afraid she kept the diagnosis to herself, she had us dragging her up onto the moors only a few days ago. She was a bit of a law unto herself was our Martha,' Rani said fondly.

'She was that alright.'

'At least you'll be able to put your solar lights out now without them being secreted elsewhere,' Rani laughed. Ronnie was far too busy thinking about the secrets that lay in Martha's walled garden to laugh.

'Have you told anyone else yet?'

'Just Arthur and Ella, they knew it was coming as Arthur kept checking in on Martha's niece, making sure they were OK. I popped around earlier to tell them the news. Ella doesn't really know exactly who we're talking about, but bless her, she makes all the right noises and says the right thing.'

'Sometimes I think that's a bit of a blessing,' Ronnie said.

'Eh, yeah... I suppose it is. I guess getting old is no joke. Well, must dash, I'm heading back to Warkworth tonight.'

As soon as Rani left, Ronnie put his shoes on and went straight around to Arthur's at 'Number Three'. The knock on the door caused the inevitable barking and when opened Ronnie was met with a huge ball of bouncing fluff in the shape of their bearded collie - Merlin. He jumped up, two paws on Ronnie's shoulders. Ronnie gently pushed him back onto the floor and said a firm 'no'. The dog knew he meant business and stayed on the ground, tail dancing around. 'You've heard the news then?', Ronnie said in a panic.

'Ronnie, don't get yourself in such a state, it's been a secret for well over twenty-five years now. No one has let it slip in all that time.'

'It's not so much someone talking I'm worried about, it's what's under that bloody fountain that worries me. Joe and Heather Weiss are dead now, so they're not answerable for any of it, your poor Ella's unwell and Gerald practices being forgetful when it suits. You're in your eighties now, it's me that's going to carry the can, and Clara of course - she's going to freak when she gets back from her mother's.'

'There's Bill and Nina from the West Wing too, they were there too... Bill helped dig and Nina helped clean up. Don't keep thinking it's you carrying the can, cause it's not, we all have quite a lot to lose should the secret get out.'

Arthur poured two glasses of whiskey. 'Now, sit,' he said. Ronnie did as instructed.

'Be realistic Ronnie, they're never going to find out we helped her. I'm sure they wouldn't believe that nearly all of Aspley knew about it and kept quiet for well over twenty-five years.'

'What about DNA, it was Joe Weiss and I who lifted him?'

'I'm not sure DNA techniques are quite that clever, anyway, were you not wearing gloves?'

'I'm pretty sure I had been wearing them whilst digging but I suppose Martha was digging after me anyway, remember? When we came to dig further down the next morning she had already done it. We just had to lift the body in and cover it over.'

'Then, of course, it was my bloody idea for the fountain.'

'Building the fountain means nothing Ronnie. If asked, you need to just admit to that, just say Martha asked you to do it. There's nothing odd about that, is there?' Ronnie often helped the older residents out with gardening jobs.

'The best thing you can do is just relax about it all. That fountain will probably still be there in a hundred years time.'

'Yeah, I guess you're right.' Ronnie just hated the idea of the police sniffing around.

'I wonder who she's left the house to?' Ronnie was starting to feel the warmth of the whisky switching off his feeling of panic.

'I guess it will go to Africa, her niece. Well, that's my guess anyway. But Martha was unpredictable, you never quite knew what she would do next.'

'I'm pleased I can put the odd garden ornament out now without it getting nicked. I grew some beautiful white roses in the front garden once and she helped herself to them one night. She got a thrill out of stealing, I'm convinced of that.'

'She had a hard life though Ronnie. Ella found her one morning covered in blood, sleeping in the courtyard, cowered under one of the bushes. We all saw what that beast did to her. She was so small and so frail up against him. He really was an animal.'

'I know, I know we did the right thing at the time. She probably would have lost her job had she admitted what she had done. But I do think people would have understood, even then.'

'It wasn't quite the same back then though, was it Ronnie? Now, in this day and age I think she'd get off with it - then I'm not so sure. She had obviously hit him with some force and I'd guess more than once. His face was in a bit of a state.'

'When my Ella spoke to her afterwards she said she had warned him if he ever touched her again she would get him back when he was asleep and bash his head in. She told me she just saw red that night and went and got her mother's skillet.'

'She sure did, that bed was covered in blood. Two tours of Iraq and I didn't see as much blood as that.'

'My Ella and Rani's mum Heather helped clean it all up. Bill and Nina burnt the bedding and the mattress in the allotments, remember?'

'Hell, I had forgotten that bit. Do you know I think some of the old rusty springs are still in my allotment. I'll have to move them, they'll be evidence now. We need to think about all those things and not leave any stone unturned.'

'I think you're getting a bit carried away Ronnie, I honestly can't think what can be left after twenty years. Some metal springs yeah, but we're always burning our rubbish around here. There's probably mattress springs all over the place and God only knows what else.'

'You don't think any of the other neighbours know, do you?' asked Ronnie.

'Sarah at 'Number Two' was on late shift at the time, thank goodness. I don't think a police officer would have kept quiet about it. There's new people in 'Number Six', the 'Chapel' and the 'Hall' now, so they won't know but I think pretty much everyone else was out in the lane that night. Then Joe asked Bob Scott at the farm to get rid of the car. Bob hated him too, they had had some sort of altercation when Bob was a lad and he never forgot it. He was more than willing to bury the car.'

They both looked pensive, wondering how the hell they had kept it quiet all those years. When it's talked about now it seems like an episode of Vera to Ronnie, when in fact at the time it was purely a way of keeping Martha in her job as a headmistress. It didn't feel like they were hiding a murder, it felt like they were putting right a great wrong, a wrong they had witnessed and a wrong they felt unable to right.

'Honestly Ronnie,' piped up Arthur, 'there was at least eleven people involved in covering it up that night, nearly all of them helped in some shape or form, helping dig the hole or helping clean Martha up, cleaning the house and burning evidence. They were all complicit and that's why everyone has kept quiet over the years.'

Chapter Eight

The morning of Martha's funeral was the windiest day anyone had seen in Aspley for years. The constant roar of the wind put everyone on high alert. The violence of the trees swaying and the noise of small branches hitting windows and roofs reminded everyone of the power of nature and the 'downside' of living in the middle of a wood. The confetti-like leaves were flying everywhere and moss balls attached to the slate roofs were rolling down and landing on the gardens and lane.

Ronnie was out 'braving the elements'. He had been cutting all the grass verges since seven o'clock in the morning, making the place look smart for the funeral. He was fighting a losing battle with all the leaves and twigs flying around everywhere. Early on he had seen Rani in the 'Chapel' gardens, picking big bunches of sage. He remembered Martha doing that very same thing when Rani's parents and brother had died. He felt a little tug on his heart strings that this young girl was so thoughtfully doing the same in return for Martha.

Ronnie's wife Clara and Maisie - his special little girl, were still at Clara's mother's in Corbridge. His mother-in-law had recently fallen down stairs, so Clara was looking after her until she could get back on her feet. He had wanted Maisie to stay with him for company but Clara insisted in taking her, saying she would make her grandma feel much better. It always made people smile to be around Maisie.

Martha's funeral service was to be held at a church in Morpeth, sixteen miles away. She had been part of their choir and that same choir were to sing at her funeral. Then it was to be a 'family only' burial in the graveyard at Rothbury, in a family plot alongside one of her brothers who had recently died.

St Mary's Church in Morpeth was packed for this little, popular woman. She had taught children for well almost forty years and had remained in contact with many of her star pupils. The church, just off Morpeth common, was quite renowned in Northumberland because it contained the grave of Emily Wilding Davison, the suffragette who threw herself in front of the King's horse.

The inside of the church was strikingly beautiful with high internal arches and stained glass windows. Martha had insisted that the congregation should enter before her coffin. It proved to be a blessing with the roaring winds outside. Ronnie managed to get a seat near the back. He looked around for fellow neighbours and saw Rani, Arthur and Ella in the second row from the front. He could hear Ella talking loudly about the beautiful windows. Gerald from 'Number Five' was there with Sarah, the ex-police woman from 'Number Two'.

The church was full to capacity, when the music started up and the choir started to sing. Martha's coffin was brought into the church by the undertakers, one smaller guy at the rear carrying Rani's huge bouquet of sage with blooms of pink hydrangea. It looked amazing and it filled the church with the smell of sage. Ronnie had a wry smile to himself when he realised the song the choir were singing - Amazing Grace. He wondered if killing your husband with a heavy frying pan while he slept would make Martha that 'wretch to be saved'.

The vicar spoke of Martha's community spirit, her passion for teaching and for children and how she'd lived her life with God by her side. Ronnie wondered if God was at her side now and was also at her side the night she killed her husband James with a frying pan. He looked over towards Arthur, who's head was hanging low. He wondered if he was thinking the same.

Martha's family were in the front row. He knew she had a good few brothers and a sister. It was a shame they never turned up when she needed them most. But it was only Africa, with a couple he'd never seen before in the front row. It was obviously her mother and father. She looked so much like a product of both of them, having her father's height and big eyes and her mother's quirky sense of dress. They all looked like they were stuck in the 1970's. Africa could be heard sobbing for her aunt.

The vicar went on to say he had a special message from Martha. Ronnie's stomach tightened - *what the hell was this going to be*, he thought. 'Martha has asked that you bring gusto to the next hymn, her favourite. She wants you to raise the roof for her, that's before it's blown off in this hellish wind'. Ronnie was not a religious man but he knew all the words to this next song. The familiar tune started up on the organ, then everyone started 'raising the roof' as requested... 'and did those feet in ancient times, walk upon England's mountains green'.

Something began to stir in Ronnie that he was fighting hard to hold back but by the time they got to 'and was Jerusalem builded here, among those dark satanic mills,' his eyes welled over. He felt stupid but when he raised his head, quite a few people were wiping their eyes. Wait until Clara hears he wept at Martha's funeral.

When the ceremony had finished, Ronnie was one of the first to jump into his car to head home. He didn't want anyone to see his red eyes but he also didn't want everyone to be confronted by a branch over the driveway into Aspley.

Tea was provided at Martha's afterwards and this would probably be Ronnie's last opportunity to get a good look at the fountain. The cars began to litter Aspley and after Ronnie had cleared some small branches from around the hamlet he made his way around to 'Number One'. When he got there, Arthur was already in the garden being blown around. 'What you thinking?' asked Arthur, as he slid the outer door shut.

'I'm thinking could we get him up before the house sells? But how would we explain that one?'

'We could offer to remove the fountain so the house sells?'

'Anyway, who gets the house? We might be worrying for nothing,' said Ronnie.

'I'm told it's Africa who'll get the house and Martha's money is to go to the St Mary's Church fund.'

Arthur looked pale and deep in thought, 'I don't relish the thought of digging that up, do you?'

'No, I think we should just hope the new owners like fountains' said Ronnie, resigned to the fact that the fountain would have to stay in place.

Chapter Nine

Clara arrived home two days after the funeral. Maisie was delighted to see her daddy and ran straight to him, jumping on his knee. Ronnie had missed her so much and just couldn't stop cuddling her. The house wasn't alive without his Maisie.

Ronnie was telling Clara all about the day of Martha's funeral, about Rani's sage bouquet and the first hymn choice. Clara laughed, 'I know she had a bit of trauma in her life but even I couldn't have smashed your face in as you slept, so I guess she was a bit of a wretch. Poor old Martha.'

'Thanks for that, I guess I can sleep more soundly now.'

'You'll never guess what though?' said Ronnie.

She stared at him over her glasses, 'What?'

'I cried during the second hymn. I wasn't the only one though, quite a few had their hankies out.'

'Stupid bugger!' she said, laughing. 'You amaze me, you can shoot Somali pirates dead at work and not bat an eyelid, yet you cry when you sing a bloody hymn.'

Clara was cooking the evening dinner. Maisie was having roast chicken but they were having Ronnie's favourite, a hot and spicy curry. He was so thankful both his girls were back. He pulled on Maisie's ponytail, 'hey cutie pie, give daddy a big love.' Maisie responded by giving him a big sloppy kiss on his cheek.

'So what's happening with Martha's house?' asked Clara.

'According to Arthur she left it to Africa but I spoke to Rani and she says that Africa didn't want to live in Northumberland, she wants to use the money from the house to go travelling.'

Clara flashed him a knowing smile, 'so, someone's going to buy more than they bargained for, aren't they? I tell you Ronnie, I wouldn't want to sleep in that end bedroom, it was a blood bath in there. Heather and Ella did a good job cleaning it but I bet there's still got to be traces of the blood, even after all this time.'

'I know, I'm going into Newcastle soon for a visit to an Internet cafe to look up what the police can find after twenty- five years.'

'Why not use your iPad?... oh my God, you're not thinking they're going to look at everyone's computer to see who's been researching dead bodies, are you? You are, aren't you? I think you're getting a bit carried away with all this Ronnie. Firstly, someone might love the fountain. Secondly, even if they dig the fountain up they might not go deep enough to find the body and thirdly, after twenty-five years, what sort of evidence would there be of someone who merely lowered the body into the hole?'

'And dug the bloody hole,' he said.

'Ronnie, you're being ridiculous.'

'I'll just feel better if I do a bit of research on forensics, just to know what we're looking at.'

'You should perhaps tell the others not to google dead bodies too,' she said, laughing.

'I've already done that,' he said.

That night, after the wonderful curry and when Maisie was fast asleep in bed, Ronnie turned the conversation back to that night.' What did Martha say to you when you were cleaning her up, you've never really told me?'

'She just said that James had overstepped the mark that night and she couldn't bear him being in her house anymore, she said the 'red mist' descended. She just kept ranting really, I couldn't make sense of some of it. She should really have gone to hospital. I had just qualified - remember, I was sure her wrist was broken.'

'What other injuries did she have?'

'Bloody hell Ronnie, you're asking something now, I was just a girl, a trainee nurse... she did have a nasty cut under her eye and a head injury - the back of her head was soaked in blood. She was also covered in bruises. Oh and she had scratch-marks on her neck, quite deep, like finger nail scratches.'

'I never knew that, how did she get scratches?'

'How the hell would I know!'

'Did they look like they had been done with finger nails or something else, I thought she was supposed to have done it when he was asleep?'

'Yeah, but he attacked her first, I guess. It was that long ago Ronnie... I don't know. I bathed them as they were still bleeding and I put plasters over them.'

Ronnie hadn't known about the scratches. He thought they must have been done by something other than fingernails, as he couldn't imagine James having long fingernails - he was a builder. He tried to think of something that might make a similar pattern of injuries.

The story Martha had given was that she had arrived home from school and James was already in the house. She knew straight away he had been drinking, as the house smelt immediately of alcohol. She said he slammed her hard against the wall with his hands around her throat. He wanted something to eat, so she had agreed to start cooking. After eating the meal he started on her. She said he threw her around like a rag doll, punched her, then when she was unconscious must have locked her in one of the cupboards in the hallway, as that's where she woke up. She said that she had managed to push the cupboard door open as the latch wasn't very big. She said she kept very quiet until she heard him go to bed. It was then that she crept into the kitchen to get her mother's old skillet.

'When you bathed her wounds you said they were bleeding,' he said to Clara, 'surely after all that time in the cupboard the bleeding would have stopped? Say she got in from school at 4.30pm, cooked dinner, let's be generous and say an hour for that…she was in that cupboard for six hours before she came out into the lane screaming?'

'Perhaps, he fought back?'

'No, she said she did it while he was asleep because she knew that was her only chance. She said he would have eventually killed her and that it was her only way out of the relationship.'

'She probably just got all the timings wrong, she wasn't really thinking straight, was she?'

'I guess, but the scratches bit doesn't quite add up, does it?'

Chapter Ten

Africa stayed in Martha's cottage for eight weeks until her aunt's will was read and all her wishes sorted out. Martha had indeed left Africa the house but all her savings and money from the sale of her furniture and possessions were going St Mary's Church fund in Morpeth. She stipulated in the will that when she had been a lost soul, the vicar and congregation of St Mary's had rescued her, giving her that reason she needed to go on. Africa had felt a sense of guilt as all her mother Julia got was a bible, supposedly the family bible but her mother couldn't ever remember it.

Although it was a generous gift for Africa, it did not give her the option to stay in her aunt's house in Aspley. The council tax alone was astronomical, never mind all the other bills, so she had no option but to sell. The thought of living a quiet life in Aspley had appealed to her at first but it wasn't meant to be. Ronnie had decided to give Africa a knock to see if there was anything he could do to help, to get her ready for the impending sale of the cottage. He had agreed to do the garden for her, which had been neglected over the last few months and help her take any unwanted items to the tip.

'The only thing I would say to you Africa is to be aware that your aunt had a bit of a habit of stealing things.'

'Noooo ....!' she said, taken aback.

'See that garden ornament there, the dog - a Tibetan Terrier to be precise, that's mine, stolen from my garden about two years ago.'

'Really?' She sniggered in embarrassment, 'she was supposed to be such a good person, it doesn't quite go with her 'churchy' image.'

'Don't be embarrassed, we all just accepted it as one of Martha's quirks. Joe, Rani's dad, used to go around every couple of weeks to talk to her and retrieve things. But after Joe died no one quite had the nerve to do it. She was quite a little firecracker your aunt, a real force of nature when she was rattled.' He looked around the small walled garden, 'I can see loads of stuff belonging to other neighbours here.'

'Well, would you mind going through it all with me and I'll take everything back.'

'I'll do that for you, there's no need for you to do it.'

'It's a kind offer Ronnie but I think it should be me representing my aunt. Anything we don't know who it belongs to I'll put outside in a box and ask the neighbours to have a rummage.'

'Sounds like a good plan,' he said.

'So when are you going to put the house on the market?'

'Actually, I have someone coming around this afternoon to give a valuation from one of the estate agents in Rothbury.' She paused, 'I hate to impose, but would you stay with me while they're here? Honestly Ronnie, they could tell me anything about how much it's worth. I just don't have a clue.'

'Yeah, no problem. Clara's home today looking after Maisie, so I have plenty of time.'

The estate agent arrived an hour later, after they had both sorted a virtual treasure trove of neighbours' possessions. The estate agent was younger than expected with long, mousy straight hair and a big smile. 'It's a bit of a mess at the moment,' said Africa, 'but I'm hoping to clear a lot of the stuff out before anyone views it. I'm only going to keep the essentials; one bed - the other bedrooms will be empty. I'll keep the sofa and the TV, everything else is going to the St Mary's Church charity. I aim to live in it until it's sold, so at least it will be aired every day.'

'That's a good idea, let the buyers see how big the rooms are. I think you should have a quick sale if the price is right, as we do have quite a few people on our books looking for a home all on one level, they're at a premium in this area.'

After the estate agent looked around, Africa asked 'what sort of price are we looking at?'

'Between £350,000 and £375,000, dependent on how quick a sale you want.'

Africa looked at Ronnie for guidance, 'Yes, I thought around that figure, why don't you go for £360,000 and see what happens? That will get you around the world a good few times.'

'Ah how lovely you're going travelling,' the estate agent said, wish I had done that.'

The visit ended with Africa saying she would give them a ring when she had made a firm decision.

Ronnie smiled at Africa and raised his eyebrows, 'you're going to be a very wealthy young lady. Even though it's money you've never had I wouldn't let the house go for too much below the asking price. I'm sure it will sell for around £375,000, especially if she has people on the books wanting ground floor living.' She started to get excited, 'wow, I'll be able to buy myself a house and travel, I wasn't quite expecting as much as that. I thought with it being in the 'back of beyond' it would be worth much less.'

Ronnie laughed, 'some people like living in the 'back of beyond' you know,' feeling slightly insulted.

Africa was true to her word and went around the neighbours, handing them back garden ornaments, lots of solar lights and some tools. Then she told everyone that on Sunday she'd be putting out some of the suspect goods and they were to take back what was theirs. It became a meeting place with neighbours congregating throughout the afternoon to see what long lost treasures were there. All the neighbours were reminiscing about when Martha had taken an item and their failed attempts to get it back. Gerald turned up looking for a statue of a lady, described as artistically holding a shawl around her midriff, in other words a topless lady.

Africa disappeared from the group and came back a few minutes later with the huge statue in her arms, 'here' she said, handing it to Gerald, who just about buckled with the weight, 'I thought it was actually Martha's, as it had the same design on it as the fountain.'

'What about that fountain, pet?' asked Gerald.

'Don't tell me that's yours too?' she said, gasping.

'No, no, of course not, I just wondered if you were keeping it?' *Subtle as a sledgehammer,* thought Ronnie.

'Of course, it's a feature. Aunt Martha loved it, so I have no reason to think buyers wouldn't like it too.'

Chapter Eleven

It only took three months for 'Number One, Aspley Stables' to be sold and the new occupants to appear on the scene. The whispers about the new residents were already resonating around Aspley. They were a couple in their late forties, the husband worked in banking in Newcastle and she worked from home, although no one as yet had managed to find out exactly what it was she did. It was obvious to the neighbours that they had bought the house because she used a wheelchair to get around and needed to be all on one level. A temporary ramp had been put at the front of the house, but she told people that a lot of work needed to be done to the cottage to make it completely wheelchair friendly.

It was the Aspley tradition to go around to new neighbours' houses and introduce yourself, perhaps take a bottle of wine or a cake. Clara was goading Ronnie to go around, 'go on, you're dying to know what they're going to do with that bloody fountain, aren't you? Just ask them what plans they have for the place.'

'I'm nearly frightened to ask, just in case I faint at the answer they give. If they say they're digging it up, well...'

Cara laughed, 'you're not going to faint you flipping big girl.'

'You think I'm getting this all out of perspective, don't you? Just wait, if they find that body you'll be passing out too'.

'Ronnie, it was years ago, you already know that your DNA won't be found. There's no way they can prove who dug that grave and you weren't the only one either. Even if someone squeals, they're going to have to send at least ten people to prison, it's not going to happen.'

'Clara darling, I'd love to think you're right but I think they take murder and assisting a murderer a lot more seriously than you think. Look, I'll go around, have we got some wine? Should I take Maisie around to meet them?'

'I don't think that's a very good idea for obvious reasons, do you?' she smiled. Ronnie just shook his head, 'you're such an arsehole sometimes Clara.'

With a bottle of red in his hand he knocked on the door of 'Number One'. It took a while for someone to answer but eventually the lady in the wheelchair opened it.

'Hi, I'm Ronnie from the 'Coach House', just around the corner. I just wanted to bring you this and introduce myself.'

'Hi 'she said, 'I believe you're the man responsible for keeping the garden tidy.'

'Yeah, it was just a little tidy up, Martha kept it very ship-shape herself until just a few weeks before she died. She was quite a keen gardener, you've got some nice plants in that garden.'

'It's a bit of a shock for us having such a small garden now, we had a couple of acres at our last place, but with my illness we just had to make the move and a big garden was no longer practical.'

'Do you have any plans for the garden?'

'My husband is going to do some work at the front here to make a permanent ramp, so we can get rid of this horrible metal thing. One of his old school mates is a landscape gardener and he says he'll come up with something in keeping with the rest of the garden and house.'

'Sounds good. I'm always willing to give a hand if I'm about.'

'Ah thanks, that's really kind of you.'

'Sorry, this is for you,' he said, handing her the bottle of wine.

There was an embarrassing pause with him holding out the bottle of wine and her not taking it. It seemed like an eternity to Ronnie. She smiled, 'you'll have to move it much closer to me if you want me to have it.'

'Oh God, I'm really sorry, I just thought your arms would be normal, I mean ...,' he had now turned puce.

'A little tip Ronnie, if you see someone in a power wheelchair they usually have something wrong with their arms too.'

'I'm so sorry. Clara's always saying I need to put my brain in gear sometimes, she's totally right of course.'

'Don't worry Ronnie, everyone does it. Usually people put out their hand to shake mine. I can still lift it a bit, look but I can't stretch all that distance. If people go to shake my hand I have to tell them to go and get it if they want to shake it. Anyway, thanks for the bottle of wine, it's much appreciated.'

'Look, can I help you with that, I'll put it away for you if you like?' he said. She smiled sweetly, 'I think you're swinging too far the other way now Ronnie. Don't worry, you'll get used to me after a while.'

Ronnie walked back into the 'Coach House' taking his fleece off and throwing it down. 'Well, I've just made a complete arse of myself.'

'Ah no, what did you say, you didn't offer to remove their beautiful fountain, did you?'

'Course I didn't, I handed her the bottle of wine. We just kind of looked at each other for what seemed like a bloody lifetime. I didn't know she couldn't use her bloody arms very well, did I?'

'So why did you think she used a 'power' wheelchair and not a push one?'

'You don't need to give me the low down, she's already told me the score.'

'Arsehole.'

'That's probably what she said when she closed the door. I need a drink' said Ronnie and reached for the whisky.

'So, what's her name?' Clara asked.

'I don't know.'

'You didn't think to ask?'

'No.'

'Do they like the fountain then?'

'I didn't ask.'

'So, that was a really useful visit then, wasn't it? Well at least she knows you're a bit of a 'dick' now. That's something at least. If they ever bring the body up you'll be the last person she'll suspect as the mastermind.'

Chapter Twelve

Life went on at Aspley with the new neighbours fitting in well. They were still mostly living elsewhere but were coming to the house regularly to liaise with workmen etc. The lady of the house, who Ronnie eventually found out was called Anna, would often be out in the front garden tending her newly raised borders. The husband, who was called Christopher, worked long hours at the bank, so it was Anna everyone got to know first. She was small with long dark hair, often tied at the back of her head. Her disability, although severe, didn't seem to stop her much. She had a car she could wheel her chair into the back of, which she said she used mainly for driving herself to hospital appointments. She had already admitted to Ronnie that her driving days were sadly coming to an end with the deterioration of her fingers and arms.

The front of 'Number One' had been totally transformed with a winding block paved ramp now running through an attractive rockery. It looked like it had always been there but some of the neighbours were of course holding their breath to see what the 'newbies' were going to do with the walled garden - Martha's pride and joy.

Arthur and Ella had the key to Rani's old house next door and Ronnie had wanted that key to get into the back garden so he could look over the wall to see what was going on.

'And what are you going to say if Anna sees you peering over the wall?' asked Arthur.

'I'll just say I'm cutting the ivy or something.'

'Ronnie, all we need to do is keep quiet! No one can prove anything.'

'I just think we should be trying to control the situation a bit, instead of sitting back and allowing ourselves to be victims of fate. Perhaps if I could say how much Martha loved the fountain, they might decide to keep it?'

'Africa has already done that, they know. That's not going to make much difference to them, is it? They didn't even know her.'

I think we've got to be prepared, I honestly believe they'll take it out - I would if I bought the house. We made a mistake that night when we buried him in the centre of the garden, we should have put him in one of the corners of the garden. They might not have disturbed him there.'

'That was my fault,' admitted Ronnie, 'I just looked for the easiest place. If we had put him in a corner we would have had to move bushes, or the rockery or the patio at the other side.'

'Have you spoken to Gerald lately, he's already made preparations for when they find the body?' said Arthur, raising his thick grey eyebrows.' He's been to the doctors to say his memory is getting much worse, can't remember a thing, he says.'

'God, he's been playing that card for years! He seems as bright as a button to me.'

'There is someone we need to talk about,' Ronnie grimaced and shook his head. 'Bob Scott...will he stay quiet about burying the car on his farm?'

'I can't do anything about that one. When Bob found out that our Fiona was still alive and that she had just pretended to drown in the river just to get away from him, he was livid. He won't speak to me or Ella.'

Bob Scott was Arthur's son-in-law, who worked the farm a couple of miles down the track. Arthur's daughter had faked her death to get away from an abusive relationship. She was now living in Scotland with Jack, her son.

'Should I go and talk to him?'

'I would say he's best left alone, I can't imagine him ever revealing anything to the police, can you?'

'No, it would probably be out of character, plus there's a huge barn over the place where he buried the car. That won't resurface for years if he keeps quiet.'

****

It was only two weeks later, when the day some of the Aspley residents had been waiting for, actually materialised. Arthur phoned to say that a skip had arrived in the car park and there were now workmen carrying bushes and large bits of masonry out of 'Number One'.

'Can you have a look to see exactly what's going on?' asked Ronnie.

'OK, I'll have a walk around for a look - but then I'd promised to take Ella out for a little walk.'

'I'll catch you on your walk, are you going to the woods?'

'Yes, see you later then.'

Ten minutes later Ronnie saw Arthur, Ella and Merlin out for a very slow stroll around the block. 'Here,' shouted Ronnie, 'come and have a seat on the bench here.' Ronnie had set a small bench in his open plan front garden, amongst the heathers and the ornamental grasses.

'That would be wonderful' said Ella, grateful for a seat.

They both sat down in the afternoon sun, Merlin on an extendable leader, enjoying his time sniffing around all the bushes where Maisie had been playing.

'So?' said Ronnie.

'Gone…so is the concrete plinth you set it on. Took a sledge hammer to it apparently.'

'So is there a hole now?'

'No, a bit of a dip but it still looks pretty flat. Apparently Anna's instructions were to clear everything out, she wanted to start from scratch.'

'Jesus Christ!'

'Language young man, I don't like blasphemy!' Ella suddenly piped up.

Bill and Nina from the West Wing of the Hall came past, 'lovely afternoon for a walk, I think we could call this a bit of an Indian summer,' Bill said. Nina walked over and gave Ella a big hug, 'it's wonderful to see you looking so well Ella.'

'Thank you' Ella said, smiling. But everyone knew that she didn't have a clue who she was talking to, although she still seemed to enjoy meeting people. 'No Maisie today?' Nina asked Ronnie.

'No, Clara's cooking. Hopefully Maisie is having her afternoon nap.'

Ronnie lowered his voice, 'we've just been talking about 'Number One', the walled garden has been completely stripped out.'

'What, the fountain's actually gone?' asked Bill, looking worried.

'Yes,' said Arthur, 'it's flattened.'

Nina and Bill had been there the night Martha killed James. Bill had helped with the digging and Nina had taken bed sheets away to be burnt. They had never spoken about the incident since - now they both looked at each other in trepidation.

Ronnie could tell that they didn't quite know what to say. They had probably tried over the years to erase the incident completely from their memory.

'I guess now is the time to practice ignorance,' said Bill, 'or go on holiday for the winter.'

Two days later Nina and Bill were off to their holiday home in Spain. They had obviously chosen to stay out of the way in case the unwanted bones resurfaced. There was nothing unusual about Nina and Bill wintering in Spain, they did it every year, but this year they were just leaving earlier, much earlier.

Chapter 13

It had been a few days since the fountain had been removed and nothing had happened except a load of block paving being delivered, which was all now stacked up neatly in the shared courtyard. Ronnie was beginning to feel less anxious about the situation, the body obviously hadn't been unearthed during the work. He was convinced the skeleton must still be about three feet or so below the level of the soil after the removal of the plinth - way more than a spade deep anyway, so why was he getting himself into such a state? He was desperate to go into the garden of 'Number One' and have a good scout around, but he knew if the owners saw him it could possibly raise suspicion.

He was in his garden removing the now crispy seven foot delphiniums from the back of the house and Clara was cooking Sunday lunch, with Maisie presumably hanging around her legs. Autumn was on the cusp and he was working hard to put the garden to sleep for the winter. He usually worked abroad in the winter months but this year had decided to stay home and enjoy being with Maisie.

He could hear the faint voice of a woman shouting 'Ronnie', coming from the front garden. He went around the side of the house to find Anna on his front drive. 'I'm sorry, I couldn't reach your doorbell and I'm not too good at knocking very loud either. I thought you might be in the back garden. I just wanted to let you know Maisie is in my back garden digging a big hole. I'm sorry, I tried to get her to come into the house but she wouldn't and I'm afraid I can't get out there to get her.'

'What!' he said, in a total panic. He looked back at the side gate - it must have been open.

'The little madam has sneaked out. The older she gets - the more crafty she gets. I swear she must have opened that gate herself.'

He left Anna behind and could hear her propelling herself as fast as she could, trying to keep up with him. He ran around the building to the outside of the cottages into the shared courtyard, then through the white open gate into the walled garden of 'Number One'. There was Maisie, hairy bum in the air, digging right where the body was - bile filled his mouth. He grabbed her and looked at where she'd been digging. He could see old, torn material at the bottom of the hole. A little bit more sick came into his mouth and he spat it out nearby. He kicked the soil Maisie had removed back into the hole.

He looked towards the cottage door. Anna was now sitting at the back entrance watching him, unable to come any further. He could feel himself colouring up. How long had this woman been sitting there watching him? Had she actually seen him vomit?

'I'm so sorry Anna, Tibetan Terriers are always digging holes. As soon as you give her a bone she's off wondering where on earth she can hide it. They also dig a hole when they want a nap. They just curl up into it.' He knew he was rambling.

'There's no harm done, it's a building site anyway,' said Anna.

'What was she so interested in, she was very intent on getting at something?' He had to think super fast. Does he deny seeing anything or does he tell her it was just an old duster or something?

'It was just a bit of cloth, probably an old duster or something from when the fountain was built. Honestly, there doesn't have to be a reason for her to dig, it's her favourite pastime - digging, eh girl.' The dog was filthy, caked in mud. Her white paws were black, as were her belly and her little snout.

'You're going to be in so much bother when your mummy sees you,' he said, holding her up so she's looking into his face. Anna watched the scene transfixed at the way this rather butch man spoke to the dog like it was a child. He obviously adored her, in fact all the neighbours seemed to love her. When Anna first arrived she had thought 'Maisie', who the residents talked about was actually Ronnie and Clara's daughter, not a blooming dog.

'You never know, I might have treasure under there, the buildings are ever so old aren't they?'

'I'm afraid all you'll find is a load of old horse shoes and a few rusty nails,' said dismissively. 'It was just a stable yard - hence the horse shoes. Joe Weiss, who used to live next door at 'Number Four', once used a metal detector on the whole area to see if he could find any buried treasure. I'm afraid the best thing he found was old rusty nails - definitely no treasure.'

Chapter 14

Jamie Jones, a Crime Scene Manager at Wallsend Police Station, was starting his early shift. His first cup of coffee of the day was consumed whilst catching up on paperwork. It was just starting to bring him around after a hard shift the day before. Early shifts were the scourge of the job for Jamie. He was a night owl and getting up at six in the morning just wasn't for him anymore. He logged onto the force computer and felt quite happy with the amount of jobs listed on the daily CSI log. *He might even get a lunch today*, he thought. He had spent over twenty-five years in forensics and had seen probably every sort of crime in his long career.

His first two jobs that morning were easy, a couple of burglary dwellings and then he was booked to attend a post-mortem later in the afternoon. The PM he was attending was a drugs death, nothing suspicious or out of the ordinary - so it hopefully wouldn't be a long day. His lunch sat waiting for him on the desk when he returned for his break. The police force was experiencing a lack of funds, the consequences of which were eating sandwiches that had sat at room temperature all morning and the lack of a cold drink. Fridges and water bowsers had been removed to save money, which meant there was only one fridge left on his floor and absolutely no water. You couldn't even drink the tap water as it was one of those new 'eco' stations that used rain water, so eating warm food and not getting a drink for hours on end was 'par for the course' - that's if you actually had time for a lunch.

He was just about to go back out when one of his colleagues shouted over, mumbling as he was tucking into the biggest sandwich Jamie had ever seen. 'Jamie, there's a new job just gone on the CSI log; unearthed bones, what's a guess someone has dug up the previous owner's dog?' He looked at the log on the computer screen. It was entitled *Bones found in garden*. 'It's right out in the sticks,' he said. 'Who's the cop that's gone?'

'It's Sally Hargreaves from Rothbury.'

'She's usually quite switched on,' said Jamie. 'I'll take a run up there for a look, I have to go to Rothbury at some point anyway as there's a car number plate waiting to be fingerprinted. Can you show me attending?'

It wasn't unusual for them to be called out for animal bones and last month they had been called out to a skeleton on the beach, which actually turned out to be part of a plastic skeleton - a medical prop.

It was a long drive from the CSI base in Newcastle up to the Rothbury Moors but at least he was now fed and he'd quickly call in at one of the petrol stations for something to drink. Twenty minutes later he stopped at the Old Farmway Garage at Morpeth and treated himself to a coffee from their newly installed machine. It was surprisingly good for machine coffee - he had identified a few good coffee spots around Northumberland. The busy and notoriously dangerous A697 wasn't too bad today. It was always full of lorries avoiding the busy A1, using it as an alternative to get to Scotland, plus there were tractors to negotiate. Turning off towards Rothbury he made his way along twisty roads until eventually he arrived at what his 'sat nav' was saying was his location, but it so obviously wasn't - there was nothing there, just old wooden barns.

Jamie picked up his radio to ask for directions. He'd see if he could get in touch with Sally, who had already attended the scene. He remembered Sally's force number and keyed it into his radio.

'Hi Sally,' he said when she picked up, 'it's Jamie from Forensics, are you still at the scene of the bones?'

'Yeah, I'm just chatting with neighbours and waiting for the Sarge to arrive.'

'My sat nav says I've arrived but I'm just looking at derelict outbuildings.'

'Did you come from the south? And does one of the derelict buildings have a huge horseshoe on the door?' He looked around the buildings, 'Yes and yes,' he said.

'You've come just a bit too far and missed the turning. It's on the brow of the hill you've just come down. There's no signpost - the entrance is on the left - it just looks like you're driving into woodland. You'll eventually see the police car if you just keep coming down the track.'

In his twenty-five years of working in the area, Jamie had no idea this place even existed. He'd driven past the entrance numerous times and never even noticed the turn off. The trees were acting as a canopy, blocking out the light. As he drove deeper into the wood he thought to himself that this would be a really spooky place at night. The van hit a few deep pot-holes and the equipment rattled around in the back of the van. He was now coming up to the white painted cottages described by Sally. They had small open-plan gardens in front, which were filled full of plants and bushes. Just past the cottages the road opened up into a bit of a square, with houses on all sides. The police car was parked on the right, outside what was obviously 'Number One', the scene of the bones.

Sally suddenly appeared, making her way over from a house that looked like an old small church.

'Hi, I've just been talking to the lady from the 'Chapel' there', pointing back, 'she says she's only lived here five years but she knew the old lady who used to live in the premises, she died about two or three months ago. Nice old lady apparently. She knew that she'd lived here a long time but couldn't say how long.'

'Can I have a look at what we've got then? It's probably just animal bones.'

'Yeah, I'll have to give the lady a knock, she's in a wheelchair so it takes her a while to answer the door.'

'Do you have to go through the house to get to the back garden, that's where they are, isn't it?'

'No, there is a back gate accessible via a shared courtyard around the corner - but I thought it was probably a good idea to leave it locked for now.'

'Yeah, good idea - thanks Sally, you're thinking they're human aren't you?'

'Looks like it to me, but be warned, I have been wrong before' she said, smiling.

The door was eventually answered by a dark haired woman in a powered wheelchair. She was struggling for ages before she managed to get the door open. Sally stepped forward, 'Hi Anna, this is the guy I told you about. Is it OK if we come through again? This is Jamie by the way, he's what's called a Crime Scene Manager and will have more idea than me what sort of bones they are.'

Jamie smiled, 'sorry we have to come through your house.'

'You're fine' said Anna, 'I must explain, we haven't fully moved in yet, in fact we're only really camping out in one room, hence the carpets - they're all pretty old, so don't worry about your shoes.'

The garden was only about twenty-five by twenty-five-metres but totally private. The house was 'L' shaped and looked like the bedrooms took up one side and the main living area the other. The third side looked like it was the back of next door's house and the fourth side was a high wall, which must be between this cottage and the one next door. Jamie thought to himself that if he had wanted to bury a body, this would be the perfect place to do it as no one could possibly see.

'Right,' said Jamie, 'you stay here, less people trampling over the scene the better.' Sally remained at Anna's side at the doorway as they watched.

'I take it it's that hole there, is it?' They both nodded - 'yeah.'

'I can see some green fabric, is it under that? Were you gloved Sally when you looked at it?'

'No, but I just used that stick to your right to pull back the fabric.'

Jamie moved the piece of torn cloth to one side. There was a muddle of small bones. 'Has anyone touched the bones... who dug it up?'

'My husband dug it up to satisfy my curiosity,' said Anna. 'A neighbour's dog originally dug the hole the other day. The dog was obviously really interested in something. When her owner came to get her he said it was an old bit of cloth the dog was interested in and he kicked some of the soil back in the hole. Apparently, his dog just loves digging but I was frustrated at not being able to get access to see for myself what exactly was in the hole. So I kept nagging my husband to get a trowel and dig to see what he could find - curiosity just getting the better of me.'

'It's only either Anna's husband or the dog that could have disturbed them,' said Sally. 'Well, what are we looking at? An old pet dog, is it?'

'I'm afraid you were right the first time Sally, it looks like a human hand to me, the wrist bones are still in situ. I can see metacarpals, they're in a bit of a jumble after being disturbed.'

'In fact', he continued, poking in the hole, 'one looks like it has tooth marks in, a wee bit chewed - your neighbour's dog I presume. Don't worry, they're probably really old. I take it your neighbour didn't see them when the dog uncovered it all?'

'I think he was just so embarrassed his dog was out loose digging in my garden. He just kicked the hole in as soon as he picked the dog up. He didn't pay that much attention to what was in the hole. Oh my God, I can't believe there's a skeleton in my new garden!'

'Honestly, it might not be yet or as I say, it could be a very old burial site. Right, I'm just going to get my camera and an evidence bag and I'll take a few of these bones off to the pathologist. He'll confirm if they're human or not. As I say, they're probably really old, so don't you worry about it - just leave everything as it is and I'll get back in touch with you in due course.'

As Jamie left the garden and walked to the van, he knew the bones were indeed human and they weren't part of any ancient burial site. They looked like they had been there for a while - but not that long.

Chapter 15

That afternoon, when Jamie attended the drugs death post mortem, he handed the bones to the mortuary staff. The Alnwick uniformed police officers were going to ensure security of the scene in the garden of 'Number One'. The post mortem went smoothly with no surprises and he managed to finish work on time.

On attending work the next morning, confirmation had come back from the pathologist that they were indeed human bones - staff were estimating they were around twenty to thirty years old. The procedure now was to send them off to the specialist laboratory in Edinburgh to be carbon dated but it looked like the body would have to be exhumed.

Jamie Jones was now in full work mode. He wasn't an expert in bones but he had already anticipated the result the pathologist had given and the ensuing workload ahead of him. The little segment of fabric he had removed was a bit of a giveaway - it looked like the type of fabric used to make a three piece suit. The rule the police worked to was if the body was less than one hundred years old they had to investigate like any other murder - so with the update, it was full steam ahead.

At 8am the same morning he was already in the van, heading up the A697 again towards Rothbury. The journey up north into the Northumbrian countryside was always one of his favourite drives, through the pretty villages of Longhorsley and Longframlington, then the twisting road through woodland and along the banks of the river Coquet towards Rothbury. It provided some of the most beautiful scenery in England but Jamie's life experiences were different to most, it gave him a very unique perspective of his beloved Northumberland.

He didn't just see the beautiful scenery but he'd see places where he had recovered dead bodies from the river, houses where people had 'blown their brains out' and scenes of horrendous accidents. Every single one was plotted like a map in his brain.

On arrival in Aspley he saw a few of the neighbours come to their windows, alerted by the sound of his van. They obviously weren't used to much traffic or indeed strangers in Aspley, he thought.

Anna Jude was propelling herself down the ramp as he was decamping his work gear from the back of the van. 'Well,' she said, 'were they definitely human... what's the plan?'

'I'm afraid it's not good news, yes definitely human and also less than one hundred years old. I hate to tell you this but the probability is that you'll have to move out. The senior investigating officer or the SIO as we call her, is on her way up here and I'm sure that's what she'll tell you. We'll be doing a dig today to see what's under there. It depends what we find really but it's looking like it's a crime scene.'

Anna was horrified, 'but there's only me staying here at the moment, my husband works away sometimes and he's down in Liverpool. We've only really set up one of the bedrooms, the rest of the house is pretty much empty. The furniture is due to arrive next week after all the flooring has been laid, plus it's currently being decorated. I haven't got anywhere else to sleep now and I need specialist equipment, it's impossible, I just can't move out.'

'I'm really sorry, but it's potentially a murder scene. We'll wait and see what the SIO says, aye?'

With that she wheeled back and shut the door - hard. Rather than going through the house again, Jamie went around the cottage and through the courtyard to use the back gate to fetch all the equipment he needed. He reached for his radio and asked where Dan, his colleague was. Then they would have to wait for the Archeologist to arrive at the scene before they could start the exhumation.

Anna was back at the door again, 'how long will it take to dig it up?'

Jamie smiled, 'it depends what we find down there, I'm afraid this might be a long job, you never know. I could be wrong, stranger things have happened, there might not even be a full skeleton or the bones might be older than we thought - they're currently on their way to a lab in Scotland where they'll be checked to see exactly how old they are.' He knew they weren't wrong but just wanted to pacify her a little.

He put down the plastic scale next to the bones still on show and started to take photographs. The scale was basically two rulers joined at a ninety degree angle. It was used to record size and placement. The area was always photographed from the four corners, so it was all time consuming work.

Sally, the Rothbury Beat Officer arrived back at the scene, now very interested in what, or who more precisely, was buried in the garden on her patch.

'Can you find out an ETA for your supervision please Sally, we need to sort out a proper cordon?' He looked towards Anna sitting watching - 'Is there any chance of having a key for this gate? I don't want to keep going through your house or keep disturbing you, but I certainly don't want anyone else entering the scene either.'

'Yeah sure,' said Anna, who was starting to realise that this was now going to have serious consequences for her. 'My husband is going to have a fit when he gets back,' she told them, 'he really didn't want to move here, it was me who fell in love with the place - he said it was creepy! I'm so going to get an 'I told you so' when he gets back. I've got people coming today to lay more flooring.'

'I'm sorry, Anna, you're probably going to have to cancel, there's no way workmen will be allowed on the property at the moment,' Sally said sympathetically. 'I'm really sorry, if I could change anything, I would!'

'This is turning into a bloody nightmare.'

Dan, Jamie's colleague, who was relatively new to the job arrived around 9am to help. They stood for a while chatting outside the van, Jamie updating him on what had been done so far. He was informing him that lab staff in Edinburgh had probably already been tasked with checking the area out on old maps, just in case there were any ancient burial sites around the Aspley area.

The two CSI's were both getting 'suited and booted' in their pale blue paper suits, totally unaware of all the eyes on them and the pandemonium created in the hamlet by their presence. As Jamie was getting the tent out of the back of his colleague's van, he was approached by an old guy walking a rather handsome and fluffy bearded collie. It pulled on its lead until it was close enough for a pat. 'Hey' he said, 'you're a bit of a live wire,' as Merlin the dog jumped and nuzzled into him.

'Sorry, he's a rescue dog and we're trying to stop him jumping on people and getting too excited, but we're failing... failing miserably. He just adores people.' There was a pause, 'am I allowed to ask what on earth is going on?'

'Well, I'm sure your neighbour will tell you soon anyway, we've found some old bones in her garden.'

'What, human ones?' Arthur said, in the most incredulous manner he could muster.

'Looks like it.'

'Well... I guess there could be bones all over this place. I've done a little research into the history of the place and there was a manor house here from as early as 1589, so I guess they had to bury their dead somewhere. These stables weren't built until around 1890 though.'

'How long have you lived here?'

'Let me see, it will be about 30 years or so now, something like that anyway.'

'Just stay there a sec, will you?' Jamie said, leaving Arthur standing and heading back into the courtyard.

Arthur stood waiting, letting Merlin sniff the hedge rows. The policewoman who Arthur had seen earlier, came out of Martha's old house, full of smiles.

'Hi, I was hoping to talk to you, you're not Arthur are you?'

'Yes,' he was trying not to look nervous but he could feel his heart starting to race a little in his chest.

'The lady at the Chapel said you'd be the best person to speak to about the woman who lived here previously.'

'Oh yes, yes,' he said, 'Martha, Martha Dickinson, headmistress at Rothbury primary school for years - lovely woman, died a few months ago, very sad, died of cancer.'

The police officer was tapping a few details into a tablet as she talked.

'Do you know how long she lived here?'

'Let me see, we had been here a few years when she arrived, I think about twenty-eight years, something like that.'

'Did she live alone?'

'Yes.'

'Always?'

'Yes... oh no wait a minute - not always, her husband arrived a good few months after Martha came. He was here for about a year or so, I think' Arthur was originally going to lie, but thought better of it, just incase someone else mentioned it and it made him look guilty. 'He worked abroad, so he was there one day, gone the next. The marriage didn't last very long, as I say they divorced about a year or so later and he went off to work in France, I think.'

'What was his name?'

'Eh, let me think... I did know it... Jimmy I think it was, yes, James Dickinson.'

'I take it he was sometimes known as Jimmy?'

'Yes, but I think Martha used to call him James.'

She tapped away on her little computer. 'Anyone else live at the house whilst Martha was there?'

'Not really, she did have a niece who used to stay with her from time to time, but not very often. She came back to look after Martha when she was dying.'

'What's her name?'

'A bit of a strange name for you, she's called Africa…Africa Wells - she inherited her aunt's house. All the money and the house contents went to a fund for St Mary's Church in Morpeth - Martha was in the choir there for years.'

She was now tapping wildly into her machine.

'Do you know who lived there before Martha?'

'It was an elderly man who lived on his own, he didn't really mix with anyone. I think he was called Peter or something like that... forgive me, my memory isn't quite as good as it used to be. He had worked on the railways for years and bought the house when he retired. I think his mother died leaving him a bob or two.'

'Do you know anyone else who knew this Peter?'

'Perhaps Ronnie' he said, pointing towards Ronnie's house, 'but to be honest he didn't speak to many people. I probably knew him better than most because we had a shared interest in trains.'

'Thanks Arthur, you've been really helpful. Can I take your telephone number please?'

Jamie and Dan almost had the white tent in situ when Sally's supervision arrived. The Sergeant stood at the gate and shouted over, not wanting to disturb the scene.

'Hi Jamie, what's the score?'

Jamie had worked with Sergeant Stevenson before and had a lot of respect for him. He wasn't like the usual cop who would walk all over a crime scene without thinking, he was particularly knowledgeable after working for several years on the Murder Investigation Team, called the MITs.

'Here Sarge, I'll show you the photos.' He picked up his camera and brought the photograph of the bones up on the little screen.

'Totally sure they're human?'

'Yeah, got an email from the pathologist this morning confirming it - look you can still see some of the wrist bones intact.'

The sergeant blew out, making his lips vibrate together. 'Are you going to be the one that tells the occupier they have to vacate, or is that up to me? It's not going to go down too well, is it?'

'Already warned her it will probably happen. She's obviously not happy, it's compounded by the fact that she needs specific equipment to function,' Jamie said to the now hassled looking Sergeant.

'I bloody hate murder investigations,' the Serge said, 'it brings everyone and their granny out of the woodwork, murders don't happen in the Rothbury area. It's a nice quiet place, a crime free place and that's why I love it so much.'

Chapter 16

The scene was secured and the cordon in place, tent erected, lights all set up - they were all ready to go. Jamie's radio suddenly burst into life. DCI Karen Foster, who was new to the team was the SIO for the bones job. She was setting up a briefing at Rothbury Police Station and said she wanted him there 'pronto' and that Sally Hargreaves was to attend too.

It only took Jamie and Sally twenty minutes to get into Rothbury but the meeting was already in full flow when they arrived. The newly promoted Detective Chief Inspector Karen Foster was certainly not Jamie's first choice to run the investigation. Over the years he'd found that the new SIOs were a bit of a liability, trying to prove themselves before really learning the job.

'Come in!' she shouted, 'you're late!' Great start thought Jamie, his hackles already up.

She told them that 'as per the book' she had spoken to an Archeologist and she would be attending the scene later this morning.

'Jamie, it is Jamie isn't it?' Jamie nodded. 'Can I have an update please, I need to fill out this pro-forma?'

'Yes, fine... we were called to the scene yesterday morning. I attended at 0915 hrs. On speaking with the occupant it appeared a neighbour's dog had initially disturbed the scene of the bones, then the new owner of the garden dug to find out what the dog had been after and found what looked like metacarpals - bones of the hand. I recovered the bones last night and dropped them off at the morgue where the pathologist confirmed they were human, probably around the twenty to thirty year mark. The scene has been secured and we're ready to exhume - just waiting for the Archeologist.'

Sally followed on, 'the problem we've got ma'am is the house now belongs to a lady who's just moved in. She's disabled and was not at all happy at the prospect of moving out. Apparently, she has specialist equipment already installed in the bathroom and one of the bedrooms that she needs because of her disability, but it's going to be a problem getting her alternative accommodation. The other rooms of the house are empty, apart from some bits and pieces in the kitchen - she hasn't fully moved in yet. But it is a problematic situation for her.'

'Well, it is a murder investigation, what does she bloody expect?'

'She really didn't expect to have to move out of her house, I can tell you that.'

'When I worked with witness protection we'd occasionally use a local hotel not too far from her, a posh one... Linden Hall, is it? Book her in there, I'm sure it's got really good disabled facilities - she'll be fine there and if she's not then refer her to me, I'll explain why she must vacate. Look, I'll phone her anyway, what's her number?'

Sally jotted it down and handed it to the DCI.

Jamie placed photographs of the found bones on the desk in front of DCI Foster. 'This is what we're looking at - some metacarpals... wrist bones. The fabric looks like suit material to me, but that's obviously just guesswork at this stage.'

'What's your gut telling you on this one Jamie?'

'I think it's a perfect place to bury a body. It's very private and apparently there was a huge water fountain on top of the site - the new owner has just had it removed. I'll be surprised if it's not a murder by a previous occupant or at least someone staying at the address.'

'What do we know about the previous occupants, PC Hargreaves?'

'An elderly lady lived there for over twenty-five years. She was the former headmistress of Rothbury Infants' School, a church goer too.

Although when I checked her out she did have previous convictions for shoplifting... bizarrely.'

'Before her?'

'Elderly man living on his own, in his eighties I believe, the neighbours didn't seem to know too much about him.'

'OK, pass details over to the DS and we'll take it from there.'

'Well, good luck digging Jamie. Have you heard from the archeologist this morning, I did tell her to ring you for directions?'

'Not yet, but I did pick up off the log that she was on her way.'

'Right everyone, thanks for the briefing. Keep me up to date with anything of note, we'll wait to see what you uncover. I'll visit the scene when there's something more concrete. 'Jamie thought she'd be itching to see the scene herself but obviously not.'

Jamie drove slowly back to Aspley, enjoying the beautiful wild and rugged scenery. It was going to be a very long day, he thought, a day with a mini trowel stuck in his hand until he got digger's cramp and a bad back. Unearthing a skeleton was notoriously time consuming.

Dan was having a cup of coffee with Anna when he arrived back at Aspley. 'Everything's done,' the young CSI said, looking a little embarrassed. 'Any news on what time the archeologist is due then?'

'She's on her way.'

'Where from?'

'Absolutely no idea, the last one we used came from Cambridge, so be prepared for a bit of a wait.'

Dan's radio started to bleep. His face dropped when he was asked to attend a job in Alnwick. With a lack of resources he had to leave the scene before it had even begun.

Emma Bould, the Archeologist arrived about twenty minutes later. Shiny black hair tied in a ponytail, she was all high cheekbones and tan. She obviously spent a lot of time outdoors, unless it was all fake thought Jamie. He could see and feel the excitement in the young girl.

He guessed it was like Christmas for Emma, who's life was full of elation at the thought of exhuming a body.

'Hey Jamie, we meet again!' Jamie knew her vaguely from a previous scene about a year ago where the skeleton had turned out to be over two hundred years old.

'I'm surprised you found us as easily as you did, it's a little hidden gem here, isn't it?'

'I didn't,' she said, 'took me bloody ages, been travelling since 5am. But I'm here now, so let's see what's waiting for us.'

'Just a minute, let me get suited up first.' Jamie caught a bit of her enthusiasm for the job, but knew this would wear off after an hour or so of removing an inch of soil at a time and his back had started to ache.

The inner cordon was policed by one of the probationers from Alnwick. He looked cold, like he had been standing there all night.

'Never mind lad, your relief will be here soon.' He looked at Jamie like he was crazy, 'you're joking, I only started ten minutes ago.'

Jamie laughed, 'sorry mate, you looked so cold I thought you must have been here all night.'

The probationer didn't find it remotely funny and just glared at him. *Honestly*, Jamie thought to himself, *the new wave of cops coming in were a right bunch of soft whingers.*

Jamie and Emma made their way into the tent, each carrying their boxes of tricks, and Jamie also armed with his camera over his shoulder. Everything was already in place to begin - the electricity negotiated from the home owner, which would be needed in order to carry on working when they lost the light.

'Give me a second or two and I'll go and get the first sample boxes,' said Emma.

She returned a few minutes later with the large plastic boxes, needed to put each layer of soil into. On the first, she wrote her initials on the side, along with the number 'one'. She placed measures around the hole and asked Jamie to take the photographs.

'Right, first inch, then re-photograph.'

They started picking at the soil around the outside of the hole and placing the soil into box number one. As they worked around the wrist and upwards it soon became apparent that a second arm was underneath the first, like they had been crossed over the body, in a specific pose. They remeasured and photographed the scene again.

'Any guess at age of bones, or is it too early for you to say?' Jamie asked.

'I'd guess at around twenty, thirty years but mind that is just a rough guess. They're definitely not over one hundred years old, just in case you were hoping we'd get an early finish.'

'Na! I guessed around twenty or thirty from the fabric.' They had sterile brown paper laid out flat between them and they were putting the bits of deteriorated cloth on it. 'Does this look like suit fabric to you? 'Jamie asked.

'Yeah, it does, it's like some sort of pinstriped fabric, and look, I got that tiny bit before, which looks like lining. Most of that must have already deteriorated.'

They worked on, painstakingly removing the soil over the body.

'Look at this bit' he said, holding it out towards her, 'mmm interesting - could be the hem of a handkerchief or something, see how it's turned over and has a distinctive corner to it.'

They continued working for a couple of hours, chatting away and Emma getting excited every time something new appeared. They were slowly uncovering their treasure.

'Right, let's photograph and get some lunch, my back is starting to moan a bit,' said Jamie. He looked at enthusiastic Emma who appeared as if she could just go on forever.

They went out to the van, removing their masks and taking the top half of their blue suits off. Jamie just had ham sandwiches but Emma pulled out a picnic hamper from the back of her car. She opened it up, 'please Jamie just help yourself if you see anything you fancy, I brought plenty.'

'Blood hell, you sure did!' he replied, looking in and seeing sandwiches, scones, packs of butter, Jaffa cakes, fruit and cartons of fruit juices. He forgot, this dig was probably like a holiday for Emma, who likely spent most of her time in a lab.

Their appearance in the car park had brought the neighbours out with offers of tea or coffee. Jamie had a rule, never to accept anything from the public, not even a cup of coffee. He always preferred to know exactly where his food and drink was coming from. He had seen how some people lived and thought he could never be one hundred percent sure it hadn't been spat in or corrupted in some way.

Anna, the home owner came wheeling around the corner. She must have been out for fresh air or she'd been to a neighbour's house. 'Hi', she said, 'I don't suppose you know how long it will take yet, do you?'

Jamie left Emma to answer. 'No, not really, all I can say is that it can take as long as four days to remove a skeleton, but it's very much dependent upon the type of soil, what we find and manpower of course.'

'Has anyone phoned you about going to a hotel yet?' asked Jamie.

'I've just been to Linden Hall to have a look at their disabled room but I can't manage without my electric bed, so my lovely new neighbours got together and carried the bed from my house to the 'Coach House' around the corner there. I'm staying in their spare room. It has an en suite wet room so it's actually a perfect set-up. My husband will go to Linden Hall at the weekend when he arrives home, if you're still here of course.'

'You've got very good new neighbours,' Jamie commented, thinking it odd that the husband went to stay in the hotel alone, leaving his wife with someone in Aspley. The neighbours would surely be virtual strangers to this woman so it was an immensely kind gesture they'd made.

After lunch, Jamie's mobile started to ring - it was Dan, 'I'm back boss, OK to come into the scene?' Jamie could see young Dan's face change the minute he walked through the garden gate and cast his eyes on the beautiful Emma Bould. She looked up and smiled at him revealing her amazingly white teeth and he could see Dan literally melt - the young lad was gone. 'Hi,' she said, 'lovely to meet you, I'm Emma.' His face immediately coloured up into a mottled red, 'yes, nice to meet you too,' he stumbled.

Chapter 17

In the afternoon there were the two CSIs and the Archeologist working hard on bringing up the body. Emma gave Dan the talk about what to do and what not to do and showed him some of the insect casings he was meant to look out for. The three of them now working proved to be a real bonus, they were starting to get somewhere. Dan had been working on the area where Emma predicted the legs might be and they were all now starting to see the full skeleton emerging. The skull and teeth were also becoming prominent. Emma commented that the bone structure suggested it was male but that she'd feel more confident when the hip bones were fully visible.

They were already on box six and there were still loads of soil to remove. Jamie could tell Dan was enjoying himself - he'd never been on a dig before and 'Enthusiastic Emma' was telling him lots of stories from past digs she had been on, and he was absorbing it all like a sponge. Dan was slowly uncovering the bones of the feet. 'I'm still having a bit of trouble working out how these bones make feet, there looks to be too many to me.'

'There's lots of bones in a human foot - twenty-six to be precise,' said Emma, not paying too much attention.

As Dan picked away at the soil, he started counting - one, two, three....

Jamie laughed, 'you checking they're all there?'

'Yeah, so that's fifty two for two feet, right?'

'Yeah that's right,' said Emma. Both her and Jamie were removing soil from around the skull, which was now showing some real points of interest.

'Fifty two, fifty three, fifty four, fifty five, fifty six - there's way more of these feet bones here...'

Jamie and Emma started laughing. Emma got up and walked around to Dan, still laughing until she saw what he had uncovered. Jamie watched as Emma's big smile vanished.

'No wonder you couldn't make out the shape of the foot,' she said. 'There are three feet there. You see, that's one, then there are two here. You're seeing the toes of the second one at a slight angle to the others.'

'Well, Jamie... I do declare we have got ourselves two bodies in this here grave.'

'Are you sure?'

'Absolutely sure, have a look.'

After assessing the scene, Jamie went to sit in the van to make the necessary calls. 'Hi, it's Jamie, is DCI Foster about? She's not answering her mobile.' He waited a while and then DCI Foster came on the line.

'Hi Jamie, what you got?'

'The body looks like it's received blunt force trauma to the front of the skull. The teeth are intact so we may be able to still get some DNA from them.'

'Right, definitely murder then?' she said.

'I'm afraid there's something else, looks like we've found a second body buried underneath the first. Only the foot has appeared at the moment but we're guessing there's another one there.'

'Shite, that's all we need, a bloody double murder! Right, I'll get the team prepped and ready. Keep me updated Jamie. If I get a chance I'll pop up but it's a bit chaotic down here at the moment. Has the owner vacated the property yet?'

'Yes, she's staying with a neighbour.'

'Good.' with that she was gone.

When Jamie returned to the tent, Emma was standing back assessing the scene. 'Another three or four hours and we could have the first skeleton boxed and to the mortuary. It's 4pm now, anyone fancy staying a few hours to help?'

Jamie looked at Dan, 'there's no money in it mind Dan, the SIO wouldn't sanction any overtime… the pot's empty, apparently.'

'Huh, yeah that'll be right, until it comes time for the bloody cops to get overtime, and then it seems to be bloody available.'

'I know, but you have to admit it's getting really interesting. I can tell you that in my twenty plus years of working in forensics, I've only been involved in two other cases where we dug up a skeleton and that was only one body, this is two. Well, at least one full skeleton and a foot so far.'

'OK, I'm in,' said Dan.

'The soil here is great for excavation,' said Emma, 'makes the job so much easier.'

They all worked on the hip area, photographing each stage as they went. At about 5pm they were working under the lights as dark clouds had swept over and the light was fading hard. The skeleton now stood proud of the ground. The three stood back, admiring their work.

'Definitely male?' said Jamie.

'Almost certainly, see the broad shoulders and narrow hips, that strongly suggests it's male.'

'Let's have a look at the fabric recovered,' said Jamie, 'it's quite strange as there were quite a few bits of suit type fabric found on top of the body. It suggests to me that it was draped over the body as opposed to him wearing it. There's only tiny bits of what looks like a part of a handkerchief. Or perhaps it could be pyjama fabric? Maybe someone put his suit jacket on before burying him or just threw it over him before covering it over with soil - the more I look at it the more it does look like striped pyjamas. Obviously someone cared as they folded his arms across his chest in the typical death pose.'

Emma looked at the fabric again, 'I think you're right about the pyjamas, as I recovered what looks like it could be some sort of cord - that could be the ties around the waist.'

'No buttons found though,' said Dan.

'Right,' said Jamie, 'how about getting him into the exhibits box?'

'Alright', said Emma, 'is it OK if I work on the feet?'

They both agreed, feeling relieved that Emma would be working on the complicated bit as neither one of them were convinced they knew which bone belonged to which body. Jamie wrote his initials on the tenth box and they started slowly to bring their guy up from his resting place.

'You do often find things when you're lifting the bones out of situ, so keep your eyes open for any buttons near the chest area or the wrist bones.'

'We need to keep quiet about the second body for now, no blurting it out to the neighbours, we don't want to spook them.' Little did he realise how much the news of a second body in the grave would actually impact on some of those neighbours.

Jamie continued, 'the poor residents of Aspley won't know what hits them when the Murder Investigation Team turns up in the morning, asking them loads of questions. I bet the people who live here haven't had anything like this to gossip about for years, if ever. Poor Anna, who owns the house, doesn't realise it's going to be ripped to bits looking for evidence. Most people think after all that time we won't find anything, but we nearly always do.'

They carefully boxed the first body and were ecstatic when they found a small button under one of the wrist bones, supporting their belief he may have been wearing old fashioned pyjamas. It could always be a shirt, but the cord which was found at the waste suggested otherwise, thus proving he wasn't just a random visitor to the house, but more than likely someone who lived there. By 8pm they were done, the body was boxed and in Jamie's van, ready to be dropped off at the morgue. Jamie phoned the SIO with an update. 'Jesus Jamie, you're not still at the scene at this time are you, there's no overtime, I thought I made that clear?'

'Crystal,' said Jamie, 'we're doing it for the love of the job', *or more likely cause we're bloody mugs,* he thought.

DCI Foster paused, Jamie realising she didn't quite know what to say. *A 'thank you' would be nice,* he thought but knew it wouldn't be forthcoming.

'So, what's the score?'

'The skeletal remains of one body, most likely male, has been removed and I'll be taking it to the mortuary in the morning. The body still has some good teeth so there's definitely a chance we could get some DNA from the pulp. The skeleton has obvious blunt force trauma to the front of the skull - there's always a chance this could have happened post-mortem, but Emma doesn't think so. We believe he was wearing pyjamas and then perhaps a suit jacket was thrown over him, or he was wearing it over his pyjamas. So our guess is that he was someone who lived there, or at least was staying at Aspley around twenty or so years ago.'

'How accurate can they be as to the age of the bones?'

'Until the bones are carbon dated we won't know for sure, it will always be guesswork, but the archaeologists are usually reasonably accurate. She said her guess would be around the twenty, twenty-five years mark.'

'How long to carbon date it?'

'It takes ages. The neighbours might yet all give you the name of who they think it could be, although they were staying quite tight lipped when they were talking to Sally Hargreaves who did the preliminary enquiries.'

'Right, get yourself home, you'll be bloody dreaming of skeletons tonight.'

Chapter 18

Dan was 'suited and booted' by the time Jamie arrived the next morning, keen to get working on the second skeleton. Emma's car was already there too, she was probably already working. Jamie quickly got into his pale blue paper suit and joined Dan in carrying around the heavy metal cases and exhibits boxes. In the tent, as predicted, Emma was already hard at work on the foot area of the skeleton. 'There's loads of bits of fabric around the foot and the leg. The foot is quite small, I would say around a size four or five.'

'Morning Emma,' said Jamie, grinning at Dan - he could see his colleague was already smitten with this beautiful, rather over-enthusiastic young woman.

'Yeah…sorry, morning. I'm engrossed already.'

'Would you guess at female then Emma?'

'Yes, most likely.'

'Would it be alright for Dan and I to start at the top end, where the skull may be? This is a bit of guesswork Dan mind, as this body is probably much smaller than the first,' said Jamie, 'bearing in mind what Emma is saying about the small feet.'

'And,' said Emma, 'this one looks like it's face down. Go in around the five foot mark.' Emma didn't raise her head, totally engrossed in a small piece of metal she'd found near the foot. 'Look, it's a small silver coin. What the heck, there's more. Get photos Jamie.' Emma put all the measures in place and Jamie took the photographs.

'It's a bracelet,' he said, 'you know one of those gypsy types, with all the coins hanging from a chain.'

They were now starting to put together a picture of the woman in the grave. 'It takes a particular type to carry off an ankle bracelet like that' said Jamie, imagining layered skirts, skimpy tops and long curly wild hair.

The second body emerged even quicker than the first, with only a small amount of soil between the two skeletons. Emma pointed out that a lot of the detritus between the two bodies had been fabric, the first body had been covered with clothing before the second body went in. They removed tiny little silver hooks and eyes from around the chest and stomach area. It didn't take much imagination to guess at the type of garment she had been wearing at the time of her death.

'Look' said Jamie, 'on that rib bone there.' There was a triangular chunk missing. 'Looks like a stab mark to me, what do you think Emma?'

'Yeah, does to me too.'

As they started to bring the body out of the earth, it became clear that a knife had been used on the second body, but there was no evidence of a knife used on the first. The first body had most certainly received a blow to the front of the head.

Two plain clothed officers from the Murder Investigation Team had been knocking on the eleven doors in Aspley all morning, trying to gather as much information as possible. Jamie was waiting for a briefing from the SIO as to what they'd found out.

By 4.00pm they had the body boxed and one of the MITs officers had offered to take it to the mortuary, as it was on his way home. After two very long days' work, Emma's outdoor adventure was over and after a preliminary one foot central dig, she agreed they were unlikely to find any further bodies. The fact that the fountain had been built over the top of the two skeletons suggested that the probability of other body sites within the garden was slim.

Jamie spent the rest of the time looking at tool marks used by whoever buried the bodies. They had unearthed the original sides of the grave and could see the patterns left by the tools used. It looked like two different spades had been used and one had very interesting damage on the bottom where it had obviously hit a rock, the bend in the metal having scored a very specific pattern. Jamie wondered after twenty plus years whether it was possible that this spade was still in existence - probably not, he thought, although he still had some of his dad's old tools from years ago, so he guessed it was a possibility. He spent the next half hour making a cast of the unusual tool mark around the grave.

Jamie phoned DCI Foster to see if the MITs officers had uncovered anything relevant. She said that the previous occupant, Martha Dickinson, did have a husband who used to frequent the residence but he worked in France and when they split up about twenty-five years ago he moved to France permanently. 'So,' she said, 'we need to try and find a James Dickinson in France. We've got people going through missing person reports for any missing females around twenty years ago but there's nothing in the immediate area. Due to the age of the remains we've decided to go for publicity straight away on this one, to see if we can get a quick lead. Would you let the homeowner know of what we're planning, she seems to like you?'

'Yeah, OK. Are you sure we're not a bit quick getting the media involved?'

'Probably, but I just want this one off the books as quick as possible. It's going to be running media coverage, so we're literally giving them the absolute basic information to start off with. I just have a feeling someone will come forward with the names of our couple.'

Tomorrow Jamie would be working on the interior of the house with Dan. Any new flooring put down by Anna would be ripped up. He guessed she was now regretting her burning curiosity to see what had interested her neighbours' dog so much. He had seen her a couple of times wheeling around the hamlet but hadn't yet spoken to her about the forensics he needed to do inside the house. No time like the present he thought.

Whilst Dan cleared away some of their equipment, he took a walk around to the 'Coach House' to see if she was there. The door was opened by a slightly pale and anxious looking middle aged man holding the cutest dog ever. Jamie loved dogs but this one looked like it wanted to rip Jamies throat out. Its teeth were bared and it was ready to take him on. The man stepped back to let him in.

'Come in, take no notice of her, she's all bark and no bite.' Jamie looked at those sharp, little white teeth and wasn't totally convinced.

He walked into a large kitchen/diner with Anna sitting at the table with a laptop.

'It's Mrs Jude I'm after,' he said, looking at Anna, 'is your husband with you today?'

'I'm afraid you'll just have to make do with me,' Anna answered, raising her head.

'Do you want me to leave?' said Ronnie, looking between Anna and Jamie.

'I've just come to give you an update.'

'Would you stay Ronnie please?' asked Anna, quietly.

Ronnie agreed and to Jamie's horror he put the fearsome ball of fluff down on the ground. It immediately ran full pelt towards him but then stopped and started sniffing him all over. Then it made its way off around the corner and brought a teddy out of its basket, dropping it at Jamie's feet.

'She likes you,' Anna said.

'It's probably the smell of bones she likes. Was this the little tyke who started all this?' he said, now stroking her under the chin. 'There were little teeth marks on one of those bones, you little terror.' Jamie quickly changed the subject when he saw the horror on the man's face.

'I have some good news Mrs Jude, the bodies are up now.'

'Bodies?' she questioned in horror, 'I was only expecting one.'

'No, there was a second underneath, they're going for publicity straight away, so you'll probably read about an appeal for any missing persons in the paper tomorrow.'

Jamie watched as Ronnie suddenly sprung up and made his way to the sink to get a drink.

'The bad news is that it definitely looks like a double murder, so the house will have to be thoroughly and forensically investigated and that could mean carpets or new flooring taken up I'm afraid. We have to be really thorough in a murder case, we have no option.'

'Surely there'll be nothing after all these years?' she said.

'You'd be surprised.'

Chapter 19

'Which room are we going to start with?' asked Dan, moving down 'Number One's' long corridor, keen to get going.

'I think the end bedroom,' replied Jamie, 'that room has a strange feeling to me... and then I think we'll work our way backwards to the living room. The end bedroom looks like it has the original flooring and it's stripped ready for decoration, so it should be quite straightforward - no big bits of furniture to consider.'

The Aspley cottages were all 'L' shaped, the bedrooms were in one wing and the living space in the other. There was a long hallway with doors off to each of the bedrooms and the family bathroom. It reminded Jamie more of a hotel corridor than a home. The master bedroom was huge and freezing cold, mainly due to the fact that it had windows to the floor on both sides. The window on the side of the secret walled garden doubled up as a doorway, giving easy access into the private enclosed garden. Jamie looked out into the garden, contemplating the actions of the offender, thinking to himself that if he had committed the murder then this was definitely the easiest egress to remove the bodies.

The floor was concrete and covered with plastic square floor tiles. They looked really old fashioned and Jamie was almost sure they would have been here since the cottages were first converted some thirty or forty years ago. It would be nice to get a quick break on this one, he thought.

'Right, usual photographs Dan,' said Jamie, 'then we'll swab.'

Jamie thought the old tiles were a bit of a gift - if they were going to get twenty year old blood from anywhere, the cracks in these old tiles were the perfect place. He had already noticed an area of interest when he walked towards the far window and wanted to see if he was right. His instincts were usually good.

Photographs done, he and Dan started a presumptive blood test on the area using the Kastle-Meyer technique. They used round circles of absorbent paper, folding them in half, then quarters until they had a cone shape. They then pushed the point of the cone between the cracks before opening out the circle of paper. In their metal equipment cases they carried the agent used to detect signs of blood. Once it was poured on the centre of the paper, it would turn pink if there was a positive reaction - a reaction to blood. Both of their samples turned immediately pink. They both smiled at each other, 'a hit straight away, I think we've found our murder scene Dan.'

'You see, at least twenty plus years and it's still here, great stuff. This looks to me like there's been a huge pool of blood. See, if you stand back, the cracks do look ever so slightly darker. Let's see if we can block a bit of this light from the window and use the torches to see if we can get an idea of scale.' The ultra violet light would hopefully detect any sign of blood spillage.

They tried different filters and eventually they could see the scale of the area of blood. It was huge and went all the way to the window. It looked like a body had possibly been dragged out into the garden through the UPVC door. 'Let's get this door swabbed, let's see if there's anything trapped in the rubber seals.'

They worked all morning on the one room, removing samples of blood for profiling, all taken from the floor towards the courtyard window and from inside the door frame. Paint was scraped off the wall where it shone a slightly different colour. They eventually sprayed the whole room with luminol, looking for a reaction with any traces of haemoglobin, taking photographs of the outcome. There was little doubt, they had found the scene of the crime. Something had taken place in this bedroom over twenty years ago and more than likely when the now deceased school mistress lived here.

'I'm going to test to make sure the blood is human, just in case someone slaughtered a pig in here or something daft.' Jamie took out the equipment to do an immuno-chromatographic procedure, which looked similar to a pregnancy testing kit. He ran a dampened swab along one of the cracks in the flooring, then put the end of the swab in the small plastic indicator. He waited a few minutes until the control line came up first, indicating the test was working, then the second fainter line came up, indicating it was human.

Jamie phoned the SIO to update her.

'Hi Jamie, found anything yet?' she answered.

'Looks like the murder took place in the master bedroom at some stage - I'd say there's been a bit of a bloodbath in there - the blood is definitely human. Blood spatter on both the walls and the ceiling and a huge area towards the glass doors that lead into the walled garden. Looks to me like someone bled out there and then was dragged out through the doorway. There were blood traces in the seals of the door frame.'

'We've also looked at the other bedrooms, which are all clean - and the bathroom has been totally stripped back to brick, re- plastered, floor redone and has new fixtures and fittings. At some point tomorrow we're going to need help from the search teams. The loft will need searching and it's a huge area. After all this time I'm sure the murder weapon or weapons will be long gone but we'll have to check just in case. The new occupants haven't actually been up there yet, just the guy who did their survey. We're looking for a large, heavy blunt instrument and also a knife - used on the second body. There wasn't anything left in the kitchen when the new occupants moved in, so that's a waste of time.'

'OK.'

Jamie continued, 'you know the woman who lives there is disabled? She's just had an oak floor fitted in the living room. Due to the timeframe and the fact we've already found the crime scene, I'm saying we should leave the floor in situ.' Jamie knew the reaction before it came.

'Bloody hell Jamie, are you going soft in your old age?'

'Ah, it's just life will be so hard for her and we're just adding to it. Every instinct I have tells me there's nothing under that floor, we've found our scene.'

'Lift it Jamie! I'm sending you some help this afternoon to go through the loft and help you with the floor. There's a briefing at 9am tomorrow in the MIT's conference room.'

'The pathologist hasn't even done the PM yet, it's probably prudent to wait for the result before we charge ahead.'

'No Jamie - get it done!'

Jamie sometimes wondered about their current working practice. Over the years they had systematically wrecked peoples 'houses, pulling them to bits and also using the 'virtually immovable' silver aluminium powder used for lifting fingerprints, dusted over people's treasured furniture and possessions, knowing victims would be scrubbing for weeks to try and remove it.

This time, seeing this woman in her power wheelchair, who'd obviously bought her dream home - all on one level and turning it into somewhere suitable for her to live, tugged at his 'seldom pulled' heart strings. How unlucky to have a master bedroom where two people had been murdered and two dead bodies recovered from your new garden. Plus, now she's had to move out of her home and have work she'd already done totally wrecked. He just thought she had enough to deal with.

The afternoon went as planned. The floor was removed, exposing the same plastic tiles as the bedroom and after two hours of work and as predicted, there was no forensic evidence in the living room or dining room. He definitely would be saying 'told you so' to Detective Chief Inspector Karen Foster.

Chapter 20

Ronnie was sitting chatting with Anna in his kitchen, but all the time his mind was not on what she was saying but on what he had just been told - 'two bodies', 'two bloody bodies'... he could not for the life of him comprehend what was going on. How on earth were there two bodies in that grave? He had helped put the one body into the grave, there was no other body…who was the other body? His mind was whirling and he felt nauseous.

After spending two days with Anna he had found her pleasant to be around, for someone with so many problems she was a very positive and happy person. They were now, unbelievably to him, discussing the making of the perfect Yorkshire pudding but all the time Ronnie could feel himself sweating, vomit rising in his throat. He really didn't want to be sick in front of Anna.

Could that officer have previously read his feeling of pure terror? thought Ronnie. After all, weren't police trained for that sort of thing? In his job in the special forces he'd killed people before, shot them but then they would move on away from the scene. They didn't see the aftermath and to be honest knowing they were 'bad guys' always made Ronnie feel like it was OK to kill them - that he was somehow doing a service to society. But this was a whole new ball game, he knew at the time they should have just called the cops but Martha was crying, saying she'd lose her job as a teacher. Her tears were very persuasive... too persuasive, he now thought. Had she known at the time there were two bodies in the grave, surely not? But someone must have helped her with another body, surely? Who the hell was it? He wanted Anna to stop talking so he could go straight around to Arthur's, to share his panic and confusion - *but did Arthur know more?*

When the forensics officer had left, promising Anna she'd get her house back in two days time, he had asked Ronnie if he was OK. He obviously noticed he wasn't but anyone would be shocked at two bodies being found in a neighbours' garden, wouldn't they? But Anna didn't react as badly as him and it was her garden. He wished he was a much better actor.

'You're very pale,' said Anna, 'I'd have a sit down and a cup of hot sugary tea, if I were you. I'll make you one if you like, you've already kindly put everything in reach for me. I can manage.'

'No, no, it's fine, I'll make it, you want one?' Ronnie couldn't bear watching her struggle getting cups and then trying to manoeuvre the boiling hot kettle.

'Yes please. I think I'm in shock too, shock at what state I'm going to find my new house in. I don't care what he says they need to do when there's a murder, they're getting the bill for that oak floor to be relaid and any damage they've caused. I know it's only a job to them but their callousness actually makes you feel a bit anti-police, doesn't it?'

'I guess in a murder they have to be thorough.' When he said the word 'murder' felt wrong, it hadn't been a murder, it had been a fight that had gone wrong, an accident... that's how it had felt at the time, but the word 'murder' was now slowly sinking in to his psyche.

They sat sipping their tea, pontificating on the found bodies, with Anna wanting to know all about Martha and her life when she first moved into Aspley and whether he thought it was her husband in the grave or perhaps another family member. She told Ronnie she had been talking to Sarah, the police woman living next door and Sarah had said her money was on the ex-husband being in the grave. She said he was a bit of a bad guy by all accounts, but also how he'd always been pleasant to her.

'You must have known Martha's husband quite well Ronnie, as you were both living here at the time, weren't you?'

'Honestly Anna, I'd be lucky if I had one conversation with the man. He would just grunt at you as you walked past. I know they didn't have a great marriage, obviously... hence the divorce, but he wasn't around very much to get to know.'

'The police told me that the neighbours who had been here the longest seemed to know less about him than the ones who never met him.'

'Really! That's because they're just repeating gossip, not actually telling them any facts - there wasn't that much to know. He was a normal sort of guy, bit grumpy, kept himself to himself, liked a drink mind. Basically, that's all I know about him.'

'Listen' said Ronnie, desperate to get away, 'I've got some garden tools to take back to 'Number Three'. Would you be OK whilst I did that? I'll leave Maisie with you, if that's OK? She's a bit of a 'workie ticket' when I take her, she chases poor Merlin all around the house or the garden. You can see he gets fed up with her.'

'Sure, no bother at all. She's fine with me, aren't you sweetie pie?'

Chapter 21

Ronnie was trying to look as normal as possible whilst walking around to Arthur and Ella's cottage - he actually felt like running but knew all the neighbours were on heightened alert with all the police hanging around. He wiped the sweat from his brow before he arrived, admonishing himself for being so over emotional. His life working in the army and then in private security should have prepared him for this. He had worked on merchant ships tackling Somali pirates who were desperate to board. It had made him feel like he could cope with any situation but shamefully this situation panicked him. He realised he had fought many enemies in his career but he had never fought the British Justice System. He had never felt like anything he had done before was breaking the law but he knew hiding Martha's dead husband's body was wrong and had never been comfortable with it.

He could see Arthur in the kitchen as he approached, so knocked gently on the door. Arthur had a big smile when he saw him but it soon dropped when he saw shock in Ronnie's eyes. He walked in and waited until Arthur shut the door behind him.

'There were two bodies in that grave Arthur, two... did you know that?'

'No man, don't be stupid! There was only one, I was there when we lowered him in, remember?'

'Tell that to the bloody forensics team who've just unearthed a second body from that garden.'

Ronnie could see Arthur trying to recall events of that night, his brows knitting together in confusion. They both fell silent for a while, until Ronnie's panicked voice started up.

'Can you remember, we stopped digging the hole that night when we thought Sarah next door might be coming home after her late shift? We couldn't risk her hearing us digging, could we? Martha had strangely insisted on staying in her own house that night and when we returned the next morning she had actually been digging herself and she said she had thrown James' clothes in the bottom of the hole and covered them over with a little soil. What if there was a body under there Arthur, what if she had put another body in?'

'God Ronnie, hold your horses man, you're getting a bit carried away there, aren't you? Martha was about eight stone wet through. You're telling me she had hidden another body in the house and then carried it into the garden…and then dragged it into the grave and covered it over? Don't believe it, she couldn't have done it, anyway, who on earth was it?'

'Well, what other explanation?'

Arthur stopped and thought for a moment, moving his head back and forward... 'No, no, surely not. Well... you know,' he paused, 'there is one thing I never quite got my head around about the whole thing, it was the amount of blood in that bedroom. There were large pools of blood on the floor near the window, remember? And splashes all up the walls... and even on the ceiling. She told us she hit him a couple of times, but we all knew it was more than that, his face was mashed. I'm no expert Ronnie but I did think it strange at the time. I thought perhaps she had hit him standing up near the window, then he must have bled, then got back into the bed or she had somehow put him back in bed. She was so confused and distressed at the time, we didn't push it.'

'Has it really taken us twenty years to come to the conclusion that things weren't right that night,' said Ronnie.

'We all knew it wasn't right, but we'd also seen for ourselves what James had put her through, the man was a monster. Black eyes, broken wrist…remember when he threw her down the front door steps in her night clothes and left her out all night in the rain? She was in a right state.'

'I know, I know what you're saying, but I hope she was telling the truth. No one really asked James for his side of the story, did they?'

'We'd have had a hard job, he wouldn't talk to any of us. Anyway, the evidence was there man, she was always bruised. You'd hear him screaming at her.'

Ella walked into the kitchen so they both clammed up and smiled.

'Enjoy your snooze my darling?'

'Yeah, I heard you talking about James…is that Martha's James you're talking about?'

'Ah, it's nothing my love, just reminiscing.'

She dropped her head and put her finger to her mouth, 'he's under the fountain.'

Arthur's heart dropped to the floor, 'you can't go around saying that Ella.'

'It's OK Arthur, nearly everyone knows, we dealt with him, remember? He shouldn't have taunted Martha with his new girlfriend, should he? That was a recipe for disaster. Martha would take a beating and a bit of humiliation but she never took another woman being on the scene.'

Ronnie and Arthur glanced at each other. 'Who was the new girlfriend Ella?' Ronnie asked.

'Some tiny ginger piece from behind the bar at the Shoulder of Mutton, big teeth, like me, 'she laughed, showing off her pony sized teeth.

'Can you remember her name Ella?' asked Ronnie.

'She had a strange name, she wasn't from around here, broad Scottish I think she was… painfully thin, ginger hair but big boobs, that's why the men all followed her about.'

'Come on sweetheart - I'll make you a cup of tea,' - that was Arthur's prompt to Ronnie to stop asking Ella questions.

'Dizzy... Fizzy'

'What?'

'That's her name, James' floozie - no wait a minute…Didi, yes that's it, Didi Fisacherly. I knew it was something fizzy.'

'Well done love.' Arthur was astonished she could remember, but he now hoped she'd forget it just as quickly. Ronnie watched on, thinking how dangerous it could be if Ella started remembering things about that night and she was in the wrong earshot.

'Now you've got to forget all about Dizzy Fizzy,' Arthur said. Arthur and Ronnie's eyes locked for that split second and they knew exactly what each other was thinking.

Arthur made Ella a cup of tea and sat her back down in her comfy chair, cats climbing on her knee and dog at her feet. Ronnie couldn't imagine that he would be quite as attentive to Clara in the same circumstances, but he guessed you just had to get on with it.

'So,' said Ronnie, whispering, 'do you think this second body could be this Didi woman?'

'I haven't a clue but as soon as Ella described her I could picture her behind that bar and I think she's possibly right with the name. Her long term memory is sometimes pretty good, better than mine to be honest, it's her short term memory that's shot.'

Ronnie contemplated the second body. 'If this woman was really small and slightly built, it's not beyond the realms of possibility that Martha could have dragged a body into that grave in the night and then covered it over, is it? Then us gormless buggers come along and drop James on top.'

Ronnie could tell that Arthur was starting to come to the same conclusion. 'I agree, there were a few things that night that were odd,' said Arthur. 'Firstly, Martha insisted on staying in the house that night - that surprised me, there were a few of us offered her a bed, but she wouldn't. Joe Weiss was insistent that she should not be left on her own but she just wouldn't budge on it. Then, when we arrived early the next morning, the grave was disturbed, it was actually a bit deeper... remember? I can hear her saying that it was her mess, so it was the least she could do. Then there was the bedroom layout…it's a huge bedroom and they always had the bed in the middle of the room but for some reason the bed was pushed up against the wall that night…I thought it strange at the time. The girls had pulled the blood soaked bedding off the bed but the mattress was badly stained too, so I told them just to leave everything and we'd have a garden fire early in the morning - we'd collect it before everyone was knocking about. I'm wondering if Didi could have been between the wall and the bed... I think we probably have been mugs Ronnie, all of us.'

'Please don't tell me anymore Arthur, I can feel my chest tightening.'

'That's just the problem lad, there is more, I'm sure of it, quite a bit more.'

MARTHA'S CHILDHOOD

Chapter 22

The Rothbury tracks are all covered in mud,
but disturb the devil and they'll be covered in blood.
He lives in the moors, up in the mist,
waiting for a fare maid's neck to twist.

Seven year old Martha repeated the rhyme as she took a moment to play 'twosies' - bouncing two old balls against the farmyard wall of Gorfen Letch Farm. Life was so unfair, she thought to herself, her brothers got to do nice things, but not her. The boys were allowed to go to the local gathering, but not her... no, never her. Her dad said she had been touched by the devil as a baby and would never bring anything but trouble to their door and she had lived with this curse all of her short life. Her teacher at school had assured her it was all rubbish and told her that her dad was just ignorant for saying such things. When she had repeated this to her father, she had spent the night alone in the dog kennel, stripped naked and only with the three sheepdogs for company. It was so cold she thought she would die. She secretly wished she had died, then her dad would be in big bother - that would teach him.

Poor Martha always tried hard to please her father. At school she was by far the brightest child, even working on the farm she could keep up with her older brothers and sometimes even outdo them. All of her efforts still led her to live on the fringes of the family - she never felt part of it. Daily beatings and nights locked in cupboards or the dog kennels had just become accepted within the family - that's what you did with a 'child of the Devil'.

Martha stood looking in the only mirror in the house. She had dark gingery hair, coarse and wayward and if you parted her hair you could see her scalp was purple. Her teacher, Miss Dunlop, had told her it was a kind of birthmark, something called a port wine stain, nothing to worry about at all. But worry she did. It was the source of all that was wrong in her life. The rest of her wasn't bad, she had a pretty enough face and striking blue eyes and unlike her brothers, her skin would colour in the sun, making her look more healthy than her siblings. She always had a smattering of freckles across her nose but also the odd black eye, bruised arms from being grabbed and whip marks across her back - made with the bull's tether.

The teachers at her school suspected her father but Martha would tell them her injuries were caused by fighting with her brothers. Miss Dunlop, her favourite teacher, told her she was bright enough to go to the grammar school when she was twelve but only if she worked hard. Martha knew her father would never allow this, so she would have to come up with a plan before then - that's something she was really good at - making plans.

The only thing on young Martha's mind was getting to the summer gathering. All the local farmers and their families from the village of Thropton and the town of Rothbury would get together. There were livestock parades, fairground rides, 'hurdy gurdies', shooting games and lots of stalls with candy floss and other goodies. She was so excited. All her family were going but she had been told she had to stay behind to feed the animals…the sheep needed water out on the fells and her father's pride and joy, 'Rollo' the bull, needed walking in. He was an enormous beast of a bull but a gentle giant in nature. There was no doubt her father loved him more than her, as he had no mark of the devil for a start.

Martha had to work out a way of persuading her parents to let her go to the fair. Her mother might let her go but her father certainly wouldn't. She remembered the tin can on the very top shelf in the pantry, a little of that added to her father's food should work wonders. Her father would be in for breakfast soon and her mother was collecting eggs, so she got a chair, pulled it into the pantry and grabbed the old tin from high up on the shelf. The lid was difficult to remove, her little fingers not quite strong enough to get it open. She quickly put the tin on the bench, put the chair back in its place at the table and ran up to her room with the tin. With the help of her brother's knife she managed to prise the lid free to reveal the little pellets inside. She put a few in her handkerchief, then listened to hear if anyone was back in the house yet. She ran downstairs, putting the tin under her jumper. If she was caught it would have been obvious she had something hidden beneath her clothes.

'What you got there our Martha?' said her youngest brother, Billy.

He was lurking in the corridor outside the bedrooms. Martha always felt the little sneak was watching her every move. 'Nothing to do with you Billy Curry, you little rat.'

'Mam!' he squealed.

'Shut up Billy, it's a surprise for Mam, don't spoil it.'

'What is it then?'

'It's a cake, so keep your big trap shut.'

She somehow had to distract Billy so that she could get the tin back in its rightful place in the pantry. 'You can help,' she said enthusiastically.

His eyes grew bigger, 'OK,' he said.

'Go into the kitchen garden and get some of those pansies that are next to the path. You can put them around the cake to make it look pretty.'

He shot off, skinny legs appearing to go in different directions as he ran.

By the time Martha's mother came back into the house, the tin was back in its place and she was putting logs on the kitchen fire.

'Set the table Martha!' Never a please or a thank you but this time she set the table with pleasure. Her brain was in overdrive…should she put the grains in the posh jam or the first slice of bread? She decided for the first slice of thickly buttered bread as the children weren't allowed to eat before their father. Her handkerchief was up her sleeve so it was easy, her mother was too busy frying eggs to notice.

The kitchen started to fill up, the heat of the fire making everyone's cheeks shine red. Martha's scene was set, it was perfect. Then Billy, who'd already forgotten about collecting the pansies, reached for the slice of bread first. She looked to her father, who hadn't noticed but the arm of her mother reached over and slapped little Billy's greedy hand.

'Wait!'

Martha had purposefully put the biggest wedge of butter on this slice, knowing her entitled father would think this was his. Sure enough, the big grubby hand reached for the exact slice she had predicted. Martha was thrilled that her plan was coming together. He stopped chewing half way through and her breathing stopped. 'Where's that fancy jam?' Martha jumped out of her seat and pulled the jam off the dresser. He stared at her… she hoped he didn't have the power to read her mind.

Chapter 23

The Curry family lived in a beautiful part of Northumberland in the Coquet Valley, but it was harsh, especially in the winter when they were often cut off from the rest of the world. Gorfen Letch Farm consisted of two small farmers' cottages knocked into one, so there was enough space for their ever increasing family. The house had a paddock at the front of the property, which ran down to a large lake on the valley floor - it was their own swimming pool in the summer, even though the children would emerge covered in leeches. They would all spend the next ten minutes screeching and checking each other's bodies, picking off the black shiny leeches attached to their skin.

The house had a farmyard at the side where 'Rollo', their prize stud bull, was housed. There were lots of outbuildings - barns and byres, a paradise for the children to disappear into. The one place they were banned from and learnt never to go into was the grain store - and they took that ban very seriously. A girl at school had fallen into a grain store once and died - drowned in the grain. They didn't find her body until the sheep dogs started to pick up on the ghastly smell and began to fuss around the door to the store. Martha had already decided no matter how she died, she didn't want to smell like the dead animals she would find in the woods.

The nearest neighbours to Gorfen Letch Farm were the Foggo family, who lived in the neighbouring farmstead some two miles away, further up the Coquet Valley. The Foggos only had one son - unusual for a Northumbrian farming family. He was called 'Burt' and he was in Martha's class at school. He was different to the other children in the local school - in the winter he always had warm clothes and shoes - not like most who would turn up in the snow in little jackets and thin jumpers. He was big for his age too - stocky, well made, not at all like the skinny Curry children. His mam and dad were different to Martha's parents - they were warm and friendly and always greeted you with a smile. Martha had been to their farm several times on errands for her parents and each time she had cried on her way home, comparing her life with that of Burt and realising just how bad her life actually was. She wanted to stay at the Foggo home so, so badly. Burt's mother was a large lady with a pretty face who embraced you in the most miraculous cuddle ever. Martha had never felt anything like it before. She felt like she disappeared into the warmth and security of this ruddy cheeked, soft bodied woman.

It was obvious, even to eleven year old Martha, that Mrs Foggo had wanted more children, especially a daughter. She made such a huge fuss over Martha and the young girl lapped up every ounce of this affection, which was so obviously missing in her own family.

She would lie in her bed at night plotting how she could go and live at West Forest Farm with the Foggos and last winter she saw her chance. Rollo the bull had managed to get out of his pen and wander off. It was snowing heavily and they needed to get him indoors. He was her father's pride and joy and made money being hired out to stud. Martha had spotted him earlier in the kitchen garden behind the sheds but seeing her chance to abscond, she pushed her coat on and shouted 'I'll go and check the top field!'

Their top field connected their pastures to those of West Forest Farm. By the time she got to the farm's boundary the snow was bleaching down and lying heavy on the freezing cold ground. The wind was starting to whip up through the valley. She could no longer run as the snow was drifting up the hill and accumulating deep around her wellies. She could see faint lights at the Foggos' farmhouse shining through the blizzard, so she headed that way. In parts, the drifting snow was now around two feet deep and she was starting to wish she had turned back, scared she wasn't going to make it. But Martha was built of sturdy stuff and her determination kept her going. Mary Foggo knew nothing until she heard a light tap on the kitchen door, which caught her attention.

'Jesus, Mary and Joseph!' Mary cried out, when she saw the state of the little thin girl standing soaking wet and covered in snow at her door.

Martha stood there, wellington boots far too big for her, glowing red knees open to the elements and wearing a thin grey cotton dress underneath an old coat. The coat had seen better days, even when her mum presented it to her. It had been gifted to her by one of the neighbours who was throwing it out.

'Oh my dear!' Mary cried, throwing a warm towel from the hearth around her. Martha immediately started to relax, her plan had worked - she was now in a safe and warm place. Her knees were stinging in pain with the drastic change in temperature. Burt came flying down the stairs, alerted by his mother's cries. He stopped when he saw the bedraggled girl - his school friend, standing on the clicky mat, dripping water everywhere.

'Burt, run and get the big towel from my bedroom, will you son?' He ran back up the stairs and returned with a huge white towel. Martha was scared when she saw how white the towel was - she knew she'd dirty it. If you rubbed her too much she'd leave dirty marks on the lovely white fabric.

The towel was placed around her head so she looked like she was wearing a big cape. 'Them wet clothes are going to have to come off pet, you'll never warm up with them on.' Martha's eyes swung immediately to Burt, who's face turned puce.

'Never mind about him pet, he's going to go and get you some dry clothes. Right lad, go into the chest of drawers in the spare room and fetch a few of my old nightdresses, the smaller the better and get some of your old jumpers out and we'll see if one of them will fit, OK pet?' Martha smiled, overjoyed at the attention she was receiving.

By the time Burt came back, his little school friend looked altogether more human. She was now burning pink - he thought she looked much healthier than she had for ages.

The girl with the titian hair was dry by the time Burt's father came in from ensuring the animals were all locked up safe in the barns.

'Holey, Moley! What have we got here then?'

'It's one of the Curry children - said she was looking for that bull of theirs in the top field when the snow kicked in. She saw our lights on after getting lost in the blizzard and headed here.'

'Your dad's going to be mighty worried about you, young lady. You shouldn't have been out in this weather - no place for little girls.'

'No, he won't,' she answered matter of factly. 'As long as Rollo is OK, he'll be just fine. He doesn't worry about me, none of them do.'

Both adults looked at each other and raised their eyebrows before turning to Martha, smiling at her sympathetically. They had heard from Burt that she was developing into a feisty lass but they already suspected that life for the young girl at Gorfen Letch wasn't easy. Living amongst all those boys would be difficult and they knew that Ernie Curry was notorious for being a bit quick with the fists.

'You're still going to have to get news to them Albert, I'm sure they'll be wondering where she is,' said Mary.

'You're joking lass, I wouldn't even get a hundred yards in this, it's drifting so bad with that wind blowing out of the north. It's whipping through the valley at about a hundred miles an hour.'

'They'll be going spare Albert.'

'They're just going to have to, there's nothing I can do about it tonight.'

'Honestly, don't worry, I've been missing before and they didn't even notice I wasn't there. They'll think I've just sheltered in with the animals.'

'Not all night pet, I'm telling you they'll miss you at bedtime.'

'Honestly, I've been out all night quite a few times… slept in the barn with the cows, then I'm sometimes in with the dogs… so, you see, they'll just think I'm around the farm.'

Mary looked at Albert knitting her dark eyebrows together, both trying to believe what the child was relaying to them.

Martha spent two blissful nights in the spare room of West Forest Farm, whilst the blizzard continued to rage. She would sit and stare at her surroundings, her mind being blown by the fact that there were sheets on the bed, white, lilac and light blue striped ones at that. A beautiful soft pillow cradled her head and a hot water bottle kept her feet warm. She knew she had to come up with a plan to come and live at this farm with the Foggos. She could be their servant, she could work on the farm, she could teach Burt his schooling - she knew she would be an asset to have around. Although Burt was a year older than her, it was Martha who was always top of the class or winning all the local school competitions. She was regularly tasked with helping other children and had often helped Burt with his spelling and grammar.

Her adventure ended thirty six hours later when Albert Foggo announced that the blizzard had subsided and although the snow was still deep in parts, he thought he could get her home. They reached a point where she thought he might not manage but he and Burt, who insisted on coming too, had managed to dig through the drift. Eventually, all three were at the door of Gorfen Letch and the experience ended with a crack over the head from her father and him explaining to a rather concerned looking Albert that she had the devil inside her.

Chapter 24

It was the morning of the Rothbury Gathering - the best day of the year for the locals who lived in the Coquet Valley. The fairground was coming to town and there would be animals for sale, prizes for the best farm stock, vegetable shows and lots of stalls containing home produce for sale.

Martha was watching her father eating his breakfast of bread and butter, laced with her special grains. She had hidden them in the big chunks of soft, freshly baked bread. Large lumps of butter were melting on the still warm bread and she was entranced, eyes fixed as the stupid, greedy man was pushing it into his mouth as quick as he could. She sat watching the fat dripping down the corner of his mouth - *'may God forgive you your sins, you ignorant man'* she thought, with some relish. She decided to follow him around today, watch her 'long thought out' plan come to fruition - he deserved everything he got and she knew she was doing the right thing - anyone would do the same.

'That bloody breakfast is causing me some bloody gyp woman!' he said about an hour later, as he trundled into the kitchen after yet another visit to the 'netty' outside. The Foggos' had an inside toilet but they still had to brave the weather to do their ablutions. 'The taste in my mouth is awful, are you sure that yeast was alright, it's paining me something rotten?'

'Well, me and the bairns are alright, it's only you who's ill, the lads finished off the loaf – look.' Nancy Curry was becoming a little concerned at her husband's ashen face, but more worried that she would get a slap for making him ill.

He glowered straight at Martha as if he knew everything she had done. She stared straight back without blinking, although inside she was panicking, her heart racing. She returned his fixed gaze with a sweet smile, making him glare at her further - smiling at her father sometimes made him even more bad tempered.

The plan had worked and by ten o'clock that morning her father had taken to his bed, with her mother fussing about him. 'What about the gathering?' Nancy said.

'Well, I can hardly go like this, can I, shitting every ten minutes? You've done this to me with your sloppy cooking woman, or that little devil child of yours is trying to see me off. She grinned at me like the devil itself - I don't trust her Nance, honest, she's up to something - I can just tell.'

'Don't be ridiculous Ernie.' She was simply trying to pacify him but knew she had chosen her words badly.

'Don't tell me I'm ridiculous woman, I'm telling you that lass is as crafty as a bitch fox! We should have drowned her at birth!'

'Ernie, may God forgive you!' Although she chastised her husband for his thoughts, Nancy Curry didn't quite trust her eleven year old daughter either. She was far too clever, much cleverer than any of the boys and she could never quite work out what the lass was thinking. The boys were easy to read - but Martha was different, completely different.

'The bairns can go to the gathering,' Ernie grimaced, fighting another bout of stomach cramps, 'but not that little heathen, she's staying on the farm, there's work to be done - the hens need cleaning out - set her to it!'

Martha was listening at the door. This was anticipated, she needed to implement the second part of her plan. When the boys came in from their chores, their mother told them that they'd be going to the gathering on their own. The two oldest ones smiled, thinking they might even get some beer this year.

'You must look after the younger ones mind, that's the deal.'

Martha danced around the kitchen with pretend joy.

'I'm afraid you won't be going Martha.'

'But why? I haven't done anything wrong! I'm top of the class at school, I always do my chores and I look after Rollo and keep him company.' Her eyes were now filling with huge tears.

Nancy looked at her only daughter, a daughter she had longed for until the very day she actually got Martha. Still, the child had a point, there was nothing obvious to punish her for. She'd actually prefer for her not to be around so she'd get her to clean out the hens when she got back.

'OK, you can go, but don't tell your father, any of you.' Martha always knew she could sometimes get around her mother. It was easier to get into her head and mash it up a little. She had, over the past few days, asked her mother lots of questions that she knew her mother would not be able to answer. She was relentless, she knew this irritated her mother and that it would make her hate having the little girl around. She could get into her father's head sometimes but she didn't like even going there. She knew her father hated her with an absolute passion and he'd snap way quicker than her mother. Her dad was best avoided.

The spring gathering was everything Martha had hoped it would be - there were stalls, rides and lots of games. She had managed to accumulate a small amount of money, some found ages ago and hidden in her room and some stolen from her mother. Her brothers got the blame as it coincided with one of their nights drinking - Martha had planned it that way. Her dumb brothers were like lambs to the slaughter.

One stall at the fair was just books, rows and rows of them. Martha's eyes grew when she saw 'The Secret Garden'. She asked the portly, rather posh lady behind the stall how much it was. It was far too expensive for her, so she held it for a while longer, stroking the cover longingly and brought the necessary and well practiced tears to her blue eyes.

'How much money have you got darling?' asked the stall holder.

'I only have two thrupenny bits, it's all my mam could afford to give me,' she said, before she brought the tears forward again. She stroked the book for good measure and placed it back on the stall and turned to walk away. One pace, two, three... she wasn't going to cave - *the old bitch wasn't going to bend,* she thought - she'd remember her alright. She then heard a shuffling behind her, 'here, little girl,' she shouted, handing her a brown paper bag. 'Keep your money pet' she said. *'What a sweet old lady'* Martha thought, so kind, she'd remember her forever.

Martha now had enough money to go on some of the rides, she was thrilled. After the rides she realised she hadn't seen her brothers almost the whole time she had been at the fair, not even her younger brother Billy, who she was supposed to be watching out for. If they all trundled home drunk without young Billy there'd be big bother. She headed to the beer tent and as predicted there they were, her three elder brothers outside, 'three sheets to the wind' and her little brother nowhere in sight.

'Where's Billy?' she eventually had to shout through their stupor.

'Doing the little job we set him, he's in the tent.'

She hated to think what they had Billy doing. He was under the large beer table, which was covered in a huge white cloth. His job was to watch for really drunk people and steal their beer when they were distracted. Then the boys would get to drink the remnants of someone's pint. It worked and by the end of the afternoon her brothers were drunk, so drunk she worried how she would get them all home.

The journey back to Gorfen Letch involved her middle brothers both throwing up every five minutes and Joe meandering all over the lane. Martha was hoping that her elder brother Joe, who was supposed to be taking care of his younger siblings, would sober up before they got home. She wondered how her father had fared with the rat poison. She hadn't put too much in, just in case he detected it. She was new to poisoning but knew she'd have to slowly increase the dose. But she needn't have worried, it had all gone to plan, her father was still in bed writhing in agony and she had simply had the best day ever.

Chapter 25

Whilst at school, Martha had been told by Miss Dunlop that poor Jewish people in Europe were being 'targeted.' She explained that a politician called Hitler was trying to 'eradicate' the Jewish population. Martha liked the word 'eradicate' - she rolled it around in her mouth... *'errrr.. a.. di.. cate'*. She pondered to herself how the word sounded so much kinder than the word 'murdered', as to her a murderer was someone who was out of control, but to eradicate someone demonstrated an absolute necessity to get rid of them. She had that need inside her, a need to eradicate, just like this man Hitler.

The rat poison had worked in keeping her father away from her for short periods of time. She had no 'punishings' for weeks but it was getting risky. The doctor had been called and she heard him ask her dad if he had been using any chemicals and not washing his hands. He even asked about rat poison. Did they use it on the farm?' he had said. Her father's beady eyes had followed her around after the visit, as if he knew, or at least suspected what she was doing, so she needed a different course of action. She needed an entirely different eradication plan.

She had decided that Rollo, the family bull, was going to play a major role in her new plan. She had been spending so much time with the amiable beast that she felt she could anticipate his every move. He was such a gentle giant. The only time she ever saw him buck or thrash around was when his 'privates' came into contact with stinging nettles in the field. Nettles made him simply lose his mind, he'd jump around like an idiot until the stinging ceased.

She would have to wait a few months before her plan could be put into action though, as she needed her second eldest brother to reach the age of sixteen, so they were more likely to be able to keep the lease on the farm after her father died. Plus, she needed the nettles to be in season and at their very best. She ran every detail of the plan through her head whilst in bed. It was the last thing she thought about at night and the first thing she thought about in the morning. She'd stand in the barn as Rollo was fed and groomed, then when her father was in the perfect position between Rollo and the barn brick wall, she imagined sneaking forward, unnoticed, with stinging nettles in her gloved hand.

The only person who knew or cared about what her father did to her was her friend Burt Foggo and perhaps his mam and dad, who she knew had their suspicions. Burt had rescued her on more than one occasion when she had been locked in the dog kennels. She sometimes wished he hadn't bothered, as she was always stripped naked and totally embarrassed. The first time he had given her his coat to hide her embarrassment and then taken her back to his mam and dad's farm. They had no idea what to do as their son relayed the awful story to them. Ernie Curry was a formidable character to accuse of such crimes, especially when they only had their thirteen year old son's word for it. Burt had told them that Martha's dad touched her in a way a father shouldn't. They were so shocked they asked no further questions. It was unbelievable to them - things like that didn't happen in their world. It became the norm that Burt would skulk around Gorfen Letch before bed, to ensure Martha wasn't tied up by the neck, just like the sheepdogs.

Martha learnt how to love someone from watching the Foggos' with their son. She watched Burt's mam cuddle him for no reason at all, and how he responded to that. His dad would ruffle up his hair and say 'that's me lad', even after a simple task. She wanted that sort of life too. Why did she belong to the Currys? They made it clear they didn't want her. She wasn't sure they really cared that much for any of their children, except when they could help them with the work around the farm or in the kitchen.

Over the last few weeks, Martha had watched her mother's belly begin to swell, yet again. She knew the signs now but she had lost the last two babies. Martha secretly hoped she'd lose this one too. When her youngest brother Billy was born, life was much harder for her as she had to look after him.

She knew her mother was hoping for a daughter this time, a proper one, not another 'Devil's child' like her. She watched as her mother's wish slowly came to fruition when her little sister was born. They called her Julia but her nickname was 'Dolly' because she was beautiful, like a little china doll. Dolly brought great conflict into Martha's life. Martha thought she loved her and hated her all at the same time - she was confused by her feelings. She loved babies but this baby brought so much joy to her mother and even her otherwise emotionless father, that it was hard to watch. But she was also protective of her little sister and she knew for definite now that her eradication plan had to be soon. She had felt so unwell lately that at one stage she thought her father was using rat poison on her now, but when her belly started to swell, she knew what was happening. She too was now going to have a baby. She had watched her mother in the months she was expecting Billy, the dead babies and then Dolly. She remembered the baby that was almost fully grown, the one that died in a hot bath. She knew how it had died because she was eavesdropping at the door and heard the midwife tell her mother it was for the best. *Sometimes*, she thought, *death was for the best.*

Martha didn't quite know how the baby got there but suspected it was her father's 'punishing.' She couldn't see what he was doing because she was pushed face down onto the ground and then just felt immense pain. But she had watched Rollo enough time with the cows to suspect what was going on.

This had to be a secret, she knew that much. Twelve year old girls didn't have babies. Even Burt couldn't guess this secret. When the baby was born she'd hide it until she had eradicated her father, then bring it back to the house. She knew she could potentially get around her mother and elder brothers.

She managed to hide the bump although it was more difficult at school. The bump though wasn't actually that big - nothing like the size of her mother. Then one night the pains started and she needed to get up onto the moors, out of the way of prying eyes. It was a warm night, muggy even and she knew exactly where she was going to give birth. She headed up to the two stones in the heather and gorse as it was far enough away so they wouldn't hear her scream. Her mother would scream, so she knew what to expect. Martha hadn't anticipated how hard the journey up there was going to be and she felt utterly exhausted. Every few minutes she was falling to the ground in agony. When she eventually made it to her secret place, she sank onto the heather between the stones, as if they were protecting her.

The pains kept coming, faster and harder and she was moaning, trying her best not to scream. It seemed to go on for much longer than her mam's pains. She then froze as she heard someone coming, footsteps crunching through the heather nearby, and then a figure blocked out the moonlight. Her heart raced, at first thinking it was her father who had followed her, but as they knelt down next to her and spoke with a caring voice, she realised it was Burt Foggo.

'You can't tell anyone about this Burt,' she begged. 'No one, not even your mam and dad. Promise me Burt, promise me!'

'But you're ill, you're going to die if we don't get you help, you're in pain, I can see you're in pain. I checked the dog kennel when I didn't see you at the farm. I searched everywhere, then I thought I'd better check up here.'

'I'm not ill Burt, I'm having a bairn!'

'Na, you're too young to have a bairn, you can't be!'

Martha was screaming in agony. 'You're going to have to help Burt! You help your dad during lambing, don't you?'

'Ya joking! It's not the bloody same thing Martha,' he said, panicking.

'It is, it's exactly the same, help me Burt - please!'

Martha had managed to get her hands on some leaflets from the doctor's surgery in Rothbury that explained about birthing babies.

'Can you see the head Burt?' she asked, directing him to look up her dress.

He closed his eyes, pink and embarrassed. 'Stop Martha, stop!'

'Oh for God's sake Burt!' She started to scream again and he did what he was told.

Now fascinated, Burt shouted 'it's coming Martha! It's coming, I think I can see the top of its head!'

'When the pains start again I'm going to try and push it out.' It wasn't long before the pain did kick in again. 'Have a look what's happening Burt.'

After a few minutes and several bouts of contractions, Burt shouted 'Oh my God Martha, the head's out!'

'Right,' she said, 'you're going to gently pull the head on the next lot of pains, it should come out.' She was panting, terrified at what was to come next.

But she was right, the next push and the baby was out. Burt had wrapped it in the towel she'd brought and it was crying. Martha told Burt the well rehearsed plan for cutting the umbilical cord and that they had to wait for the after birth to come out. Martha was spent, all her energy gone. The baby was tiny, much smaller than her sister Dolly and now it was totally silent. She looked down, noticing even in the light of the moon that something was wrong… the baby's lips looked blue.

'Burt!' she shouted, handing him the bundle, 'it's not breathing!' He grabbed the baby in panic and started to swing it in his arms. He then started to pat its back but nothing was working.

'I can't Martha... I can't do anything, it's not breathing, nothing's working, it's gone, it's just too small.' Martha hadn't even considered what sex it was.

'What is it - a boy or a girl?'

'It's a girl,' Burt said, his face wet with tears, shining in the light of the full moon.

Chapter 26

The moonlight shone on the sad scene of a dead baby and two confused children trying to deal with a situation no child should have to.

'I know one thing about giving birth,' said Burt, 'the afterbirth is going to have to come out. Look, stand up, see if that helps.' He had one arm around her and with the other was gently pushing her tummy. It eventually worked and the afterbirth came away. She flopped back down on the heather, totally exhausted and fell asleep whilst Burt watched over her. Then, on the other side of the small stone he pulled the heather back and using his bare hands and with the help of a sharp stone he found nearby, he started to dig into the earth.

It was difficult at first as the peaty ground was fibrous but it soon became more manageable. The hole was deep by the time Martha was fully awake. Burt had put a layer of grass at the bottom of the grave. She slowly passed her daughter to him and he gently laid the tiny child on a bed of green. He put the old worn towel over the beautiful little face and then filled in the hole.

By the time Burt was finished you couldn't see anything untoward. He had even tried to replant the heather over the grave and found some small boulders to lay on top to stop any animals digging.

'This needs to be our secret Burt, if anyone found out they'd take me away and I don't want to go. God only knows where they'd take me.'

'I think it would be better for you if you weren't at Gorfen Letch Martha. If we tell Mam and Dad I'm sure they could help.'

'Don't worry Burt, it isn't going to happen again, I can promise you that. With the best will in the world I don't think your mam and dad could do anything. Dad just doesn't listen to anyone.'

Burt knew for certain now how the baby got in her belly and he felt sick at the very thought.

'How are we going to get you home without anyone noticing?'

'You don't need to worry too much about that, I let Rollo out so that they'd know I was out looking for him.'

'Why don't you come back to my house for breakfast, I could tell Mam you've been up all night looking for the bull and it's made you poorly?'

'What about my clothes, is there blood on them?' She shakily stood up, turning around and letting him inspect her.

'Only on the front there, where I laid the bairn. But it could be anything. I could run in and get you one of my jumpers to wear if you like?'

'No, that's OK. I doubt anyone would be able to work out what had happened from that anyway, it could be food or even chicken blood for that matter.'

The trek to West Forest was hard for Martha. She was in awful pain down below but didn't want to tell Burt in case he wanted to carry her. They eventually got there with Mary Foggo fussing about her as soon as she walked through the door.

'Why child, you look fit to drop, what on earth is wrong?' she said, glancing at Burt for an explanation.

Burt explained that Martha had been out all night searching for Rollo, their bull and how he had been helping her since the early hours. Thankfully, they hadn't noticed that Burt had been out all night as well.

Mary Foggo knew this child was sick, really sick. She could see it. Her skin was unusually pale, she was glistening with the heat and she had a definite tinge of blue around her mouth. 'I think I should call the doctor pet,' Mary said. Both Burt and Martha both said in unison 'no, don't do that.'

'Please Mam, Martha's dad will kill her for being out all night and he'll blame her for the bull getting out in the first place. Come on Mam you know what Ernie Curry is like, he'll whip her real good. We've come up with a plan.'

Mary looked at them both suspiciously. She knew this wasn't going to be Burt's idea, her son didn't usually come up with plans to deceive.

'Aye, and what's that then?'

'I'll run over to the farm and tell them she hurt her ankle searching for Rollo last night and she can't walk. I'll help Mr Curry with the bull and even Martha's chores, if necessary. This gives Martha time to pull herself together.'

Mary looked at them both suspiciously. There was a lot more to this story than these two were telling her but she reluctantly agreed.

'Right lass, let's get you undressed and into bed and we'll get some food into you.'

'Please, I'd like to get undressed myself if that's OK?'

Mary's eyes perused Martha, and Martha knew exactly what she was thinking. Ernie Curry was known for using his fists, it was surely bruising that was being hidden.

When Burt came back from the farm, Martha was hanging on his every word. 'Your dad wasn't bothered,' he said, 'Rollo was in the barn when he got up but the door was open, so he knew he'd probably been out.' *Rollo, the clever old bull, must have gone back of his own accord*, thought Martha. 'He didn't even want me to do your chores,' continued Burt, 'he said one of the lads would pick up the work. He did say as long as she's back to school on Monday when it starts up again. So you've got four days to get your strength back.'

'Four days staying here,' Martha said with glee, 'are your mam and dad OK with that?'

'You know my mother, she loves having another lass about the place.'

Martha relaxed in the big feather bed, feeling the clean sheets and smelling the clear air. She had been well fed and watered, but still in pain. Burt had fetched her some old rags to put under herself in case she was still bleeding. But she was the most comfortable she could possibly be and she drifted off into a perfect sleep.

Martha knew nothing until Mary Foggo woke her. 'Come on pet, it's getting near tea time, you're gonna have to eat something.' She must have been asleep for ages, she thought. Mary gave her a tray and on it was a bowl of lamb broth, thick with lamb, pearl barley and vegetables with two slices of homemade bread, thickly spread with butter. Every spoonful of broth had a piece of lamb in, not like her mam's soup - that was more like one tiny slither of lamb per bowl.

Mary came up later and took the empty bowl away and replaced it with a piece of Victoria sponge cake. Martha felt like it was her birthday and this was just the start of her four days. *This was how life was meant to be*, she thought.

Chapter 27

The days of bliss at West Forest Farm came to a crashing and abrupt end. It was Sunday afternoon and Burt had been given the job of walking Martha back home, their pace slowing the nearer they got to Gorfen Letch. Emotions were running high.

'I don't want to go back Burt,' she said, tears welling in her eyes. She hated to cry but she was completely overwhelmed with a feeling of pure dread and sorrow.

'I know pet, but you've just got to. My mam did try, honest she did, she went down to the farm to speak to your mam and dad about keeping you at West Forest to help her around the house. But your dad said you were needed to look after your baby sister and insisted you return immediately. He was nasty with her too.'

'I knew it would be him that would stop it, my mam couldn't care less, but he takes great pleasure in punishing me and making my life a misery.'

They both looked at each other, Burt feeling her pain and understanding her hatred towards her father. He was nothing but a monster in Burt's eyes.

They stood at the kitchen door, hesitant to go in. Martha took a deep breath, turned the handle and went inside. Two of Martha's brothers and her mother were seated in the kitchen, her mother nursing Dolly. No-one spoke to the in-comers or even raised their head, it was almost like they didn't exist. Burt got a taste of what it was like to be Martha.

Eventually the silence broke. 'Ya back then?' her mother said, stating the obvious.

'Yes, I'm back.'

'I think your mam and dad wanted to keep her Burt. I told them she's trouble that girl, you'll have her a few weeks and then you'll realise she's an evil little madam.' Nancy Curry glared at her daughter. Martha suspected that her father had been planting more unkind information into her mother's head when she had been away, as her mother was not usually quite this cruel, just neglectful. 'Your dad wants you here to help, he says you have it too good at the Foggos' farm.'

Martha glanced at Burt and she could see his eyes filling up with tears, he was such a sensitive soul. He was often teased at school for being a 'cry baby'.

'Come on' she said to him, grabbing his arm. 'I'll show you Rollo,' hoping she'd get him out before the floodgates opened.

'Ah man Burt, don't cry for me, I'm as hard as nails really. Don't think anything that stupid woman says hurts me at all, I just pity her ignorance. Miss Dunlop says it's just stupid ignorance saying that I'm the Devil's child.'

'But she's horrible, she's your mam, she's supposed to look out for you. She's supposed to love you no matter what.'

Martha looked at her friend, her only friend, the only person who she thought just might understand her. Should she tell him about her plan, her 'eradication plan'? *Probably not* she thought. *He's too soft hearted to understand that some people just have to die, just so that others may live.*

'Eradication' had to happen soon. She was still in pain down there and the thought of her father's punishments made her shudder with terror. Her mother was so wrapped up in looking after the new baby - the beautiful Julia, that she knew her father would come looking for her soon. She knew Burt had worked out exactly what was happening to her, but wasn't sure he fully understood the 'punishings', his mam and dad protected him somewhat from real life.

Tomorrow was going to be the day. Before school she'd go along to early morning feed and when Rollo got his first morning brush down she'd do it. She hated using poor Rollo in her plan, but needs must. She didn't sleep all that night in excitement. She had already found the patch of nettles, all she had to do was grab a bunch and stick them under Rollo when her dad was standing beside him next to the barn wall.

She heard her mother cleaning out the stove to get breakfast ready. She put on her school uniform and slipped out the back door. She put socks on her hands and grabbed a few long stems of nettles. When her father came into the barn, she was stroking Rollo and giving him a handful of freshly picked green grass. 'What you up to you little demon?'

'Just giving Rollo some grass, he likes it – see,' she said, handing him more.

Her father got a bucket of feed and placed it before the animal, pushing Martha hard out of the way.

Martha made her way to the dark corner of the barn whilst her father brushed the great beast. He was in the perfect place. She grabbed the nettles, came forward out of the darkness and stuck them under Rollo. Instantaneously he bucked and smashed into the wall on his right hand side, pinning Ernie Curry against the wall, pushing all the air out of the man's chest until Martha saw red trickling from his mouth. His eyes glazed over, like a doll's. He looked her way as if he knew what she had done. She smiled sweetly back, knowing that this would hopefully be the last time she ever saw that evil face again. Her plan had worked better than she could ever have imagined. It was one hell of a push the bull gave him, she just prayed he couldn't recover from it. She watched as her father slid down the wall. For good measure and by God's own grace, Rollo trampled over him, stamping his big hooves down hard on her father's chest.

She ran out of the byre, put the nettles back where they came from and went inside for her breakfast, smoothing herself down to bring back her composure.

'Where's ya dad?'

'He's giving Rollo a good rub down. I think Rollo knows he's going in with the cows soon, as he's a bit more frisky than normal,' she added, planting the seed.

Dirty looking scrambled eggs were dropped in front of her. She ate heartily, her appetite for her mother's offerings returning for the first time since the baby was born. Her only hope now was that he was dead, she prayed he was or she'd be in big bother. He looked dead to her but she wanted to be well on her way to school when her father was found. She didn't want to be number one suspect - as usual.

School was really interesting. Miss Dunlop taught them about Red Indians. Martha had already worked out that her teacher had a thing about 'underdogs' and she was currently manoeuvring herself into that very position, not that she had to try very hard. Daughter of a poor farmer and abused - she always made sure Miss Dunlop caught a glimpse of her bruises and injuries. She had considered going to her teacher when the baby was in her belly but Martha thought she could lose control and end up somewhere she really didn't want to be.

She was practicing her 'upset' face when Miss Dunlop came up to her in the school yard. 'You look a little down in the dumps Martha, are you OK?'

'No Miss, I'm fine, just thinking about all those poor Red Indians, they really didn't have much of a chance against all those people coming into America, did they?'

'No Martha, they surely didn't.' She paused for a second. 'Martha, I have some books here I'd like you to work through tonight, they're what we call intelligence tests. There's two books and I'd like you to spend one hour on each, do you think you'll be able to do that?'

'Yes, no problem. I'd love that.'

'I'll give you a note for your parents if you like.'

'No Miss, no need, I'll do them after my chores and before bed, they won't even know.'

'That's fine, but I do think you should tell your parents about it.' Martha smiled and nodded. 'Good girl,' she said, touching the child's freckled cheek.

What a day, thought Martha, it looked like she had finally got rid of the evil bastard and now Miss Dunlop was priming her for her 11+ exam. Life really couldn't get any sweeter but if her plan didn't work she knew she'd have to run, move from Gorfen Letch and leave her family behind. Not even West Forest Farm would be a safe haven.

Chapter 28

At lunchtime, Martha's eldest brother Joe turned up at the infants' school, asking that Martha and Billy be allowed to return home immediately. There had been an accident of some kind. Martha felt pleased when the message was repeated by Miss Dunlop, specifically that the teacher had used the word 'accident'. Everything was so far going to plan. Billy was removed from his class and Martha took his little hand and said 'come on rat face, we better get home to see what's going on.'

'What do you think's happened?' he asked, looking all worried.' Do you think the baby has died?'

'No, don't worry, I'm sure the baby is fine.'

He stared at her with huge eyes. 'Actually, I'm not that keen on the baby, it just screams all the time and Mam hardly lifts her head from it.'

Martha smiled at her little brother and ruffled his hair, just like she had seen Mr Foggo do. 'You're a strange little rat, aren't you?' she was actually pleased her little brother didn't care that much for the baby.

There were a few neighbours in the farmyard when they got back. Her eyes fell first on Mr Foggo, who gave her a little sad smile when she arrived back.

Joe shouted for them to get into the house.

The kitchen was full of women. Martha's mother was sitting with Julia on her knee, eyes red and bloodshot. 'What's going to happen to us now?' she kept repeating, rocking the child in her arms.

'What's happened?' Martha asked. The kitchen went quiet as the two children entered.

'That bloody stupid bull of yours has squashed ya dad to death. Looks like he pinned him up against the wall. We're going to have the beast shot,' her mother said venomously. This was not in Martha's plan, she hadn't even thought that they'd actually shoot poor Rollo.

'No, you can't shoot him, he's worth too much money. He's the best stud bull in the area.'

'He's a killer, he can't be controlled, are ya not bothered about ya poor dad, you little minx, only about that damned bull? Ya dad was right about you, evil you are, evil.'

Everyone in the room was silent, watching the strange proceedings taking place. Martha felt hot as all eyes fell on her. She thought the only thing she could do was cry.

'I'm sorry,' she said, wiping the tears away, 'of course I'm bothered about poor Dad, but shooting Rollo won't bring him back, will it?'

Martha ran out of the kitchen towards the byre, tears streaming down her face. 'Joe... Joe, you can't have him shot, he's worth too much to us.' She ran to Rollo. 'Look' she said, walking underneath him, ending up between him and the wall, exactly where she'd earlier watched her father crushed to death. The farmers looked on in horror, fearing she'd go the same way as her dad if she wasn't careful.

'Joe, be sensible, you know how gentle he is. Dad must have really spooked him.'

Joe eventually spoke out, 'she's right, he's the gentlest bull we've ever had, not a bad bone in his body.'

'Ya missing the point lad, once they've killed you can't have that trust in them again' replied one of the farmers.

Then Mr Foggo came into the conversation, 'the bull here helps pay the bills, without it they'd struggle. He's too good a stud to just get rid of him.' He looked towards Martha and smiled.

Martha felt everything shift after Mr Foggo spoke. 'Aye, ya right but they're gonna have to be careful with it' muttered another. Martha relaxed as the general consensus of opinion had shifted. Rollo was to live.

It wasn't long before young Burt arrived at the house too. He'd be in big trouble if he had sneaked out of school, thought Martha, when she spotted him skulking near the barn. In fact he had explained to Miss Dunlop how his mam and dad would be helping at Gorfen Letch Farm and that he was probably needed there too. Miss Dunlop had let him go.

Martha told Burt exactly what had happened. She took him into the byre and showed him the very spot where Rollo had slammed his massive body into her father.

'I was so upset, I thought they were going to kill Rollo, but your dad stepped in to help Burt, he was fantastic.' She kissed the bull on his shoulder. Burt looked at her inquisitively and she noticed straight away he suspected something. She knew exactly what he was thinking. 'Poor Dad,' she said quickly, 'not a good way to go, was it?' demonstrating what she knew she should actually be feeling.

As the pair left the farmyard, Burt turned his head towards the nettle clump at the entrance to the yard - lots of healthy nettles and a few strands of wilted nettles in the centre, like they had been picked and then pushed back into place. Martha noticed and wondered if he had guessed what she had done. He looked down and kept walking, so she presumed not.

The funeral took place three days later at the Church of All Saints in Thropton. Her dad's family attended, most of whom she'd never even seen before. Her paternal uncles and aunts came and even her eighty year old grandmother, a woman she had never clapped eyes on in her life. Her dad's family all had one thing in common, they all completely ignored Martha, just like she didn't exist. Her brothers and baby sister were remarked upon, 'isn't he like our Sam', 'isn't she pretty', 'he's got his grandfather's nose…,' but none even glanced in Martha's direction. She knew it was because they believed she had been touched by the devil - they had all been told in advance. She remembered what Miss Dunlop had said and recounted to herself that they were an ignorant family, probably couldn't even read or write.

During the 'after funeral tea' at the farm, she stayed with Burt and her younger brother Billy. Joe was now the new master of the house and he was enjoying his new role. It only took a couple of days before the transformation into a younger version of her father had taken place. He was now free from his father's dominance, ready to create his own domain but Martha's punishments had stopped. She may not be treated quite as well as the others but she could cope with that, just so long as her dad's filthy hands were consigned to history.

Her 'eradication' plan had worked. The two elder boys had been allowed to keep the tenancy for a trial period, just to make sure it would work out. She knew it would, as Joe was a much better farmer than her dad ever was. Her father was stuck in the old ways but Joe was willing to learn and try new things.

Now all she had to do was get a place at grammar school and her master plan would come into fruition. She knew Miss Dunlop would be even more supportive now she was fatherless. *What a lovely word* she thought to herself, *'fatherless', nearly as good as 'eradication'.* She looked into the bedroom mirror and practiced her very sad face.

Chapter 29

School was always Martha's number one priority, her safe place and her means of an escape from a life of poverty. But she was aware of always hiding her devil's mark from the other pupils at school. It was mainly hidden on her scalp but a small part eked out onto her neck. Wearing her hair in a very loose ponytail covered the small part on her neck and usually the thickness of her hair rendered the rest invisible.

Her father's death had transformed her into a top class actress. Just the mention of the word 'father' in class would make her big blue eyes fill with tears and spill over, always just as Miss Dunlop came into view, pulling at the heart strings of the young teacher. Martha soon began to learn that this ability was worth its weight in gold.

The lovely Miss Dunlop asked her to stay behind after school one afternoon, just to go over her reading for that week. Martha suspected something was amiss and felt a little nervous as she sat there waiting as the rest of the pupils piled out of class.

'Martha, I have something for you,' she said, handing her a big brown paper parcel, tied neatly with string. 'When you get home you must tell your mother that these were my younger sister's clothes and that she had outgrown them, is that understood?'

'Are they for me to wear?' Martha asked.

'Open it and see.'

Martha opened the large parcel with vigour. Inside was a blue skirt, two white blouses, a striped blue and yellow tie, blue beret and some shoes, the likes of which Martha had never possessed in her life. Martha was known for just wearing either wellies or an old pair of very scuffed lace up boots, given to her by one of their neighbours. The shoes looked brand new, no scuffs or scratches at all. They were black patent leather, all shiny and beautiful - the nicest shoes Martha had ever seen it her whole life.

'The only other things you really need now is a blazer, duffle coat and science and gym outfits, the headmistress has agreed that the school will provide you with these.'

Martha looked at her with anticipation.

'Yes Martha, you're the only pupil from the Rothbury catchment area to pass their 11+ examination, congratulations!'

For once Martha didn't quite know what to do or say, she just stood there gripping tightly onto her shiny new shoes.

Martha's 'happy bubble' continued until the moment she reached the old farm gates of Gorfen Letch. She knew her mother, and possibly even Joe may not be quite as pleased for her as her young teacher.

'Not going to happen!' her mother said, as she announced the news. 'You'll be needed on the farm. I'm not having your bloody nose buried in a book, it's hard graft you need lass, not swanning around at grammar school, thinking you're the bee's bloody knees. Both your father and I left school at ten, it did us no harm. We learnt what hard work was early on. For God's sake, what would you do with bloody qualifications anyway? No, you need to work on the farm and that's it, finished with.'

'Joe – please!' screamed Martha, 'please Joe, please!' Her eldest brother was her only hope now.

Joe stared at his sister, panic all over her face. He knew she had had a terrible life and he knew exactly what his cruel father did to her, perhaps this was the time to put it all right, to make up for all the abuse, all the beatings. He didn't believe in all that 'devil's curse' lark his Dad was always on about, that was just old wives' tales that his father had stupidly believed.

'Come on Mam, she's a clever lass, perhaps she could make something of herself? Give her a chance.'

Martha jumped in 'I'll work on the farm too, when I get home from school.'

'No'

'Come on Mam, be reasonable. You know Dad made her life a living hell, let's put that right.'

Joe had over-stepped the mark, his mother's face was like thunder. 'No he didn't, if anything she made his life a living hell. He never took to her, she's the Devil's own, she deserved everything she got.'

'We both know that isn't true, don't we mother, and we both know who did the evil acts. Perhaps people should know about that, don't you think?'

Martha looked at Joe in astonishment - they both knew about the 'punishings' she thought. Did they know about the baby as well? She felt embarrassed and horrified at the very thought of it.

'Alright!' her mother screamed in temper, 'you can bloody go, but one step out of place and you're done, you're out to service or back working on the farm.'

The headmistress was true to her word and she was given a brand new blazer, duffle coat for the winter, a wrap over science coat, gym skirt and pale blue top. Although Miss Dunlop said the clothes she bought were her little sister's she knew all to well this was a lie, you could see everything was brand new.

The grammar school was an hour's journey each way. Although Martha was tired at the end of the day, she still had to work on the farm as promised. Her mother had her chores ready for her as soon as she walked through the door. Even so, she loved her new life. The only thing she couldn't cope with was not coming top at everything. She had always been top at the infant's school and it was a change she didn't like. Her main rival was one rotund girl called Regina Cresswell.

Regina, or Reggie as she was known to her friends was good at everything - except games. Martha hated this. Reggie's parents were incredibly wealthy and paid for extra tuition for her, so Martha felt she didn't have a chance against her in certain subjects, like French. Reggie even had holidays in France to practice her language skills and she had tutors for both Maths and English. Martha used to practice her French in the cowshed. She wasn't even allowed to do it within hearing distance of her mother.

Despite the rivalry, Martha and Reggie eventually became unlikely friends. Reggie lived near the school and always went home for her lunch and one day took Martha with her.

'Oh my goodness, is this all your house?' Martha could not believe how big it was. The house was a 'stone's throw' from the school and Alnwick Castle. It was accessed through wrought iron gates and the front garden was full of roses. It had three windows either side of a huge oak door, set into an archway and was three stories high.

'Come on' said Reggie, 'I'll introduce you to Kate.'

'Is that your sister?'

'Good grief no, she's the help.'

The children walked through the house to the rear. Martha's eyes were on stalks. There were big beautiful settees, huge grandfather clocks, stuffed animals in glass cases and the hall floor was shiny and in beautiful symmetrical patterns.

'Come on, hurry up Martha,' Reggie shouted as Martha dawdled through the passageways.

They ended up in a large kitchen with a big scrubbed table in the centre. A big hipped woman with dark hair was smiling as Reggie walked into her arms.

'Hello pet, are you hungry?' she asked, in an accent not unlike her own.

'Famished, what have we got today?'

'I see you've brought a little friend, who's this then?'

'This is Martha. Martha lives on a farm in the back of beyond and she actually helps out there.'

'Does she indeed!'

Martha felt the woman's eye on her with interest. She had the overwhelming feeling that this woman thought she wasn't good enough to be Reggie's friend.

'Hello Kate' she said, holding out her hand. She gave her the best smile she had, just like Miss Dunlop had taught her. 'It's lovely to meet you.'

'Are you both hungry?'

'Starving!' Reggie announced.

Kate produced an amazing lunch - a pie filled with chicken, a current bun and a beautiful jelly and blancmange, the likes of which Martha had never seen before. There was a pink blancmange rabbit sitting on a bed of green jelly - it looked too special for Martha to even put her spoon into it. She looked at Reggie's plump body and realised why this girl was fat - eating like this every day would definitely make you fat.

Martha soon realised that although her friend was one of the most intelligent girls in her class, she was certainly not the most popular. Her squidgy face and body, topped off with bright ginger hair, left her open to being teased by the other girls but to give Reggie credit it never seemed to bother her. She could definitely hold her own and had learned to be thick skinned. She had a massive vocabulary, with swear words that Martha had never even heard before.

The two girls were soon an item at school. Lunch was the highlight of the day and Martha soon became more rounded in both her psyche and in her body, morphing from her original 'skeletal' frame.

Martha became a constant feature in the Cresswell family home. She loved Reggie's parents, who although she thought were very 'posh' were always kind to her and treated her like part of the family. Being part of a loving family was alien to her. She'd watch in fascination when they would put their arms around their daughter and smother her in kisses until she would ungratefully scream in protest. Martha thought her friend to be a complete idiot at times, she was shockingly unappreciative of the love her parents showed her. She began to dream at night that if Reggie was out of the picture they might adopt her and take her away from the farm. Yes, they'd be grief stricken for a while but Martha could show them just what a 'good daughter' really was.

She would have to make one of her plans. Martha was good at plans.

Chapter 30

Everyone in the class was told to clap their hands together for the cleverest girl in the school; Reggie Cresswell had come top in every subject at the end of term exams. Martha grabbed her rotund friend and hugged her, just as Reggie did to her, but Martha was secretly seething with rage. '*For God's sake*!' thought Martha, *could this girl not have let her be top in at least one subject?* She vowed she'd have walked away from their friendship if it wasn't for the fact that Mr and Mrs Cresswell were taking her on holiday with them in two weeks time. She knew she was purely there to keep their daughter amused while they were off playing golf, but she'd never been on holiday before. She found a book in the school library on the town they'd be staying in - St Andrews in Scotland.

The Cresswells had arrived unannounced at Gorfen Letch Farm one day, to ask Martha's mother if she could go on the holiday with them during summer term. She had been so shocked at the presence of the beautifully dressed and very well spoken couple that she was unable to disagree that Martha 'so deserved this holiday' and it would be wonderful for their Regina to have company. They were taking their hired help with them, so she should feel assured that the children would be well cared for. After they had left, Martha's mam had immediately sent her to bed with nothing to eat and she could hear her pacing the floor saying 'Oh my God!' 'Oh my God!'

The St Andrews holiday beckoned and Martha was just so excited, even coming second in every subject at school didn't put a damper on it. She looked in the mirror at her wild auburn hair and taking her mother's scissors cut off the straggly ends and made herself a fringe, *that's better*, she thought. Mrs Cresswell had sorted out some old summer clothes Reggie had outgrown - coloured skirts and cardigans, not grey or brown like Martha normally wore. They even provided her with a suitcase. They were to travel by train to Edinburgh, then a driver would pick them up and take them the rest of the way by car.

The day soon arrived. Martha was picked up the night before their departure for Scotland by a smartly dressed driver. Her mother hadn't spoken to her at all since the Cresswell's visit, except to bark orders at her. Martha left, saying goodbye to total silence. Joe had previously given her a little money for treats, which she had hidden in the lining of her coat for fear her mother would take it from her.

At exactly 6am the next morning they all headed off. The train journey was spectacular, passing castles, beaches and beautiful towns. She hadn't realised that Northumberland was quite so beautiful. She had only seen the sea once before on a school trip and she found the spectacular blue scene mesmerising. Reggie slept the whole journey, missing everything. She could tell the Cresswells were delighted at her enthusiasm, so she embellished it as much as she could, just to please them. Seeing them happy made her feel good and helped with her future plans.

Waverley Railway Station was bustling and frighteningly busy. She grabbed her case and stayed close to Mrs Cresswell, scared she would lose them.

'Come on darling!' Mr Cresswell shouted at Regina, who was dawdling along with a face like thunder.

'I'm tired, getting up so early is awful, I don't feel well,' Regina protested.

Mr and Mrs Cresswell looked at each other with concern and she could hear them mumbling something about 'bad turns', expressing concern for their daughter.

Reggie stared at them, 'don't worry, I'm not going to have a fit, I'm just tired and hungry.'

Martha was enthralled by this conversation. She had heard of people 'having fits' before and she had once seen a sheep 'fitting' on the farm. She wondered if this was the same thing. The sheep eventually died. It had recovered from its original fit and just got up and walked off, but it had been found a few days later dead in a ditch. Joe said it had probably died because it had taken a fit and fallen into the ditch, which had about six inches of water in it - the sheep had drowned.

'Here's our car, come on, hurry up!' called Mr Cresswell. It was a huge Bentley, all four of them climbed in. Kate 'the help' had travelled up the night before to 'air' the house for their arrival.

After a couple of hours, Mrs Cresswell excitedly announced' here we are' and pointed in front of her.

'There's the club house and that's St Andrews, beautiful isn't it?'

Martha looked out at the approaching town. All the houses looked squashed together in one lump as they rounded the corner, but as they drove into it, it started to open out a bit more. She could see the golf course on the left, with all the players, and the town itself was busy with strangely dressed people and full of very posh houses.

The car indicated and squeezed through a tiny opening. It then took a tight turn to the right, then a tight left and then they were in a lawned area, with five houses in a street. All had little gardens at the front surrounded by ornate iron fences and gates. The driver parked up and was soon out of the car, carrying their cases into 'Three Dalbeattie Street', in the middle of the row. It was a stone built house, three stories high, with gable windows at the very top. They entered through an open porch into a large hallway. There was a formal dining room on the left and then a large kitchen at the rear. The kitchen had servants' bells high up on the wall and a big range oven, which was in full use and giving off lots of heat.

'Top floor girls!' shouted Mrs Cresswell, excitedly. 'You're sharing the twin room at the front.'

'Oh God, that's too many stairs!' huffed Reggie, now in a very sullen mood.

Martha looked at her red headed, moody friend and thought how ungrateful she was. How could she not be happy being taken on holiday? She was given everything - lovely food, clothes, toys, tuition and she still wasn't happy. Did she even realise what sort of life Martha led? She would last five minutes doing her chores and what about her father's 'punishings'. She knew Reggie wouldn't be able to cope with that. She thought to herself that Mr and Mrs Cresswell must be very disappointed in their daughter and she knew she'd make a much better go of it.

That night, Kate cooked the most amazing meal Martha had ever tasted in her whole life. They didn't just have one meal, they had three. They had fish to start - lots of little weird looking things that tasted of the sea, slices of different types of fish and a sauce that made her mouth water. Then it was beef, covered in pastry. It didn't taste like her mam's beef at all - this was easy to chew. Then apple pie with custard. Martha ate every bite, whilst Reggie refused vegetables and said some of it tasted like snot.

'Look at Martha, she's eaten everything.' Reggie glared at her, as Eleanor Cresswell continued. 'If a little skinny thing like Martha can eat everything, I'm sure you can too.'

'I refuse to eat snot mother dearest.' Reggie exclaimed loudly and in a spiteful manner.

Martha tensed, waiting for tempers to flare. But much to her amazement, nothing happened. *These people were angels,* she thought to herself.

Chapter 31

It had rained the first two days of their summer holiday in St Andrews. Martha and Reggie had been in the care of Kate, whilst the parents golfed. The Cresswells' would come back soaked, but were always full of their tales of how wonderful the course was, who they'd met and their best shots. It all bored Martha but she knew that learning what they did out there would endear her to them, so she had found a book in the dining room entitled 'The Noble Art of Golf 'and she intended to take it to bed with her tonight.

The girls spent their days either indoors playing games or with Kate, shopping on Market Street. The shops were fascinating to Martha - the prices of some of the clothes and fancy goods just blew her mind, nothing like the little shops in Rothbury.

On the third morning of the holiday they were greeted with sunshine peeping through the curtains. Excitedly, Martha bounced out of bed.

'Reggie, get up, we can go swimming! Look, it's beautiful out there!'

'Shut up, I haven't woken up yet!'

Martha quickly got dressed and bounced down the two flights of stairs to the kitchen where 'the parents' were eating breakfast, all dressed in tweed, ready to go off and play their favourite game.

'Well, we've got the weather for it today Martha. What are you girls planning to do today?' Mr Cresswell smiled.

'We thought, or rather I thought, as Reggie is still sleeping, that we could go to the beach and then perhaps watch some of the golfers. I've been reading all about golf.'

'Have you indeed? That's good, there's a putting green if you're interested. You children could have a go. Here, take this.'

Mr Cresswell put his hand in his pocket and handed Martha about six coins. Her eyes lit up, she'd never had that much money before.

'Thank you so much Mr Cresswell,' she said, beaming at him.

The Cresswells looked at each other and laughed, obviously amused at her pure delight.

The parents were off and out of the door, shouting at Kate to watch over the girls at the beach. Reggie took another full hour before she appeared. Martha felt rage towards her friend but tried very hard not to let it show. She wondered if she could quietly keep hold of the money in her pocket, but then thought if the parents found out she hadn't spent it they'd think she was a swindler. No, she could perhaps keep a few pence but she'd have to spend it on their day out. She saw Kate eyeing her with suspicion and hoped this woman couldn't read minds.

'Right girls, get a towel each from the bathroom. We're going to the beach first, then ice cream, then apparently we're watching golf, isn't that right Martha?'

'Yes,' she smiled, a little sheepishly.

'We'll sit at the eighteenth green, it's quite nice watching all the golfers coming in - got to watch for flying golf balls though.'

The beach was an unbelievable site for Martha, who had spent her life in the Coquet Valley. She had only seen the sea properly once before, so these were just amazing sights, smells and sounds for her. The beach seemed to stretch for miles and there were lots of people milling around, building sand castles, paddling and some even swimming in the North Sea.

'Come on Reggie!' Martha was stripping off before they'd even settled in their selected spot.

'You go first, I'll stay with Kate for a while.'

Martha was now in her second-hand bathing costume. The tide was out so she had a long sprint to get to the water's edge. The feel of the sand on her feet was strange, soft and warm. When she hit the water the cold was shocking. She had expected it to be warm, but the further she went - the colder it got. She was up to her neck in seconds and her teeth were chattering together, but after a while it became warmer. She had learnt to swim at Gorfen Letch after her older brothers had hurled her into the lake near their house. This was so much colder than the lake.

'Reggie,' she shouted loudly, 'come on, it's lovely!' She doubted they could hear, they were so far away. This was perfect she thought, her new plan was all coming together. Every few minutes she shouted for Reggie but her friend was engrossed in chatting with Kate. Eventually she came to the water's edge. 'It's far too cold Martha,' she said, hardly putting a toe in the water.

'Don't be soft, it's lovely once you get in - come on,' she shouted.

Reggie stepped further in and was now up to her knees.' Ahhhhh!' she screamed, as she raced back to the safety of the sand. 'No, it's too cold. I'm going back to sit with Kate, she's got some jam and cream scones.'

Typical, thought Martha - *she's thinking of her big fat stomach as normal.*

Martha eventually came out of the water and dried herself off, the feeling of the sun on her skin was such a wonderful feeling after the cold water. She wasn't that disappointed that Reggie hadn't gone into the water, at least she could enjoy the rest of this wonderful day. After all, there were four days of the holiday left.

Kate made sure that her young, fair skinned charge was well covered. They had a parasol that she made Reggie balance over her head. Martha had brought the book on golf and read the chapter on St Andrews itself. She'd be able to dazzle 'the parents' with her knowledge of the course they obviously loved so much.

Lunch followed with egg and cress sandwiches, more scones, tinned fruit salad and jelly with evaporated milk. Martha felt like she had eaten more in the last three days than she would eat in a whole month at home.

'Doesn't your mother feed you properly at home?' Kate asked abruptly, shattering Martha's pleasant thoughts.

'Yes,' Martha lied, not wanting this woman to know her mother would often send her to bed hungry for being 'the Devil's child.'

'You certainly like ya food.'

'Well,' she said smiling, 'I like your food much better than my mother's, you're such a good cook.'

'Right,' Kate said, raising her eyebrows slightly. This wasn't the reaction Martha wanted, she was hoping that Kate would be flattered - but it didn't seem to work on this woman.

After lunch they made their way back towards town and sat on a bench near the 18th green where there were lots of people wandering around. They could see the golfers on the 18th tee, a term she was proud she had learnt, then they would watch the ball as it came about half way towards them...then another shot and then the golfers would make their way onto the green.

Eventually, they saw a group of eight men coming towards them, one of which was Mr Cresswell. He was good thought Martha, three shots and he was nearer the flag than any of the others. He put the ball straight into the hole from quite a distance away and everyone around started to clap. Mrs Cresswell followed much later when all the groups of men had finished. There were several sets of ladies playing and eventually she pitched onto the green. She wasn't as good as her husband but not bad she thought. All in all, although the day hadn't gone exactly to plan, it was a very good day for Martha.

Chapter 32

Martha felt happier than she had in her whole life, everyday spent either walking around the beautiful and bustling town centre of St Andrew's, building sand castles on the beach or watching the golfers. No matter how hard she tried she could not tempt Reggie into the cold North Sea, so any swimming was done solely on her own.

'You'll never convince me you actually enjoy that' said Reggie, as Martha reappeared, shivering from her swim.

'Of course I do, the pain makes you enjoy the sunshine even more.'

'I'd rather miss the pain bit out thank you.'

Kate piped up - 'quite right my darling, even if it's red hot, the North Sea is always freezing and full of nasty fish. I don't like the thought of being so close to the slimy things, they look much better on your plate.'

The final day of their holiday arrived and Reggie said she was happy to be going home, but Martha was utterly bereft. How could she face going back to the farm after this? She wanted so much to stay, she had a burning need to be part of the Cresswell family. The last thing in the world she wanted was to go home.

Mrs Cresswell came into the girls' bedroom before dinner - 'right girls, pack your suitcases and just leave out what you're wearing in the morning. Kate has enough to do, packing all the kitchen things and doing the bedding in the morning.'

'I'm so ready to go home,' Reggie piped up.

'Have you not enjoyed your holiday, sweetheart?'

'Yes, but it will be nice to be back in my bedroom and just to be alone with my books.'

Martha felt wounded, as if her friend had stuck a knife in her. She also felt rather humiliated in front of Mrs Cresswell. She had 'bent over backwards' for her spoilt friend, who could be so rude and didn't appreciate anything anyone did for her. The only person she showed a modicum of respect for was actually Kate and that was only because the woman fed her, or rather 'over-fed' her! She remembered all the times she had wanted to argue back, to give her over-privileged fat friend a slap or a kick and she had stopped herself. *No*, she thought to herself, *Regina Cresswell did not deserve a friend as good as her, or indeed parents like the Cresswells'*.

Dinner was special that night - *Lobster a la Newburg* to start with, followed by lamb cutlets with creamed potatoes and then trifle. Martha had felt in a low mood all day, knowing they were returning home in the morning but the food had helped to lift her spirits. The creamy lobster dish was something she had never tasted before and the lamb just melted in her mouth. But it was the trifle that was her favourite - puddings weren't something she got that often at home - the odd bread pudding, mainly to use up the stale bread or apple pie when the tree in the garden was in season.

Mrs Cresswell sat watching the pleasure on their young ward's face. 'Did you enjoy that Martha?'

'It was simply marvellous,' Martha replied. Everyone at the table started laughing... *she didn't like being laughed at.*

'You sound just like Mama,' Reggie chuckled.

Mrs Cresswell stopped laughing when she saw Martha's red face. 'Stop it darling, you're embarrassing your little friend. I can't think of anyone better to sound like me than Martha,' she smiled.

Martha sat seething. She was only trying to be polite so why did they have to laugh at her? She knew she'd have to watch her language once she was back at the farm or she'd get a slap for putting on airs and graces, but she hadn't anticipated the Cresswells' reaction.

After tossing and turning all night, the girls were woken early in the morning. Reggie was excited at the prospect of going home whilst Martha was very quiet and sullen.

'Come on Martha, get moving.' Reggie was pushing Martha out the bedroom door. 'A quick breakfast and we're off back home.'

Breakfast soon came and went and within a short time they were sitting in the car on their way to Waverley Station. The train was running on time and the journey all went to plan. They arrived back at Alnwick late afternoon, Martha's mood obvious to the Cresswells. Whilst their daughter was now smiling and singing in happiness to be home, their young guest was morose. Mr Cresswell was scheduled to take her back to Gorfen Letch Farm in the morning but felt sad seeing the young girl's face.

That night Mr and Mrs Cresswell were sitting in their drawing room after the two girls went to bed.

'Martha obviously doesn't want to go home Reg,' Mrs Cresswell said, looking concerned.

'I know, she looks really unhappy, unless there's something else bothering her.'

'No, I don't think so, I think she's just had a taste of how life can be and she doesn't want to go back to her old life. Do you know she works on that farm when she gets home from school? She does about two hours before she even eats, that's what she says anyway.'

'Ah, she might just be exaggerating a bit, you know what children are like.'

'I don't think she is, have you noticed she often has bruises on her arms Reg? She says it's from dealing with the animals, but...'

'But you're thinking something else, aren't you?'

'I don't know, it's like there's something else hidden behind those eyes sometimes, something she doesn't want you to know. She's a strange little thing, bright as a button, takes everything in, really clever at school apparently.'

'Well, I had heard that her father was a bit of a 'sort', very hard on his children,' Mr Cresswell confessed.

'Yeah, but he's been dead for ages now, anyway who told you that?'

'Kate.'

'I didn't know Kate knew anything about the family!'

'She doesn't really, she's related to some people who live on a nearby farm. She came to me concerned when Reggie started to bring her home, thought she wasn't good enough to be around our Reggie.'

'She never said anything to me, why ever not, was it just because she comes from a poor family?'

'Well, I'm not sure, just some sort of prejudice and gossip about the family. The parents sound a bit uneducated to me. They apparently see that 'port wine' stain on Martha's head as some sort of bad sign from God.'

'You're joking! To be honest, I only noticed it the once when she was brushing her wet hair. The mother sounds a bit crazy Reg. I wonder what they would have made of having a child that takes fits - beggars belief!'

'Indeed.'

The next morning, Mrs Cresswell insisted on going to Gorfen Letch too. Reggie said she'd stay at home with Kate. She was just happy to be home in her normal surroundings. Martha was determined she wasn't going to cry but she was fighting back tears the whole car journey.

'Here we are then,' said Mr Cresswell as they entered the gate onto the dirt track.

'Just drop me at the lane end,' Martha said quickly, 'I can easily walk from here.'

'Absolutely not, I want to tell your mother how good you've been.'

Martha's heart sank. *This was going to be gut wrenching.*

'Right, you get the suitcase Reg and I'll take Martha inside,' said Mrs Cresswell, as they pulled up in the farmyard. She then followed Martha into the farmhouse kitchen. 'Ah, ya back then madam?' Martha's mother said, before noticing Mrs Cresswell was there. She froze when she saw the 'well heeled' woman in her kitchen.

'Hello Mrs Curry, I just thought I'd pop in and let you know how wonderful it was to have Martha with us, she was an absolute delight to be around.'

'Right.'

Martha knew her mother wanted to say more and to tell Mrs Cresswell what she was really like, but was too scared.

'She really is a credit to you.'

Martha felt sick, knowing this wasn't going down well by the hard, ashen look on her mother's face.

'Well, we'll leave you to it,' said Mrs Cresswell, embarrassed at this woman's reticence to speak. 'See you soon Martha darling, your suitcase is just in the porch there,' she pointed.

'Bye, thank you ever so much, I've really enjoyed it.'

'You're welcome darling, take care.'

Martha's mother went to the window to watch the car leave, 'bye, thank you ever so much,' she mimicked. I suppose you think you're bloody landed gentry now, do you?'

'No Mam, I'm just being polite, but I did have a really nice time,' she said, as tears started to well up in her eyes.

'Well, ya back now, you can forget all ya airs and graces madam and buckle down to some work. Julia needs feeding and then you can go out and help Joe. Why he persuaded me to let you go I'll never know, and how them people think you're a good girl is beyond me. They haven't seen the devil in ya like I have. Crafty as a bitch fox, aren't ya?

Got them idiots convinced you're as good as gold. Ha! If only they knew the truth!'

Chapter 33

Over the next few months, life at the farm was torrid for Martha. Her mother would taunt her about trying to be something she wasn't, and how she'd tell the Cresswells about her being sent by the Devil. Her chores were increased whilst her little sister Julia was kissed and cuddled by their mother.

'Get up!' her Mam screamed early one morning, as Martha lay in bed.

'What time is it?'

'Never mind about that, ya sister's poorly, been sick all over the place - get up and help.'

Martha dragged herself out of bed. Looking at the clock it was three o'clock in the morning. Her mother was now screaming at her, 'if you've poisoned our little Julia I'll get the police on you! I swear to God I will, I know you've done it before you little bitch, I know you have!'

'Don't be ridiculous Mam, course I haven't poisoned her, I wouldn't poison anyone.'

A slap landed on Martha's head, making her stumble forward. 'Ridiculous, am I? We'll see. Rub down the cot, then run and knock on the doctor.' It was freezing cold and pitch black outside. Martha wasn't happy at the thought of going out.

'Will the doctor come out this early?'

'Of course he will.'

Martha looked at her little sister and thought she didn't look that sick.

'Don't you dare come back without him mind,' she said to Martha as she was putting her coat on. *Oh God* she thought to herself, *she was never going to stay awake in class*. It was hard enough at the best of times, never mind being dragged out of bed this early. Today was a maths exam too.

Then Joe walked into the kitchen in his night clothes. Alongside him was her 'bleary eyed' youngest brother Billy.

'What the hell is going on?'

'It's Julia, she's awful sick Joe. I'm sending Martha for the doctor.'

'Ah Mam, she looks alright to me, can't it wait until morning? Doc O'Driscoll isn't going to be too thrilled getting out of bed at this time.'

'I'm worried that this little bitch fox here has given her something to make her sick.'

'Don't be stupid Mam, course she hasn't, have you Martha?'

'Of course I haven't, I've already told her,' Martha smiled at her mother.

'You see, she's smiling, she's done it alright.'

'Mother, you're just being stupid. No one is going for the doctor, Julia only has a bit of an upset tummy. It's probably those sweets you bought her yesterday, stuffing them into herself she was. Maybe liquorice doesn't agree with her?'

Joe was really starting to dominate in family traumas. Martha noticed her brother was becoming a man - and a man capable of controlling her mother's hysteria.

School was difficult for Martha that day. She looked around the class at the other girls. She bet they didn't get dragged out of bed in the early hours and being accused of being a 'poisoner'. It was so untrue she thought - yes, she had poisoned her dad - but she had not poisoned Julia. Anyway, the poisoning hadn't killed her dad, only made him sick, it was Rollo who did that... lovely Rollo! Bet the other girls didn't have to do chores either. There were very few girls from poor families at her school. They were nearly all from wealthy families, certainly none as poor as Martha.

The only thing that brightened Martha's mood was that she was to spend the night at Reggie's house. The Cresswells' were having a party and they asked her to go to keep Reggie company, as they were to be the only children there.

Reggie was waiting for her at the school gates as arranged. Their last lesson was games and Reggie didn't do games, so she was allowed to go to the library instead.

'Right, you ready to go? I want to go to the sweet shop first.'

'Of course,' said Martha who had to watch her friend stuff her face on the way home.

When they arrived, the big town house was festooned with bunting and the smell of cooking hit her as soon as they went inside. It was a cold day and the warmth of the house soon seeped into her bones. She felt so at home here, it was such a beautiful house - this was where she was meant to be, not in a cold farmhouse, stuck amongst the yellow gorse bushes in the middle of the moors.

'Right girls, people are arriving in about an hour's time, so Kate has made sure the water is hot. Go and have a bath. Reggie, I've put your new dress on your bed and Martha, there's a selection of Reggie's old dresses and some belts if you'd like to find something suitable. But you don't have to, you could just wear your school uniform if you'd rather... it's up to you.'

The girls both raced upstairs. Reggie was so excited, 'I love parties, Daddy is fifty. Fifty! He's so old, isn't he? Look at my new dress,' pointing at the green satin dress on the bed.

'It's beautiful.' Martha was far more interested in the other second hand dresses that Reggie had outgrown. There was a pink one she had her eye on. It had tiny little dusky pink flowers sewn onto the hem and larger pink flowers on the shoulders. She'd never had a proper party dress before, nothing like this. She wondered if she'd be allowed to take it home.

'Right, bath first,' said Reggie, now turning pink with the heat of the house.

'I'll run it for you,' Martha offered. She loved the bubbles, something she'd never have at home but Reggie's mother obviously indulged her little princess with the latest toiletries.

'It's far too full Martha' said Reggie, looking at the bath.

'Don't be soft you scaredy cat, it will be lovely. Really Reggie, you're right soft sometimes.'

'Alright,' she said, not wanting her friend to think she was a baby. 'Sit there, keep your back turned until I get in, then you can turn around. You promise, don't peak till I'm in?'

'Yes,... I promise!' Martha did as she was told, she always did what Reggie told her, even when it enraged her.

She suddenly heard Reggie thrashing around in the water, 'what the heck you doing?'

Martha broke her promise and turned to see her friend having a fit in the water. She froze and watched. Her previously thought out plan immediately kicked into action. She hadn't managed to even get her into the water at St Andrews but here she was lying in about ten inches of water, already drowning all by herself. Her head was just above the water, but if she gave her just a little push she'd be completely under.

Martha looked towards the door - *safe* she thought. She reached forward, put a hand on Reggie's face and pushed her down. She slid further down into the water. It was hard to hold her under with all the thrashing and she kept popping back up. But Martha was strong from carrying all those bales of hay and bags of feed, and it had made her muscles defined and hard. She was now soaked through, arms getting sore from holding her under. Her school uniform was drenched and there was bath water all over the floor. The thrashing eventually stopped and Reggie was still. She tried to pull her back up into more of a sitting position but couldn't. Now she knew she had to convince everyone she'd tried to help her best friend.

She ran down the stairs screaming hysterically 'Reggie's gone funny in the bath!'

Mrs Cresswell dropped everything and ran.

'I tried to get her out but I couldn't. I heard her and went in, she was under the water kicking and her arms were dancing about!'

Martha knew it was better that she didn't let the Cresswells' know that she was aware that Reggie took fits. She had researched the condition in the school library and thought it best that she just describe what had happened.

'I tried to help her! I tried so hard!' Martha was now crying, tears rolling down her cheeks… *this had always worked well for Martha.*

'Take the child out of here!' Mr Cresswell yelled as he entered, trying to pull his daughter out of the bath.

'Hit her on the back Reg, try and get the water out!' Mrs Cresswell screamed.

Kate now came into the bathroom too, alerted by the screaming. She was out of breath from running up the stairs. 'Oh God Miss! What the hell happened?'

Martha sat in the corner watching everyone panicking, trying to wake Reggie up. She knew it was futile, her friend was gone. Her best friend was dead.

'I'll get the doctor.' Kate ran past her, face ashen, tears already rolling down her white face.

Doctor John Barker, who lived in the next street, came within five minutes and at precisely five o'clock that afternoon he pronounced Regina Cresswell dead. Martha listened from another room and to her relief she heard the Doctor say that it was common for this to happen and that no one was to blame. It was just one of those things and that they had to understand Reggie was quite an ill girl.

'But she hadn't had a fit for so long,' Mrs Cresswell whispered through her sobs, 'and she wouldn't allow us to mollycoddle her.'

'You can't be with your children all the time Eleanor,' the doctor said.

Martha didn't quite know what to do. She eventually went into her little bedroom, which was a tiny room off Reggie's bedroom and sat on the single bed, waiting. Would they take her home or would she be allowed to stay? She hoped she could stay, after all, that was her plan.

After about an hour, Kate came into the room. 'I want to know exactly what happened in there, everyone is devastated. Why didn't you just hold her head out of the water you stupid girl?'

'I did,' said Martha sincerely, 'but she was thrashing about so much I didn't know what to do, her head kept slipping out of my hands. I didn't know what was going on, so I left her and ran for help.'

'Was she under the water when you left her?'

'I don't know, I just ran. She must have slipped under again. I tried my best - honest I did Kate.'

'Yes, I'm sure you did,' Kate replied, staring coldly at Martha.

Martha felt she was failing to convince Kate of her innocence. The woman had never liked her much, she thought. The Cresswells would be easier to convince, they liked her... *they liked her very much.*

'Right, get to bed, you'll be taken home in the morning. I'll organise a driver to take you back.'

'Won't Mr Cresswell be taking me home?'

'I think Mr Cresswell might have other things on his mind, don't you?'

'I want to tell them how sorry I am,' she protested, 'and to let them know I'll help in any way I can.'

'I think you've helped enough Martha, don't you? Now go to bed.'

Martha sat for a while, pondering over what Kate had said. She then started thinking about her maths exam, which she had taken that morning. She suddenly had a wonderful thought, she'd now be top in maths, her competition was gone! *Wow*, she thought, *she now had the chance to be top in every single subject at school!*

She opened the door and stared at Regina's bed. Was this beautiful bed now to be hers? She felt sure that the Cresswells' would still want her around, they'd be a bit lost without their Reggie. She could fill the gap, she knew she could, she'd be a much better daughter than Reggie. She wouldn't 'strop' when they took her on holiday, she wouldn't be greedy and get fat. She'd even help around the house! She'd need to get rid of Kate of course, Kate really didn't like her. Yes, her plan was coming together. Coming together very nicely indeed.

But the next morning, much to Martha's dismay, she was taken home by a nice man called Arnold. She had wanted to see Mr and Mrs Cresswell but wasn't allowed. She was told they were too upset to talk to her. She'd see them soon she thought, she'd pop around after school or see them at the funeral.

Arnold dropped her off at the road end as she requested. His car was lovely and clean. He took one look at the muddy lane and agreed that it was fine to drop her there as she only had a small bag anyway. She had taken the pink dress as it was hers after all - Mrs Cresswell had said to take her pick.

'You're early,' her mother said, as she walked into the kitchen, 'sick of you, were they?'

'No, Reggie wasn't very well so I came back early.'

Her mother was happy with that. 'Well, you can help do some baking now ya back, I'm making a cake for Julia's birthday - get them dishes washed,' she ordered, pointing to an enormous pile of dirty dishes.

Just as planned, on the Monday after school, Martha went around to Reggie's house only to be told by Kate that the Cresswells' were still too upset to see her. She went on the Tuesday to be refused yet again. On the Wednesday she was told by Kate never to come back as Mr and

Mrs Cresswell did not want to see her and that she was not to attend the funeral. It was close friends and family only.

Martha was furious, 'I'm sure if I could just talk to them, they'd be fine,' Martha pleaded.

'For the last time I'm telling you to go. It is far too painful for Mr and Mrs Cresswell to see you. They are absolutely destroyed at losing Reggie. Go!' she told her, pointing up the street.

Her plan had failed and she just couldn't understand their reaction. She thought they'd welcome her and she'd help them get over their loss. The eradication part had worked stupendously but she had failed to anticipate their reaction. She knew her mother would just have moved on if anything had happened to her, in fact she knew she'd secretly be pleased. The Cresswells were obviously very different! She'd have to hide Reggie's death from her mother, as she knew once her mother got wind of what had happened, she'd accuse her of being responsible. *It was all so horribly unfair*, she thought.

Chapter 34

Eleanor Cresswell sat on her daughter's bed, gently sobbing. She reached for Reggie's pillow, holding it against her face and taking in the smell of her dead child. The sobs became uncontrollable and she started to rock backwards and forwards, feeling that life was no longer worth living, not without her Reggie.

Reginald, alerted by the noise, entered the bedroom.

'Eleanor darling, this isn't helping' he said, as he sat next to his wife, cradling her in his arms. She was physically convulsing with grief.

'You'll make yourself ill.'

'We shouldn't have left her Reg, if only... if only I hadn't organised that stupid... stupid bloody party.'

'She was with someone Eleanor, we thought she'd be safe. She was always told not to put too much water in the bath - just in case, and to make sure Kate or one of us knew she was in hearing distance if she needed help. She was with Martha.'

The couple clung to each other, both quietly sobbing and holding between them the now damp pillow, sodden with their tears.

'I only had one child Reg, and now she's gone, gone forever. I just don't know what to do, what do I do now? She was my life, I'm lost without her.'

'There, there my darling, we'll go abroad for a while... Italy, would you like that? We'll go for a month, get away from this place.'

'I just want my baby back Reg.'

The door bell rang and they heard Kate answering the door, greeting someone. Then the gentle footfall on the stair carpet and a gentle 'tap, tap' on the door followed.

'Mr Cresswell, Dr Barker is here, he's come to talk to you.'

'Yes Kate, tell him I'll be down in a minute.' He left his wife as she lay down on the bed with her head on the pillow.

'Dr Barker…John, thank you for coming,' he held out his hand to the family doctor and the man who had brought Reggie into the world.

'Have you come to see Eleanor? She is in a rather awful state I'm afraid, as to be expected I guess.'

'No, I've just come to ask you a few questions about what happened yesterday. Just a run down of the circumstances. Nothing to worry about.'

Reginald immediately started to worry, 'please sit down..., is this normal, do you usually do this?'

'There's just a few things I needed to clarify about the circumstances. I just wanted to ask you exactly what position your daughter was in when you found her. Was she on her back or on her front?'

'Well, it was Eleanor who went in first but I was only about ten paces behind. She was on her back under the water. We always told her just to put a few inches of water in the bath but this time it was quite deep and there was water all over the floor.'

'What about this young friend of hers, Martha is it? Was she in the bathroom too?'

'I believe not, well not at that exact moment. She said she had been outside and heard strange noises and went in and found her thrashing about. She said she tried to get her out but couldn't. The poor child didn't know what was going on, she was unaware of Reggie's illness.'

Mr Cresswell watched the doctor as he pursed his lips and nodded slowly. He was getting an uncanny feeling as to how this conversation was going.

'Did you bang Reggie's head when you removed her from the bath... specifically the front of her head?'

'Of course not, no, my wife pulled the plug out as I scooped her up out of the water. We sat her up and banged her back trying to get her to cough... to get the water out but she was awfully floppy and it was difficult. We just didn't know what to do.'

'You did your best Mr Cresswell, I'm sure of it.'

The drawing room fell silent for a few seconds, deathly silent. 'Your daughter had some quite noticeable bruising to her forehead and around her mouth... now, it's not inconceivable that this happened when she was having the fit, but if she was lying in the bath on her back it would be more likely that the damage would be to the back of her head, not to her face. Do you see what I'm saying? Was there anything that could have fallen onto her face?'

'What, no... what are you trying to say?' Reginald was now very confused and shaking his head from side to side.

A long pause ensued. 'How long have you known Martha Curry, Mr Cresswell?'

He stared at the doctor in disbelief, now working out just what he was getting at. 'Oh God!' he said, half laughing, 'you're not trying to say that you think a thirteen year old girl, my daughter's actual friend had something to do with this, are you? Why ever would you think she would do such a thing?'

'Jealously, perhaps?'

Reginald jumped out of the armchair and walked towards the window, 'you've got this all wrong John, Martha's a good girl. We've known her for over a year now. She comes for her lunch on school days, she's polite and very intelligent. Yes, she comes from very poor beginnings I know but she's beating the odds - getting herself a place at grammar school. We took her on holiday, she was delightful to have around.'

'What was she like with Reggie?'

'Great, always lovely to her. Reggie could be so bossy but Martha never got angry with her, honestly John you're barking up the wrong tree.'

The doctor shuffled in his seat, looking awkward. 'Did you know the girl has quite a reputation in her local area... they call her the 'Devil's child'?'

'Oh my God, not that again! Do you know why they call her that John? Do you know? It's because the poor child has a birth mark on her scalp - that's why! Bloody ridiculous!'

'I know that Reg, but it's not just that. I contacted the doctor over in Rothbury - Dr O'Driscoll. He says that the father was ill a couple of years ago, swore it was arsenic poisoning, could even smell the tell-tale almond smell on him. When he mentioned it to the wife, she immediately said it was her daughter Martha who would be responsible. She said it was just the sort of thing she would do. The father picked up after his visit and to be honest, Dr O'Driscoll didn't take the mother's accusations all that seriously - so just forgot about it. Then not that long after that the father was killed in a bit of a bizarre accident.'

'Yes, a farming accident - he was trampled by a bull, I don't think his daughter could be blamed for that, do you?'

'It was apparently a very docile bull.'

'Ah come on John, this is all rubbish, you know it as well as I do.'

Eleanor Cresswell entered the room. She had obviously washed her face and had composed herself to greet their guest.

'Dr Barker... John, thank you for coming, it's nice that you're concerned about us.'

'That's not quite why he's come dear.' Reginald was pondering whether or not this should even be discussed in front of his wife. He had kept most of Kate's earlier concerns about 'the Devil child' to himself, thinking it was too ludicrous to even concern his wife with.

'He's come to tell us that he thinks Martha is somehow responsible for Reggie's death.'

'I'm not quite saying that Reg, I'm purely exploring why your daughter had bruising to her face.'

Eleanor was silent. The two men held their breath waiting for her reaction.

'Did you hear what I said darling?'

After some time she answered, 'yes of course I heard, I'm just thinking... I must admit, I thought at the time it was strange why she didn't just scream for help whilst she was in the bathroom. We'd have heard her and why didn't she pull out the plug for God's sake, she's an intelligent girl?'

Reginald looked at her in disbelief. 'Are you telling me you're taking this seriously? Really? She's a child Eleanor, a child who we know, a child who was your daughter's best friend!'

'Something didn't feel right that afternoon Reg. Looking back, she was acting a little odd.'

'What do you mean, odd?'

'Well, although she was crying she was still quite composed, even though she apparently didn't know that Reggie took fits. She never asked any questions. She told me she didn't know - but you would have thought a child would question what on earth was going on... and she was cold, the tears had nothing behind them. And why didn't she just hold her head out of the water Reg, why?'

'Eleanor, listen to yourself, I can't believe what you're saying - it's Martha, little skinny, polite Martha.'

The room was totally silent now, Reginald Cresswell sitting with his head in his hands and not believing what was going on. He felt like he was in a dream, a living nightmare. His wife now actually thought the child was responsible for his daughter's death. Was she just looking for someone or something to blame? He could not get his head around it.

Doctor Barker was the first to break the silence. 'Could I speak with your housemaid Kate please?'

Reginald raised his head. 'Why, she can't tell you any more than we can?'

'I really think it would be prudent to find out what Kate thinks about Martha. I know she can't tell us any more about the actual proceedings in the bathroom but she can tell us about Martha.'

Reginald was starting to suspect that it was Kate who had put this into the doctor's head. He knew that Kate's sister Beth worked for the Barker family. Perhaps she had mentioned it to him? He also knew Kate never liked Martha but he thought it was because of her background. Maybe she didn't think it fitting to be running around after some ruffian's child? She had once told him that it wasn't good for Reggie to be friends with someone like Martha but he had dismissed it, thinking her overly protective of Reggie. He was a politician and he liked to think of himself as progressive. He liked the idea that Martha came from a humble background and he was helping her to progress, by showing and teaching her the finer things in life.

Eleanor rang the bell to alert their maid. Kate entered looking rather flustered. Reginald knew at that very moment he was right, she knew why the doctor was here.

'Doctor Barker wants to ask you a few questions about Martha. Answer the questions as truthfully as you can, don't feel there is any agenda Kate,' said Reginald.

'Yes sir.'

The doctor cleared his throat. 'Do you like Martha, Kate?'

'No, I think she's sly.'

'What do you mean, sly?'

'Watching her it's like she's up to something all the time, even when Reggie was awful to her - sorry ma'am,' she added, looking apologetically towards Mrs Cresswell. 'Reggie could be awfully bossy at times and you could see Martha was angry but she'd bite her tongue, like she didn't want us to see the real Martha. I had a cousin like that, bad she was, but when anyone tackled her she was all sweetness and light.'

'Do you think she was jealous of Reggie, Kate?' Eleanor was now involving herself in the interrogation.

'Absolutely, you could see it in her eyes. Do you know she's actually taken that dress of Reggie's - the one with the pink roses, the one she wore for all the parties last year?'

'I did tell her to take her pick.'

'Yes, for the party, but not after Reggie was... gone, sorry ma'am.'

Reginald was uncomfortable with the situation. 'Perhaps she just wanted something of Reggie's to remember her by?'

Both women looked at him, unconvinced.

'You do know they call her the 'Devil's child' over in Thropton, don't you?' She looked towards her mistress. 'I did tell Mr Cresswell all about it.'

Eleanor looked at her now red faced husband, who said embarrassingly, 'I didn't tell you the full story because it was rubbish. It was only because of the birthmark, that's all.'

'Na, sir, it was more than that, you know it was. Her parents said she was evil, her very own parents. They said she was far too clever for her own good… had ideas that she'd be rich one day and leave them all behind. Poisoned her dad with rat poison and some say she got that bull of theirs to trample him to death.'

'That's enough!' Mr Cresswell had heard sufficient detail, it was all just speculation. 'Thank you Kate, you can go.' Kate left the room, obviously wanting to say more.

'I need to know what you want to do about this,' the doctor asked.

'Nothing!' said Mr Cresswell. Eleanor's head swung in the direction of her husband.

He continued, 'I'm sorry but I've heard nothing but ignorant peoples' thoughts and rumours. The child has had a hard enough life as it is. Plus, just think of the publicity Eleanor… we'd be open to scrutiny, it would be in all the newspapers. I don't want my daughter remembered in this way. I do not want the police involved, do you hear me?'

The doctor agreed that there was nothing evidential and that the bruising could of course have been caused by the fit. He would keep quiet and they should go ahead and organise the funeral.

'I don't want to see that child again! 'Eleanor piped up through her anger. 'You might think she's innocent Reg, but I'm sorry - like Kate, I have my doubts now too. I can't believe that you didn't tell me ages ago about the rumours. Please make sure she's not at the funeral for all our sakes, as I will not be accountable for my actions. You may think this can be brushed under the carpet Reg, but I don't.'

Back to the Bones

Chapter 35

The Newcastle mortuary was based in the grounds of the Royal Victoria Infirmary in the middle of the bustling city centre. Jamie Jones and his colleague Clare managed to find a parking space for their van right outside the morgue. They grabbed their photography gear and suits from the back of the van and walked towards the main entrance. Jamie pressed the door bell and waited for one of the mortuary assistants to let them in.

He wondered if Dan was already here. He hadn't seen any of the other CSI vehicles when he parked up but it was possible he could have found a space somewhere else. It was a nightmare parking in the city and he was sick of hearing about staff being 'ticketed' and having to pay the fines. It was often a CSI's dilemma - either meet the cost of getting a parking ticket or holding up a crime scene because you couldn't get parked.

Young Dan had been very keen to be part of the bones post mortem when Jamie had mentioned it, but he suspected that Dan's enthusiasm for this job had more to do with being in the presence of the lovely Emma Bould, than the actual case itself.

DCI Foster had also promised that she was going to be there but only for the post mortem briefing. She said she'd provide a 'stand in' for the examination itself. The post mortem was to be carried out by Doctor Roger Artem, one of the regular Home Office pathologists, who was to be accompanied by a trainee pathologist called Paul.

One of the mortuary assistants eventually came to the door and let them in.

'How ya doing Jamie, OK?'

'Yeah, not bad, not bad.'

They followed the technician down the sterile corridor. The office they used for 'briefings' was small, with a table in the centre and eight chairs around it. Dan was already sitting there chatting to Paul the trainee and Emma Bould about the trouble he'd had when uncovering the foot bones, and how he didn't realise there were quite as many bones on a human foot.

'Hi Jamie, we're just waiting for DCI Foster and Doctor Artem, the doctor is running a wee bit late today,' said Paul, checking his mobile phone at the same time.

'Ah, he says he'll be here in about ten/fifteen minutes.'

Detective Chief Inspector Karen Foster entered the room in a bluster, 'right, what's happening?'

'We're just waiting for Doctor Artem.' Jamie said.

He looked at the rather dishevelled appearance of this thirty something woman, her dirty blonde hair tied loosely at the back of her hair and dodgy blue eye liner under her eyes. He thought to himself that he was no make-up expert but that surely wasn't a good look for any woman. Even her suit looked like it had been slept in the night before.

He knew very little about this new DCI other than she was incredibly ambitious. He had apparently worked with her years ago when she was just a PC, but he had very little recollection of her. It was only her reputation that he'd really heard about. She'd been described to him as 'very rude and a bit crackers' by the sergeant from Rothbury, who had previously worked with her quite closely. He also said that she'd throw anyone under the bus to get on, so he knew the score.

Jamie watched her as she manoeuvred herself into the seat at the head of the table, obviously and mistakenly ready to take control of the situation. Dan started up his chat with Paul and Emma again but she interjected, 'sit,' she said, pointing at the chair to her right. Dan coloured up and did what he was told, looking over at Jamie who just raised his eyebrows.

'I want to start, I don't have much time' she said.

'With all due respect, we have to wait for the pathologist' replied Jamie, as politely as possible.

'Ah to hell with that, he's late. This guy can update him later,' she said, pointing at Paul. 'I really don't have time to sit and wait.'

Paul looked very uncomfortable. 'I'm sorry,' he said, 'I'll go and see where he is,' and with that he quickly fled the room, leaving the disgruntled DCI sitting shaking her head in temper.

About five minutes later Paul arrived back with Doctor Artem in tow. This was after Jamie and Dan had sat there being lectured to about how the world fell apart when people didn't do what they were supposed to.

Doctor Artem had quite obviously been briefed by Paul and when he entered he lowered his glasses and glared over the top of them at the woman sitting in what was his usual seat at the head of the table.

'Well now, who do we have here?... another fresh young face.' His professional demeanour and cultured accent made Karen Foster sit up.

'I'm afraid young lady you're in my seat, I like that one... bad back you know, comes with the territory - all that stooping over dead bodies.'

Jamie tensed, waiting for the fireworks but to his surprise they didn't come. DCI Foster got up and moved into another chair.

The pathologist started the briefing. 'OK, is everyone here who needs to be? How about we introduce ourselves as we have a few new faces? I'll start, I'm Doctor Roger Artem. I'll be conducting the post-mortems today.'

'I'm Paul Green, trainee pathologist and I'll be assisting Dr Artem.'

'Emma Bould, Archeologist, I assisted on the dig.'

'Clare Charlton, CSI, photography.'

'Dan Clarke, CSI, taking samples.'

'Jamie Jones, Crime Scene Manager.'

'Detective Chief Inspector Karen Foster, Senior Investigating Officer.'

'Carol Gould, Coroner's Officer, I'll be taking notes.'

'Right, now we all know who each other is, what's the story with this one then?'

Karen Foster reached for the completed pro-forma placed in front of her. 'OK, we received a call from the occupier of One Aspley Stables, Aspley near Rothbury at 1630 hours on the 15th, stating she had found bones in her back garden. A local officer attended, believed them to be suspicious and asked for forensics to attend. The occupier had only just moved in to the property... the previous elderly owner dying a few months prior.' She sifted through her notes. 'Neighbours thought the old woman had lived there around thirty years. She was an upstanding member of the community, very churchy, erm... she was a former headmistress, I believe. The previous occupant to that was a Peter Sudbury and he bought the house when it was first converted from an old stable block. He was actually in his eighties when he bought it, he only lived there a couple of years before he died.'

'Jamie, would you like to expand on that?' said the rotund Pathologist.

'Yes, certainly. On attending I found a small hole which the owner of the property had dug, removing loose soil to see what a neighbour's dog had previously been so interested in. It revealed four metacarpals and a small section of old material. On further examination I found what looked like an intact human wrist underneath. The metacarpals were removed, bagged and dropped off at the mortuary. The next morning they were then confirmed as human. The scene was secured by local officers, Emma was notified and together we spent two days bringing up what we initially thought was one set of remains but we uncovered a second set of remains that had been placed under the first. The primary skeleton had what appeared to be blunt force trauma to the front of the skull and the second had damage to parts of the rib cage, which is consistent with the use of a knife.'

'Emma, would you like to interject here? Anything else of note during the dig?'

The young woman smoothed back her shiny dark brown hair and shuffled forward in her seat.

'Well, the bits of clothing we found were quite telling. There appears to have been some form of plastic sheeting over the bodies which helped significantly with preservation. Firstly, we found what looked like bits of material from a suit... a pin striped suit would be my guess, also tiny bits of what looked like lining. The recovery of the fabric was more consistent with it being draped over the body as opposed to the article actually being worn. We found two clothing labels, currently being investigated.'

'Any significant fabric under the remains?'

'I believe both wore some form of clothing but most of the fabric we recovered was actually between the two remains, scant amount below the second. The suit fabric was purely above the first.'

'On the first remains we found what appeared to be what was left of a threaded cord near the waist area. This was recovered both above and below the ilium - the hip bone. We also found plastic buttons and very small amounts of a cotton fabric, which if I had to guess... I'd say were pyjamas.'

'What about the position of the first corpse?'

'First remains - the positioning consistent with being placed in the grave, arms were actually placed over the chest.'

'Mmm, someone cared then!'

'Yes, I'd say so.'

'What about insect life Emma, in respect of the first body?'

'We found insect casings consistent with the area and consistent with bodies being placed in the grave some time after death.'

'Right, how far was the second set of remains below the first?'

'Well, the foot bones of the first and second were jumbled together, that's what confused Dan here, wasn't it?' she smiled.

'Yeah, couldn't make sense of how many bones there actually was. I've never been on a dig before, well, never actually uncovered a skeleton before anyway.'

Jamie watched the young CSI as he spoke and could see he was totally and utterly mesmerised by Emma and it was probably obvious to everyone around that table. He glanced at Karen Foster to see if she had noticed but she was now head down, fiddling with her phone.

'There was a four inch maximum depth between the bodies, with the feet and legs slightly raised.'

Jamie spoke up, 'this one hadn't been carefully placed, the body was face down, one arm under the body, one to the side, legs raised upwards from the knee.'

'Dumped in other words?'

'Yes, I'd say so.'

'Insect life around this one Emma? Consistent with the first?'

'Yes.'

Dr Artem looked towards the now disinterested Karen Foster. 'DCI Foster, anything to add? Do we know who the bodies could be yet?' He had obviously noticed her lack of concentration.

'Yes... certainly. Sorry, I'm dealing with a very important job at the moment, I'm a little distracted.'

'It must be really bad if it's worse than a potential double murder!' he said, raising his eyebrows at her.

She put her phone down on the table. 'The neighbours have all been spoken to, no one has really come up with anything concrete, although there is a question mark over the headmistress's husband. He lived with her for a few years when she first moved there but then they divorced and he apparently went to live in France. I have officers checking that out at the moment. We're going for publicity as soon as we can get an accurate estimate on how old the bones actually are.'

'We won't be able to tell you exactly I'm afraid, you'll have to wait for the carbon dating for that, but we will probably be able to give you a reasonable assessment as to how long they've actually been there. I take it there's no 'stand out' missing persons from the area?'

'No, not that we're aware of.'

Jamie was just pleased she'd held back on going to the media. He had been worried about that, somebody in the MITs had obviously had a word with her. This was probably going to be a very steep learning curve for the new DCI.

Chapter 36

The post mortem was to be conducted in the usual room used for Home Office examinations. Jamie and Clare went in together. They had initially been held back by Karen Foster explaining that her 'bag man' was on his way and he'd be filling in for her at the PM. They made their way down the corridor, finding Dan already there, chatting with one of the mortuary assistants. They both took off their fleece jackets in the changing area and put on their pale blue paper suits, overshoes, hair nets and their two pairs of rubber gloves. The blue rubber gloves were the bane of Jamie's life. Over the years the skin on his hands had suffered, becoming red and sore with the constant moisture.

On two separate stainless steel tables sat one plastic box each. This wasn't the usual sight of a post-mortem and Jamie commented on how sad the scene looked. Usually he was confronted with at least a body bag containing the actual body, but these lives had been reduced to a single plastic box of bones, without anyone even knowing who they were... *well apart from the person who put them there of course.* The room was glaringly bright which strangely made it feel even more somber with the light bouncing off the sterile silver surfaces.

In contrast to the rest of the scene, Dan was hopping about like an enthusiastic puppy dog, chatting with the mortuary assistants and Paul, waiting for the PM to get going. However, when Emma, Dr Artem and the Coroner's Officer entered he immediately stopped talking and calmed down, so obviously trying to look cool and poised in front of his new infatuation.

Emma and the pathologist chatted for some time, waiting for the SIOs 'stand in' to arrive. The conversation was about their pet dogs - both having greyhounds, and the trouble they had taking them on holiday.

'I brought mine on holiday up here in the summer,' she said, 'it was so beautiful, I stayed in a cottage that looked over Druridge Bay. It was just perfect for the dog…short stroll, then we were straight onto the beach. She'd just run and run, chasing the sea gulls - she loved it. A bit of a change for her, it's usually a park walk in Leeds and I have to keep her on the lead as she's rather partial to chasing furries.'

'Yup, mine too. I go to that beach with my two sometimes as well, it's such a lovely spot. There's a cafe nearby at Cresswell, very dog friendly. It actually encourages dogs and has an agility playground for them, lovely cakes too. I'm partial to a nice bit of sponge cake,' he said, patting his pot belly. 'The owner has two dogs of his own - collies who potter about the place... beautiful dogs, really well behaved - not like mine. You'll have to try it next time you're up.'

'Yeah, sounds great.'

Jamie glanced over at Dan who was obviously taking this conversation in. *Bet he was planning on buying a bloody greyhound now*, he thought. At that point the DCI's bag man - Inspector Nigel Lowther walked in ready for action in his paper suit, profusely apologising for holding up proceedings. Unlike his new boss, he was a quiet and polite man. He made his introduction and stood back to watch the post mortem.

Right,' said Dr Artem, clapping his hands together, 'we're all here, let's make a start.' He walked towards the first lonely box of bones. He read the label Jamie had originally filled in on the side of the box - 'sealed box JPJ16 opened at 11.15hrs. Seal number B60167112 removed,' he began.

He started to remove the seal and open the tight lid of the plastic box.

'Right, let's see if we can work out what happened to you then, shall we!' he said, conversing to the actual bones inside the box. 'Paul, fancy helping me get this in anatomical position please?'

'Yes, certainly.'

He stepped back, letting Clare whose role was the allocated photographer, to take photos of the bones in situ within the box.

The pathologist removed the skull first. 'Yes, Emma, I agree almost definitely male.' He handed Paul the skull, who placed it carefully at the top of the table. They worked together, Paul placing the bones in situ until they got to the feet.

'This doesn't seem quite right here Roger. Some of the metatarsals don't match, these must be from the second body.'

Emma spoke up, 'yes, as I mentioned earlier they were in a right muddle, the lighting wasn't that great in the tent either.'

'Just leave the unmatched ones to one side... photographs, please Clare.'

'Do you have the chewed bones I dropped off earlier?' asked Jamie.

The mortuary assistant picked up a sealed box from a side bench and placed it on the table. The pathologist removed the bones, giving the Coroner's Officer the box and seal numbers.

'My two boys would have made a better job than this' he said, examining one of the chewed bones. 'Small dog was it?'

'Yes,' replied Jamie, 'fluffy brown and white thing... a Tibetan Terrier I think they said.'

'Ah yes, the Tibetan monks used to keep them on their knees, under their robes to keep them warm you know - lovely little dogs.'

After about ten minutes the two doctors had quickly placed the bones into position.

'Right, no bones left in the box, we've definitely got a male here, clear by the robust bone structure, the narrow pelvic inlet, narrower hip bones - you see... all consistent with it being male.' He moved back to the skull, 'quite a square shaped jaw, bone structure... again all consistent male traits.'

'OK, approximate height…Paul, measurements please.' He followed the young doctor as he made his measurements. Clare followed, taking photographs at every stage. 'I'd say around five foot ten to six foot, do you agree Paul?'

'Yes!' he replied.

'Age - let's see... there's evidence of wear on the pelvic bone,' he moved again to the skull as Clare sidled in for another photograph. 'Teeth... teeth appear to be all still in situ, again evidence of some considerable wear. Mmm, there's a nice silver filling here in one of the molars. I would say approximate age forty to fifty.'

'Condition of bones - let's see now, damage to any of the bones? Obviously I can see damage to the front of the cranium and ribs.'

At this point Jamie and Emma moved forward, re-examining their find, looking at the skull more closely, under the specialist lighting.

'Mmm, interesting, I'd say definitely perimortem, what do you think Emma?'

'I would say so, you can definitely see the radiating fractures around the break,' she moved slightly to the side as Dr Artem asked Clare to take another more in depth photograph of the spider web patterns around the broken bones. Emma directed herself towards Paul - 'If this had happened post-mortem I'd expect a much cleaner break, bones become much more brittle post mortem.'

'Jamie, anything particular of note when you brought the body up?' the pathologist now sweeping his eyes across the remains.

'There were the obvious breaks to the rib cage and skull and the chewed foot bones, of course. We did remove more insect casings from the skull area and small fragments of plastic and material - but nothing else of note.'

'Yes, I'd say ribs were broken post-mortem, nice clean breaks, hyoid bone intact? - yep.'

He worked systematically around the body, in a now very well rehearsed dance, allowing photographs of the bones to be taken at each stage.

'Right, that's the first one examined, shall we break there for half an hour for lunch and then we'll start on the next?'

Jamie interrupted Dan as he was walking away towards Emma, 'wait Dan, you'll need to box up the skull for further examination of the teeth, we'll have it taken to the lab.'

'OK,' he replied, looking very disappointed as Emma walked out in the company of Dr Artem.

Chapter 37

After lunch it was the turn of the second box of bones to be examined. The pathologist started in the same manner as the first.

'Sealed box JPJ19 opened at 14.05 hrs. Seal number B60169237 removed,' he began.

Paul and Dr. Artem began removing the bones, laying them out in order, a few mutterings between them, interspersed by Clare photographing the placement of the bones.

'Right Paul, measurements again, it's so obviously smaller than the first.'

'Five foot one to say five foot three at most. Bones look in good condition... Paul would you like to give your observations on gender?'

'Certainly,' the young doctor started examining the hip bones. 'Pelvic inlet... open and circular, wide sub pubic angle... no doubt we have a female. Facial bones more delicate than we'd expect in a male and some traces of hair still attached to the skull on this one... it's definitely a gingery hue, quite long strands too.'

Jamie looks towards Dan who was tasked with collecting samples. 'Can you get a sample tube and we'll send a sample of the hairs off to the lab too?' The young man carefully did as requested, whilst Paul continued looking over the body.

'What age would you put on her Paul?' asked the pathologist, testing his trainee.

'There are signs of wear in the hip joint, and also I noticed the hair appeared to be lighter at the root moving to a more reddy hue towards the end. At a guess I'd say over forty years but I don't know if I'd like to commit to any greater detail than that. Evidence of wear on the teeth... appear to be no fillings, but there are several molars missing.'

Dr Artem stepped forward again examining the hair in more detail. 'Thanks Paul, I think the best we can say at this stage is the same as the first, between forty and fifty. The carbon dating will give us an accurate assessment of age.'

'Right young man, now the interesting bit, evidence of foul play?'

With this, everyone in the room became more fixed on the young doctor and the tension turned more in tune with a normal murder examination. 'The most evidential features are obviously the marks on the ribs and on the right ulna and radius... they look like penetrating force trauma - smooth, oblique angles and there is some evidence of striations. I count seven marks on the rib cage, three on the radius and one on the ulna.' Clare was honing in on each of the injuries to the ribs and arms, meticulously taking photographs.

'Emma, Jamie, anything to add?'

'Same insect casings found... soil conditions similar, perhaps slightly more clay in parts than on the first skeleton. Samples all taken and off for examination.'

'Right, ladies, gentlemen, I thank you for your time and efforts, we'll get the report done as soon as possible.' It was all vague at the moment but Jamie knew they would have a better assessment of age when the actual report was done as the pathologists never gave too much away at the post mortem.

Dan was ahead of the game and was packaging the second skull ready for scrutiny at the lab in Wetherby, whilst Jamie pointed towards a rib he wanted packaged too. 'A few things I wanted to ask you boss before we head off,' he said to Jamie as they were leaving.

The three CSI's reached the white van parked in the car park. Jamie opened the back and placed the samples in, ready for transportation. 'I just wanted you to go over the injuries to the second body,' asked Dan.

'Alright, no problem, what is it?'

'Well, we discussed at the time the knife marks and what was obviously defence wounds on the arms. It was just some of the terminology they used.'

'All they were saying was that it was sharp force trauma, consistent with a smooth blade being used. However, they found patterns on the entry points consistent with a blade having a serrated edge - striations. I'm sure you learnt that these can then be matched with any weapons found.'

'Just wanted to check, in case I was missing something, it was the striations bit I wasn't that sure of.'

'Always good to ask Dan.'

Chapter 38

Some of the residents of Aspley were shocked at the fallout following the discovery of the bodies in Martha's old cottage garden. Whilst there were several who were not astonished at all about the revelation of one body being found, they were totally horrified and perplexed at the uncovering of a second body under Martha's fountain.

Today was like no other. The police were in the hamlet to carry out their searches within Martha's house and conduct a sweep of the locality. The locals were also having to endure camera wielding media personnel milling around the lane. The police kept moving them on but there was a never ending supply who would turn up wanting that one big story.

Ronnie and Clara felt like prisoners in their own home. It was Clara's day off from the hospital, a day she would normally spend pottering in the garden or going out for a walk with Maisie - both out of the question today. Their new guest Anna had gone out this morning to visit a relative, so they were alone in the house.

'Look Ronnie, I think you're over-thinking it all, it happened over twenty years ago. You didn't kill anyone, did you?'

'Na but I bloody well helped cover it up though, didn't I?'

'Yes, me too remember and half the other residents here.'

'Yes, but think about it Clara… Joe and Heather are now dead, Nina and Bill are hiding in Spain, Gerald is pulling the old 'I've got dementia' trick and Arthur and Ella are in their eighties now. It's going to be us left carrying the can.'

'Look, unless someone talks we're absolutely fine, don't worry. They've kept quiet for years so I doubt they'd confess now.'

'When they find out who it is in that grave... and they will, there'll be even more questions. Don't forget, Ella's a bit of a liability as well.'

'I know she's got dementia but I think she's absolutely right about one thing… I think there's a strong possibility that it's that barmaid from the Shoulder of Mutton buried alongside James. She was very friendly with him at the time, remember? And there were always the rumours that she had run away with him.'

'Why don't you go around to Arthur's house and see if the police have let slip anything about the second body?'

'I don't want them to see me hopping about between neighbours.'

'Here' she said, handing him a couple of magazines, 'take these around for Ella, she likes looking at all the celebs in the Hello magazine.'

As Ronnie pulled shut his front door as quietly as possible so as not to alert Maisie, he saw two vans parked up in the square outside Martha's cottage and some men in boiler suits hanging around. His heart began to beat faster and he tried to control his breathing. 'Morning,' he shouted, as he passed.

'Morning, nice day isn't it?' a grey haired officer replied.

'Yes, it's lovely.'

The officers were going through Martha's old tool shed located against the wall in the small side garden. *What were they bloody well looking for*? he thought.

Thirty seconds later he was knocking on Arthur and Ella's newly painted front door. Arthur looked old and tired this morning. He knew his life wasn't easy dealing with Ella's illness.

'Come in,' he said, pulling back the door to let him enter.

'Clara sent these around for Ella' Ronnie replied, handing Arthur the magazines.

'She's sitting in the garden with the dog and the cats. I'm surprised the dog didn't hear you knocking. I guess he's probably just getting used to all the commotion from the police vans coming up and down the lane all the time, and the car doors constantly banging.'

'Arthur, I couldn't sleep last night thinking about what Ella said about that ginger barmaid from the pub. Do you think it's her?'

'Well, I was talking with that young officer last night, you know, the one who's stopping people from going into the courtyard, and he did let slip to me something about the second body. He said it was all going to be common knowledge soon, so he didn't think he was breaking any police confidentiality rule by talking to me. I asked him if it was perhaps an old burial site but he said he had heard the archeologist say that her guess was the second body was female. Apparently it was a small frame... not like the first and it definitely wasn't ancient remains.'

'Yeah, it's her isn't it? She was tiny, that barmaid... wasn't she?'

'She'd be seven stone wet through and I'd say at a guess - about five foot at most.'

Ronnie puckered his lips, puffed his cheeks out and exhaled, getting rid of some of that built up angst. He raised his eyes to the ceiling. 'Arthur, that second body, it must have been Martha who put it in the grave... it must have been... that poor woman's body must have been hidden in the house whilst we were all there dealing with James. How the hell didn't anyone see it?'

'I don't know lad, but at the time I did think it strange how much blood there was... remember? And the state Martha was in I thought some of it was hers. It was Joe Weiss who raised the alarm, he knocked asking us for help as Martha was asking for Ella. Then, when we got there everyone seemed to appear from nowhere. She was sitting on the front step, covered in blood. She was in a right state and then when I saw Jimmy lying on the bed... my God, I nearly passed out. His face was a right mess, smashed in and completely covered in blood.'

'His face was covered over by the time I got there - I didn't see any of that. I remember them coming to ask Clara to check Martha over for injuries as she was soaked in blood and in what could only be described as a catatonic state.'

'It was Joe who convinced us to help her. I must admit I had wanted to call the police but Joe told us her life would be over if we called them… she'd lose her job and her home. He asked us if we really thought she deserved that. Of course everyone thought she had been through enough - because all of us, at some stage, had witnessed first hand his treatment of her.'

'Did you ever actually see him be violent towards her, Arthur?'

'Well... not exactly, but I saw the black eyes. She had a broken wrist once too, and other injuries. I don't think there's any question they used to fight... you could hear them sometimes, and it did usually result in her being injured - na, he used to beat her alright… Jimmy could be a right nasty bastard.'

'I'm just scared Arthur, she has got to have been responsible for the other body... must have been! Unless someone else helped her?'

'As I say, it was Joe who was first on the scene but Joe wouldn't have helped her hide a second body. I'm sorry, I just don't believe he'd do that - it was only because it was Jimmy we did what we did.'

'Well, she did manage to get us to hide a bloody dead body in her garden though, didn't she?'

Chapter 39

Detective Chief Inspector Karen Foster sat at the head of the meeting room table. She had gathered together members of the Murder Investigation Team and Forensics to get a complete overview of the Aspley case.

'OK, ladies, gentlemen, can we start please? Let's go around the table.' The new DCI was still not totally sure of who everyone was yet.

'Detective Inspector Nigel Lowther.'

'DS Anderson, MITs'

'DC Trevor Stapleton, MITs'

'DC Susan Neary, MITs'

'DC Peter Burke'

'DC Sarah Miller'

'Jamie Jones, CSM'

'Dan Soulsby, CSI'

'I think there's still a couple of you I haven't met, so let me introduce myself. My name is Karen Foster, the SIO on this investigation. Let me just outline what I know so far.' She reached for her notes.

'A call was received on Tuesday 15th to say a resident of Aspley had found bones in her back garden. They were later confirmed as human. Forensics and an Archeologist - Emma Bould, were called to exhume the bones and they uncovered the remains of two persons. Yesterday, post mortems were conducted on both remains and it was confirmed that one was male, the other female. I've pinned the pathologist down to an educated guess at how long they'd been buried and his best guess was twenty-five years, but giving a few years each way. The MITs officers have conducted initial enquiries with residents of Aspley and as yet we have no specific leads as to who the skeletons are. DS Anderson, would you like to outline in more detail the result of enquiries?'

DS Anderson had worked on murders for years. He was nearing the end of his career and had seen many 'run of the mill' murders but this one was a little different due to the time lapse and the main suspect in the case being a very respectable elderly woman.'

'Yes ma'am. DCs Stapleton and Neary have now spoken with all residents of Aspley except a couple who live in the west wing of Aspley Hall as they're currently on holiday in Spain... something they do every year. Enquiries at the scene revealed that the premises were converted into a house over thirty years ago from an old stable block at the rear of the Hall. The first resident was a very elderly gentleman who lived there for approximately two years before he died and who didn't interact that much with other residents. The second occupant, Martha Dickinson, a former headmistress, lived there for around twenty-eight years, being in her forties when she moved there. She arrived describing herself as being separated from her husband, but shortly afterwards she got back with her husband and he lived with her for around a year before they split and he went back to live in France. Apparently he was a builder and used to work abroad a lot. The new occupants, Anna and Christopher Jude, had been in the premises less than a week when they made the discovery - they haven't fully moved in yet.'

'Well, we can rule the latter couple out. Do we have more detail on the first resident?'

'Not at the moment, but enquiries are in hand.'

'And what about this Martha... Dickinson, was it? Our former headmistress?'

'Yes, worked at Rothbury Infants' School for years.'

'Unlikely double murderer! What about this husband of hers then?'

'Peter and Sarah have more information on him but residents said he was a bit of a 'handful' by all accounts. What was interesting was that we gleaned more information from the residents who hadn't lived there very long. The ones who lived there a long time and who actually knew him had very little to say about him, said he never really spoke to them, so they didn't know much about him. It was the woman at the 'Chapel' who has only lived there five years who told us the most as she used to chat with Martha. Apparently, she told her he was a womaniser and was violent towards her. She catalogued quite a few injuries.'

'What more do we know about Martha?'

DS Anderson looked towards his two DCs - 'can one of you do a quick update on what you've found.'

The two DCs had been looking into Martha's background and trying to find out more about James or Jimmy Dickinson since he had moved to France.

DC Miller cleared her throat. 'Yes, Peter and I have been doing a bit of work on James Dickinson. He was born and brought up in Alnwick but we can't find any living relatives. He had no siblings or children. He was a builder by trade and had his own building company, it looks like he did alright for himself. There's been no record of him in this country for twenty-six years, no tax paid, no bank account - nothing. I've sent a request to our French colleagues to see if they can trace him. I've checked PNC and CIS for any convictions, again - nothing. We're still having departure records checked.'

'What about Martha?'

'Nothing on PNC, but I did find a 'community resolution' for shoplifting, which I guess is a bit interesting for an ex-headmistress.'

'When was this?'

'Six years ago?'

'Well, I guess due to her age she might just have forgotten to pay for something and walked out.'

'Not according to the record ma'am. She had a trolley full of really expensive stuff, I think it mounted up to a few hundred pounds worth. There was a note on the record that she was under the care of a local psychologist, who actually attended and spoke with the OIC. She agreed to pay for the goods and seek help - the supermarket was happy with that.'

'Interesting... anything else?'

'Yes, it appears Martha had been married before, in her early twenties to a William Wilkie, a farmer out at Elsdon. She was teaching at a school in Newcastle when they met. He went on to inherit the family farm after his parents died. Three years after marrying Martha he drowned in a lake on their land. He had initially been posted as missing, then his body turned up a week later, floating in the lake. There was a full police investigation and records state he had apparently been out fishing in a boat and somehow had fallen into the water.'

'Did Martha inherit the farm after his death?'

'She did, yes boss.'

'So, both of Martha's marriages ended suspiciously. Am I reading too much into this or is that just a coincidence? I want you to prioritise investigation into our elusive second husband's travel details.'

'Anyone spoken to Martha's family to see if they can shed any light on anything?'

'She has a sister Julia but they were estranged. She's been spoken to, said she never met James or indeed Martha's first husband. The only contact they ever had was the odd letter and through their daughter Africa, who would occasionally visit her aunt in the school holidays. Martha had four brothers, her two elder brothers died years ago, a third no one has heard from in years and her youngest brother Billy lived in

Rothbury. She did have quite a lot to do with him but unfortunately he died only a few months before Martha… so drawn a bit of a blank there.'

'Anything else with regard to enquiries?'

'Well, I thought a few of the neighbours were a little jumpy. There's an old guy, Gerald Bainbridge, who said immediately that he suffered from dementia and couldn't even remember his name some days. This was before I even asked him a question. Plus, we spoke with a middle aged man who has lived in Aspley since his early twenties. He seemed a bit overly anxious to me. I've been doing this a long time and it just didn't feel quite right to me.'

'So they both knew Martha?'

'Yeah, they both lived there when her husband lived there too. There's an old couple who live two cottages up. They lived there at the time as well. I've spoken to the guy who lives there but apparently his wife suffers dementia and he didn't want her upset. He said she wasn't lucid enough to be of any help anyway. There's an ex-cop who still lives next door but she said she doesn't interact much with the 'Aspley crowd' and vaguely remembered James. She knew Martha though - said she was the last person she'd suspect of committing a murder. The only other people who were there in James' time were the couple who are in Spain and they're uncontactable at the moment.'

'Martha's closest friends seem to have been the couple next door - the psychologist I mentioned in the community resolution file and his wife, plus after their death their daughter... Rani Weiss kept contact with her, she was mentioned on the death certificate. I've made an appointment to speak with Miss Weiss tomorrow.'

DCI Foster was concentrating on the notes she'd made. 'Anything else in relation to enquiries? No? OK, Forensics update please.'

It was Jamie Jones who was up next. 'On initial examination in the garden of the address I found a small hole apparently dug by a neighbour's dog who had entered when the gate had been left open. The occupant had later investigated the hole himself to see what the dog had been digging for. Inside were some small bones that looked like that of a human hand. On closer examination a small piece of plastic and a piece of material were removed and under that was what looked like intact bones of a wrist. The bones were packaged and sent to the pathologist to identify if they were human. They were confirmed as human the next morning. ' Jamie reached for his mug of coffee, took a sip and continued his update.

'We spent two days digging with Emma Bould, an Archeologist from Leeds. We didn't realise there were two skeletons until we started to see there were far too many bones for two human feet. When we removed and boxed the first remains it soon became very apparent we were dealing with two sets of remains, not one. There was soil between the two skeletons but in places only at a depth of around two inches.'

Again, a mouthful of coffee and he continued, 'both remains were taken to the mortuary and the post mortem was conducted yesterday. Initial findings are that the first skeleton was that of a male, middle aged, approximately 6ft tall. There was significant damage to the front of the skull - the Pathologist and Archeologist both agreeing peri mortem - the pattern of the breaks showing blunt force trauma. There were no other significant signs of damage on the skeleton. The skull is currently in our store room waiting to be sent to the lab if required... teeth were intact, so there is a possibility of extracting DNA.'

'The second body was significantly smaller, confirmed female, again middle aged, height around the five foot mark. This skeleton had a significant amount of damage to the rib cage in the form of sharp force trauma, consistent with the use of a blade - there were also marks on the bones of the arm showing possible defence wounds. Again, skull and one of the ribs removed for further forensic investigation if needed - the rib showed a specific pattern of the blade used. The only other thing of note was that the hair was still evident on the skull, it has a definite red tinge to it. From a previous case we were told that red pigment is one of the hardest colours to remove from a hair strand, as it's a larger molecule. On close examination there did appear to be a colour differential, being paler toward the root.'

'There were insect casings found around the body, particularly at the skull of the first, which may demonstrate that the bodies were left for at least a few hours before burial. Samples were removed and Emma will be in contact if anything comes to light. We did also find two clothing labels, one which appeared to be a 'Burtons' label which was found on top of the first skull and the second wasn't quite as legible but possibly 'Tam' something... something like that.'

DC Miller spoke, 'Tammy Girl? I'm showing my age a bit, but I'm sure I used to get clothes from Tammy Girl when I was young.'

'Actually, that would fit' Jamie replied, pushing the photographs towards DC Miller.

'DC Miller, could you look into this for me?' asked the DCI, 'I'd like to know when this clothing was available.'

'Yes, no problem ma'am.'

Jamie continued…

'Forensic evidence gleaned from the cottage shows the murder took place in the master bedroom. Human blood was found in the cracks of the flooring, pooling in a large area and consistent with a body being dragged over the thresh of the door out into the garden, the ceiling and the walls also showed signs of blood… The pathologist's report will obviously follow but that's the basic forensic information, we'll just need to decide what samples are to be sent off.'…

'There was one other thing... we've taken casts of the grave 'cut marks' and the spade used to dig the grave appears to have had significant damage. We could perhaps discuss the cast being sent off at a later date for an expert to look at it, maybe we should review it at the strategy meeting? Looking at the marks, you're probably searching for a slightly curved spade with damage in the form of a 'v' shape on the blade.'

'So Jamie, I take it we can safely say we're looking for Mispers from around twenty to thirty years ago, middle aged... can we not narrow that down further?'

'Forensically I wouldn't at this stage, the pathologist might narrow it down a wee bit further in his report and we're still waiting for carbon dating... mind, be warned this takes ages.'

'OK, we'll discuss all the samples etc later. So, both middle aged, one male, one female; male around 6ft tall, female around 5ft - can we say female has red hair at this stage?'

'I would say something like female may have had a red tinge to hair.'

'No rings or jewellery found?'

'Yes, the female was wearing an anklet, made up of small coins or discs.'

'Mmm interesting, is it worth mentioning the clothing labels at this stage? Nigel, what do you think?'

The DI lifted his head from his note taking, 'I wouldn't at this stage ma'am, I'd just keep it vague. I wouldn't even mention the anklet to the press either.'

'OK' she said, obviously trusting her bag man's judgement.

'Right, Jamie and I will meet about what to send off for further forensic examination. I was warned when I took this job that money was tight and forensics is an expensive field. Right, let's list what's still to do enquiries wise...

Further enquiries to find more details about the first owner of the property. This Peter guy, seems like a long shot if he was in his eighties whilst living there, but we better cover it.

I want the residents that potentially could have lived in Aspley at the time of the murders interviewed.

This niece... Africa Wells, I want her located and spoken to.

Further enquiries as to the whereabouts of James Dickinson, and I want Rani Weiss interviewed.

See if we can contact this couple in Spain, what are they called?'

'Nina and Bill Lyons, ma'am,' replied the DS, scribbling it all down.

'Oh and a long shot I know, I want older residents in the village of Elsdon spoken to, with regard to Martha's first husband William Wilkie. See if any relatives are still there or if anyone remembers him - just in case we have a woman who likes 'popping off' her husbands,' she laughed, 'let's put that one to bed quickly!'

Chapter 40

Another meeting had been planned, a strategy meeting this time, in order to decide what forensic samples should be sent off to the lab. Jamie was putting together the samples and photographs relevant to the Aspley job, interspersed with answering queries on his mobile. The phone was relentless - requests for advice and pressure from supervision to attend their specific job first - the stress levels were often intense. For Jamie, the dead were definitely much easier to handle than the living. The new DCI had surprised him in the morning meeting, she had handled it much better than he thought she would. He thought that perhaps the influence of her very experienced, quiet and professional bag man, DI Nigel Lowther, may have proved to be the key in pulling her back from charging in and making rookie mistakes.

The strategy meeting was due to be held in conference room two, a small office on the top floor. Most people preferred this one as it had the luxury of windows and a view across green fields. This 'get together' was held to explore how they were going to move the case forward. The Exhibits Officer would be present and decisions were to be made to push the detection.

The DCI, DI and Exhibits Officer all entered together. They only needed the DS and the meeting could start. Jamie was hoping this didn't run over, as he needed to get home early tonight.

'Right, let's get started,' Karen Foster was obviously wanting to get away early too. The DI leant in her direction, 'we should wait for DS Anderson ma'am, I saw him in the corridor earlier and it isn't quite 2pm yet.'

And there it was, thought Jamie - *the cool, calm influence of the quiet man, and it worked.* She smiled at him, 'of course,' she said.

DS Anderson entered just a few moments later and Karen Foster started. 'Right, I'm new to this so bear with me, I'll learn as I go along and I'll learn quick.' Jamie had no doubt she would.

'I've just come out of a meeting with the media department, who will be working with the ITV local news reporter to put out the information about our two bodies, in the hope that someone will come forward. We're keeping it very bland, two persons, middle aged, male and female, their heights and how long we think they've been there. On this occasion we're going to give the specific location, as that's obviously already out there. I've told them I want it to be released that the bodies were found in the garden of an elderly ex-headmistress from a local school, who is now deceased - just a bit of a fishing exercise. This will hopefully go out tonight.'

'Jamie, I really wanted to talk to you about the weapon used and also the spade castings you mentioned at the morning meeting. Let's talk about weapons first.'

'Alright, fine…the marks on the female were the most telling. There were crenellations in one of the ribs that showed a specific pattern. It didn't look specifically unique to me, I would guess at a pointed bladed knife with a convex v edge and... ,'

'What's that?'

'It's the tip of the blade, it's v shaped but a more rounded v, as opposed to an angular one. The knife's edge is serrated on one side, like your average steak knife. The convex v on the tip however, is slightly more uncommon. Most have an angular v, the latter is cheaper to manufacture.'

The DI nodded whilst making notes and said 'I've got officers searching for any weapons, I know it's a long shot after all this time but who knows, there might be a knife hidden somewhere? So I take it you could identify the knife used?'

'If you did find a knife that fitted the profile you'd need to send it off to the lab. They'd be able to give you a much more detailed analysis of the patterning and probably would be able to give you a definitive answer as to whether that was the knife used.'

'Could we send the impacted bone off now to identify exactly what type of knife?' At this the exhibits offer raised his head in surprise, but Jamie cooly continued.

'You wouldn't gain anything from this. We'd perhaps do this in a live case but in this instance and the stage we're at, I think it would only help if we found an actual knife at the scene.'

'What happened to Martha Dickinson's cutlery after she died?' Karen Foster asked, looking towards DS Anderson.

'We still need to track her niece down ma'am. The niece oversaw the house sale and the removal of furniture etc. I'm told a lot of it was put in a skip that stood outside the front door and disposed of that way, the rest went to an auction - but we don't know any more than that.'

'Right Jamie, what about the male?'

'Well, it was blunt force trauma, so you can't really pin it down other than a heavy object with a flat surface.'

'For example?'

'God, loads of things... a spade, an ornament, a piece of wood, the list is endless.'

'Now, what about DNA?'

'Both skeletons had intact teeth so there's the potential for DNA to be extracted from both, but it's not always that easy, it depends on deterioration.'

'Mind, must warn you, it can obviously be costly. I think it's probably prudent to wait to see if you get any response from the media coverage first, especially in a case as old as this.'

The DCI didn't look happy at this, 'Nigel, what do you think?'

'Yes Ma'am, I think that's prudent too. You could have an overwhelming response from the coverage, rendering your DNA costs as excessive. You still would potentially have to go for DNA at a later date - for proof, but at this stage it's probably a bit soon.'

She turned to Jamie, 'if I wanted to go ahead now, what would be the procedure?'

'We'd take the skull up to Berwick where there's a qualified forensic odontologist we use. He'd extract a tooth for us - we'd package it up and send it to the lab.'

'How long before they could potentially tell us who it was?'

'It's not as simple as that… firstly it's obviously dependent on how good the sample is. They might not get any, they could get traces - it all depends.'…

'If they were successful they'd match it against the DNA national database and this would take a few days, but it's unlikely there would be a match. They would need to have had their DNA taken and that's not very probable when they've been in the ground for over twenty years. We didn't start using DNA until around 1984, 85-ish and we didn't start taking it properly ourselves until 1999/2000. They'd need to go for a familial match. The cost starts cranking up when you're talking about a familial match.'

The voice of reason in the form of Nigel Lowther interjected again. 'There are some cases ma'am when we need a quick response, as we may have family desperate to hear if it's their loved one or someone held in custody, plus there's media pressure and pressure from above. This case isn't one of them. We need to protect the budget as much as possible for those cases.'

'OK, we'll wait, but if we don't hear anything after a week I want a DNA profile attempted for both,' she said, looking slightly more pacified. I was very interested in what you said about... what was it - spade casts?'

'Yeah, a spade can leave a very unique pattern and this one definitely did.'

The DCI had never been in charge of a murder before and even when she had worked on one it was never a burial, so this was all new to her. She hated showing that she didn't quite understand how they'd even be able to see what sort of spade was used twenty years ago but her curiosity over-rode this.

'Can you explain to me exactly how you get these spade casts, Jamie?'

'When you use a spade to dig, it leaves a specific pattern in the ground, for example if the spade is curved or straight. But one of the most telling things is if the spade has any damage on it, as this leaves a very specific mark on the soil as it enters. This specific spade had a 'v' shaped nick in it at the bottom, hence it can be proved to be the spade used to dig the grave.'

'But how do you know for sure it's the spade used to bury the bodies?'

'Because as we're carefully removing the soil, the actual sides of the original grave are revealed, then we look for tool marks and cast them. In this case, when the spade stopped, it left a 'v' mark at the bottom. Now, a spade could be something someone hangs on to. I've still got my dad's old spade, it's probably well over twenty years old. If something still works we tend not to throw it out.'

'OK, so I agree - we'll wait to see if we get a response from the media and from the searches currently being conducted in the loft of the dwelling and surrounding gardens. But now I think from what you've said Jamie, we need to focus on this spade as well.' She looked towards the DS, 'can we have search officers updated with exactly what we're looking for? Liaise with Jamie for this please.'

She tapped her pen a few times on the desk before turning to DS Anderson again, 'we really need to find this Africa Wells, no idea where she is then?'

'She was apparently using the money from the house sale to travel. I've got Sarah and Peter speaking with Rani Weiss - the girl who was also with Martha Dickinson when she died. She may know where she is.'

'I really want you to find out what auction Martha's stuff went to. Ring around see if you can find out.'

'Yes ma'am!'

'Anything to add anyone?' The room was quiet with everyone shaking their heads and mutterings of 'no'.

Chapter 41

DCs Sarah Miller and Peter Burke had been tasked by their sergeant to interview Rani Weiss at the beautiful location of Moon Castle, just outside Warkworth.

'I'm quite excited about this visit today,' said Sarah, 'I've never been in Moon Castle before, have you?'

'Na, I don't think many people have. You do know who Rani Weiss is, don't you?'

'Yeah, she runs that charity for the foreign kids.'

'No! She doesn't just run the charity, she owns the whole 'kit and caboodle'. That's not want I'm getting at though. Do you know who her mother is... you don't know, do you?'

'No, come on then, who's her mother?'

'Just the one and only Superintendent Caroline Hobbs-Brown!'

'Na, Hobbs-Brown doesn't have any kids. In fact, I don't think she's ever had a long term partner, let alone a husband.'

'I'm telling you, that's her mother alright. Apparently, this Rani was brought up solely by her dad, she had nothing to do with her mother. You know when they mentioned on the Community Resolution screen that Martha had been helped by a psychologist, well that was this Rani's dad. Apparently, he was Hobbs-Brown's lecturer at Uni.'

'Who told you that then, I don't believe it?'

'It was Andrea Trousdale in Criminal Justice, she's a distant relative to our wonderful superintendent.'

'Jeez you live and learn, that's a bit of a shocker. I'm really interested in meeting her now, but secretly hoping she's nothing like her mother though.'

They sat pondering, Peter driving as Sarah was stuffing her face with biscuits. She didn't get any breakfast this morning because her lazy teenage sons couldn't get themselves up for college.

'God, if this girl's anything like her mother we're not going to get very far, are we?'

'Na, not like her mother at all I'm told... she's apparently human.' They both sniggered.

The unmarked police car arrived at the castle fifteen minutes early, their appointment being for nine. The gates were closed but there was a button on a metal post nearby that you had to press.

'Yes, can I help you?'

'We're here to see Rani Weiss. DCs Miller and Burke from Northumbria Police.'

'Follow the road to the right. Please be careful as we have children out playing out.'

The gate swung open, then they hit a second gate which didn't open until the first gate closed behind them. 'Jesus, the security here's good.'

'I think it's got more to do with the security of the children than the security of the actual building,' said Sarah, stuffing biscuit wrappers into the glovebox. 'Can I lead Peter, just chip in if you think I've missed something?'

'OK, no bother.' Peter was happy sitting back, letting his colleague do all the talking.

The two detectives came out of the trees and were instantly confronted with the full impressive and quite breathtaking view of Moon Castle, with sweeping lawns at the front and children running around, playing rounders and generally looking like they were having a great time. They parked up in front of the main entrance with a big arched porch-way and in it the biggest oak door Sarah had ever seen in her life.

They were greeted by a young pretty girl in jeans and a bright yellow jumper. 'Hi, I'm Rani Weiss,' she said, 'would you like to come into the drawing room?' She led them through a huge entrance with balconies on either side overlooking the checkered floored room. They walked into the warm and welcoming drawing room with a real fire blazing in a huge hearth and comfy looking sofas either side. Nothing matched, but everything looked perfectly placed and in keeping with the building. An old spaniel snoozed in front of the fire, raising its head to investigate as they sat down.

'He's had a long walk this morning, he's flat out,' Rani said, as they looked at the cosy picture of the old spaniel warming its bones. 'Are you here to talk about the bodies found in Martha's garden?'

'Yes, I take it you know there were two sets of remains found there?'

'Yes, Arthur from 'Number Three' told me. He was really shocked.'

'I can imagine they all were.'

A woman walked in offering tea and coffee, which they both declined.

'How long did you know Martha Dickinson?'

'All my life, well, as long as I can remember anyway.'

'She was a friend of your father I believe?'

'I guess she was more than that really. In a small place like Aspley everyone looks out for each other, so Dad and my Mum would look out for her, help her.'

'Did you know her husband James or Jimmy Dickinson?'

'All before my time I'm afraid but my Dad always recounted that he was a bit of a brute.'

'In what way?'

'I don't know really, I think they used to fight... but I'm guessing really. Martha did champion women in domestic violence situations, so I guess I just put two and two together.'

'What about Martha herself, what was she like?'

'Why... you don't think it's her ex-husband James in that grave do you? He went to live in France, it's not him, surely? Sorry, back to your question - she was kind, articulate, loved reading - Shakespeare fan, loved to take us children rambling on the moors or picking mushrooms in the fields or the forest. We'd often be out in the woods picking wild mushrooms and bringing them home for tea. She was a typical headmistress type.'

Peter jotted everything down as Sarah continued to ask the questions.

'Did she ever mention her first husband?'

'First husband? She only had one as far as I'm aware.'

'No, Martha was married in her early twenties and her husband died very young, he drowned.'

'Gosh, she never ever mentioned she'd been married before.'

'You were with her when she died, weren't you?' Rani nodded. 'Did she mention anything at the time you were nursing her?'

'Actually, Africa her niece did most of the nursing. I just visited, took her some groceries - that sort of thing. I arranged a special outing for her. I asked her if she had any special wishes or things she'd like to do whilst she still could. Martha said she wanted to visit the moors before she died, some symbolic stones that meant a lot to her... she took flowers. Once she'd been she said she could die happy now.'

'Did she say what was so special about this place?'

'It was a family place apparently. She said they would often walk to the stones together. I'm afraid she really struggled with the walk back. She collapsed but luckily an old school friend of hers from the farm where we'd parked up helped us get her back into the car.'

'Who was that?'

'Er, wait a minute... Foggo, Burt Foggo!'

'Can you remember the name of the farm?'

'No... gosh, I usually have a good memory…got it, it's West Moor, something very like that anyway. If you drive all the way through Rothbury from here, you turn immediately right after the last house. It's a bendy 'one track' road, but eventually it leads to the farm.'

'Did she mention much about her childhood Rani, I can call you Rani, can't I?'

'Of course! No, not really, I know she had quite a few brothers but only one sister. She didn't really get on with her family, except for one brother, Billy I think he was called, but he died just before Martha. The only person I ever met was her niece - Africa. Africa told me she used to visit quite a bit when she was younger but to be honest I can't really remember her that well.'

'Do you know where Africa is now Rani?'

'She was in South Africa two weeks ago. She sent me a message on Facebook but there's been nothing since. I think she's planning to go further north. She did say she'd message me when she entered another country. She's planning on finishing in Morocco, I think she has a friend there.'

'Here's my card, will you contact me if she makes contact with you again please?'

'Of course,' Rani took the card and placed it on the coffee table.

'Who do you think is buried in Martha's garden Rani?'

'Oh my goodness, I have no idea! When I first heard, I was convinced it was an ancient burial ground. Dad would tell me all about the history of the old Manor House at Aspley.'

'No, the bones are relatively recent, certainly not ancient. You see Rani, we think Martha knew who was there and could have potentially been responsible. That's what all the evidence is pointing towards.'

'Don't be ridiculous! I knew her, honestly that's not possible! She was a tiny framed little woman, an ex-headmistress. Do you really think she was capable of murdering two people and burying them under a fountain?'

'Stranger things have happened Rani, I can tell you in my job I've met all kinds of 'unlikely' murderers. So she never said anything about her husband dying or even about the fountain or the garden?'

Rani stood up and went to stand next to the fire, looking worried and pensive. 'Look, I've been mulling over whether to tell you this or not. At the time I thought it was mad ramblings... and to be honest I feel stupid and even a bit of a traitor repeating it, because I knew Martha and there's no way she was responsible for burying those bodies in the garden.'

By the look on her face and her words she now had the officers excited at what she was about to reveal.

'Go on,' Sarah prompted.

'The day she died she was repeating weird poetry. I mean she was always quoting stuff from Shakespeare, Keats and the like, but she said that... *'death was in her eyes and she'd killed people'*, over and over again.'

The two officers moved forward in their seats, shuffling and ready to interject.

'Anymore?'

'God I don't know. She then started ranting about ingredients for something or talking about a special place. I don't know, she kept going on about heather, nettles, mushrooms and water - she was just so out of it on morphine I couldn't make sense of it. She was probably just talking about her special place out on the moors.'

'Think Rani, anything else, no names or anything?'

'No, she did keep saying 'seven' over and over again.'

'Does the number seven mean anything to you, what number house did she live at again?'

'No, no, that's 'number one'. I shouldn't have told you all that, it's probably total nonsense and I've only told you because of the exhumation. I feel like I've betrayed her confidence. Africa was there too, she might be able to remember more but I doubt it.'

Getting no further forward the officers started to wrap up the questioning, with Rani just repeating the same information.

'Thank you Rani, you've been very useful. Please don't worry about betraying a confidence, if Martha is totally innocent no one except the police will ever know about it. It's right that you told us, even if it is all drug induced rubbish.' The two officers made their way to the car, dying to discuss what they had just found out.

Chapter 42

After the visit to Moon Castle the two detectives were in their vehicle, making their way towards Elsdon as planned. As soon as they started to drive out of the gravel parking area they burst into conversation.

'What did you make of all that then?' said Sarah, 'the death bed scene'?'

'I know, ramblings of a dying woman, eh?'

'Yeah, but an old woman who just happens to have two dead bodies buried in her garden, not too much of a coincidence? Our sweet old lady at the very least knows something, but at worse she's a double murderer.'

'What was it she said again?' asked Peter, 'death was in her eyes... and she'd killed people?'

'It could be coincidental I suppose, people say all sorts of things when they're on morphine... and then she went on about nettles and mushrooms. And the water bit, did you pick up on that? First husband drowned!'

'Maybe there's more bodies buried in a field of nettles or something.'

They both laughed.

They were now on the main road, with the pretty village of Alnmouth glistening in the sun on their right hand side, as they headed towards Alnwick.

'I thought the 'dying wish' was interesting, the laying of the flowers.'

'I know, that made me think too.'

'Look, how about we drop off at Rothbury on the way and see if we can find this family friend, this Burt Foggo? Let's get to know a bit more about the young Martha, should we?'

'Sounds like a good plan to me.'

The farm was quite a distance out of Rothbury, but the road Rani mentioned led the officers straight to West Moor Farm, set on the edge of moorland with views across the Coquet Valley.

'Beautiful here, isn't it?' Peter was totally taken with the view across the moors.

'It sure is!'

The farmhouse was old but looked well cared for. They walked into the courtyard and knocked on the blue door but there was no answer. There was a large brass bell to the side of the door with a string to pull to make it ring out.

'Go on then,' said Sarah, 'I know you're dying to have a go ringing that bell.'

Peter laughed and started to ring the big brass bell as hard as he could. The result was an old man's head popping over one of the stable doors at the side of the house.

'Can I help you?'

'Yes, are you Burt Foggo?'

'I am, who's asking?'

'My name's DC Sarah Miller and this is DC Peter Burke, we've come to speak with you about Martha Dickinson.'

He hesitated a moment, 'you mean Martha Curry, as I knew her?'

'Yes, that's right sir. Mind if we ask you a few questions about her? I believe you knew her.'

'She's dead!'

'Yes, we know she is sir but we believe you were a family friend, is that right?'

'Well, I knew her when she was a lass but I hadn't seen her for well over forty years until she turned up a few months ago.'

'Yes, we know about that too sir. Any chance we can come in for a chat about her?'

'Come on then, if you must.'

He came across the yard, opened the front door and led them into a cosy kitchen. An old woman came into the kitchen from another room, carrying a bowlful of eggs.

'Oh, we have company Burt!'

'Hi, Mrs Foggo is it? We're from the police,' She looked at Burt in horror.

'What's this about Burt?'

'Please don't worry Mrs Foggo' said Sarah, 'we just want to ask him a few questions about an old friend of his from years ago, Martha... Martha Curry, we know her as Dickinson.'

The old woman sat down looking intently at her husband. 'It's time to tell them Burt pet, you've spent all these years worrying and thinking about that lass and what happened. It's time pet, it's obviously time... she's gone now anyway, so you're not harming anyone.'

The old man sat down with a sigh as the officers watched with anticipation as to what he was going to tell them. 'Well, it brought it all back when I saw her again. I'd buried it all to some extent but it's all been playing on my mind again... since she came to the moors a few months ago.'

'Go on' said Sarah, shuffling onto the edge of her chair, elbows on knees.

'Well, I was friends with Martha as a kid. She had a bloody hard life that lass did... with that father of hers, he'd do awful things to her. I'd find her whimpering, stark naked, locked in with the sheepdogs, covered in muck. I didn't realise exactly what her dad was doing to her until I was much older. She was only twelve or so when she had a bairn

- out there on the moors, in the middle of the night. I was there, I helped her give birth. She wouldn't let me get any help. I'm sure me mother would have helped her but she wouldn't hear of it - made me swear to secrecy she did. I think Mam suspected though, she'd ask me all sorts of questions about it. Martha came to stay with us for a while after the bairn was born. Everyone could see she was poorly but they thought she just had a fever or something.'

'So are you saying her father raped her?'

'Aye lass, she never actually said as much but it was obvious. She used to talk about her 'Dad's punishings' and I think that was exactly what he was doing to her. He called her the Devil's child because she had a birthmark on her head, said she was evil. He used to tell everyone that she was as 'crafty as a bitch fox.' He'd repeat it to anyone who'd listen. 'He looked at his wife and she encouraged him to continue, 'go on, tell them everything Burt.'

'What happened to the baby Mr Foggo?'

'Ah little thing was dead. It gave a little whimper when it was first born. I passed it to Martha to cradle but it was gone - tiny little thing it was. Buried it up there on the moors.'

'Near the two boulders?'

'Aye lass, that's right!'

'But there's more... Peggy here won't rest until I tell you something else. She's been pestering me since I told her about it last week when we saw the local news, about those bodies in the garden at Aspley.'

'I knew she was living somewhere up there, so it made me very suspicious,' Peggy chipped in.

'I think...', the old man stopped mid flow and shook his head, 'I can't believe I'm telling you this cause it's just my suspicions, I've got no proof. I think she got that bull of there's to kill her father.'

The two officers looked at each other puzzled and it was Peter who spoke up, 'a bull Mr Foggo, can you explain?'

'They had this canny prize stud bull, gentle as a lamb it was, Martha was ever so fond of it.'

'So how can you make a bull kill someone?'

Burt looked uncomfortable. 'Well, Martha's dad was in the barn with it one morning, giving it a brush down and they said that bull had slammed him up against the wall, breaking all his ribs - probably killing him outright... then trod on him for good measure. Now, I knew Martha hated her dad, so at first I was actually pleased for her when I was told. But when I heard he'd died I left school and went to Gorfen Letch to see if I could help. When I came out of the barn I saw the usual patch of nettles at the entrance to the farmyard and in the centre was some wilted ones - they'd obviously been picked and thrown back into the nettle patch. I just started to think about what the hell could have made that bull go crazy like it did. Then I remembered Martha tell me about the bull getting his privates stung when he was out in their field - 'went crackers' she said. So it just got me thinking.'

'So you think she stung the bull whilst her dad was in the barn with him?'

'Aye lad I do, it was a small stall he bedded in. If he started going crackers in there you wouldn't stand much chance against him.'

'Tell the officers her reaction Burt' said Peggy, further encouraging her husband.

'Well, I watched her over the weeks after the death, now bearing in mind I knew she hated that dad of hers. She'd be as 'happy as larry' until she had an audience, then she'd turn on the waterworks. She scared me at how good she was at it. At school, the teacher just needed to mention the word father and she'd be off crying. I stayed away a little bit after that, she frightened me. Then she got a place at the grammar school and to be honest I never saw that much of her after that.'

Now Peggy obviously wanted to join in - 'there were always rumours about Martha in the village. Her mother once told a friend that she thought Martha was trying to poison her dad with rat poison, right poorly he was. Nothing was ever done about it, she was only a wee thing at the time. I think most people just thought the Currys were a bit daft, simple folk they were in those days.'

The old man stood up reaching for his pipe on the mantelpiece, 'Martha was mighty clever when she was young. She always had a plan, it was her plan to go to grammar school and she did it. I have a feeling it was her plan to kill her father too!'

'Who do you suspect is buried in Martha's garden Mr Foggo, any ideas?' asked Peter.

'Na lad, I never saw or heard that much of her after that until she came back to work in the Rothbury school. I think I saw her from a distance a couple of times but never spoke with her.'

'Well Mr Foggo, Mrs Foggo, you've both been very helpful, thank you. If you think of anything else, give us a shout.' Sarah handed the old woman her card, 'that's my work's mobile number on there, give me a bell if you think of anything, anything at all.'

'Aye lass, we will.'

With that the two officers left the warmth of the roaring fire and made their way out into the cool Northumbrian autumn air.

'What do you make of that then... twelve year old... rape... murder, it's a bit of a stretch isn't it? Get your notes out Peter, what did Rani Weiss say she was rambling on about on her deathbed? You know, describing the place or the ingredients for something... did you write it down exactly as she said it?'

He looked through his notes. 'Yeah, somewhere, wait a minute... yeah definitely nettles!'

'I thought so.'

'What now?'

'Just a second' said Sarah and got out of the car and knocked again on the door of the farmhouse. 'Sorry, Mr Foggo, can I just ask you one more quick question?'

'Yes pet?'

'Did you ever tell anyone about your suspicions about the nettles?'

'No lass, didn't even tell Peggy until I found out about the bodies from the news. She knew about the bairn out on the moors but I never told anyone about Martha and that bull.'

'Thanks Mr Foggo, we may be back in touch at some stage.'

'I'm not in any bother about the bairn, am I?'

'Don't worry about it Mr Foggo, I'm sure it will all be OK.' As she walked away, she wasn't actually sure if it would be OK, but it was so long ago and they were just kids.

'What did you ask him?' enquired Peter, when she got back into the car.

'I just wanted to make sure Martha wasn't just repeating bad things people said about her over the years. He never told a living sole about his suspicions about her father until he told his wife a few days ago, so why mention nettles? Don't forget she also mentioned a knife and water. Didn't her first husband drown? Na... Peter this isn't coincidence or just vicious rumours.'

Chapter 43

The unmarked police car sat in the farmyard of West Moor farm as the two DCs pondered whether or not they should tell supervision straight away about what they had found out at Moon Castle and West Moor Farm. They thought better of it, just in case something else came to light in Elsdon. After all, they said a twelve year old girl 'murdering her dad by bull' was a wee bit out there!

'Let's see what we get at Elsdon, if anything,' said Peter, then we'll just update the boss with what Rani and old Burt Foggo said later.'

'Yeah, OK.' Sarah knew now there was way more to Martha Dickinson than being a kind, God fearing ex-headmistress as previously described.

'I've never been to Elsdon before' said Peter, as they trundled through the twisty road from Rothbury.

'Ah, it's beautiful, very remote. It's got a big village green in the centre and a lot of the houses look onto the green. It's really easily cut off in the winter though. I'm not sure I'd like to live there, a bit too remote for me. Of course, it's got the gibbet as well, you know the hangman's noose?'

'Yeah, sounds lovely!'

'You'll see.'

'What do you think the first port of call should be then? Where do you get your info from when trying to piece together a potential crime from over fifty years ago? Is there a pub?'

'Yeah but I doubt it'll be open, it's a bit late in the year for it to be open during the day. There's probably a village shop, we'll start there. Yeah?'

'Owt you want Sarah! I'm 'quite at my leisure', just out for a nice ride in the countryside today. A castle in the morning, then out 'in the sticks' in the afternoon. Will this shop have sandwiches do you think? I'm bloody starving!'

'I'm sure they'll have something… you've been watching Pride and Prejudice with ya wife, haven't you?'

Peter laughed, 'nowt gets past you does it… being 'quite at my leisure' is driving the wife crazy, she says if I say it once more she's leaving me.'

They reached Elsdon just after 1.30pm. Sarah had given Peter a biscuit but he was still moaning about his stomach.

'Ah, it really is pretty' he said, as they drove into the village, 'it's actually bigger than I thought.'

'I think it looks bigger than it is - as it's all spread out, there's only a couple of hundred people live here.'

'It's pretty but a bit too green for me - give me a city any day. There's nothing wrong with a bit of concrete and lots of places to get something to eat.'

'God, you and your bloody stomach!'

The two officers drove around the village but couldn't find a village shop. 'Let's try the pub. 'It was open and the lady behind the bar of the 'Bird in Bush' was around forty or so, too young for their enquiries. As Peter went looking for a toilet, Sarah introduced herself. 'Hi, I'm DC Miller, Northumbria Police, bit of a strange request but I'm after speaking with someone who's lived in the village for over fifty years.' Sarah always held off in telling people she was from the Murder Investigation Team as it usually freaked them out.

'Well, that is a strange request. Let me think,' she said, eyeing Sarah with suspicion, looking like she was dying to ask what it was all about.

'There's old Betty Tate, she's in her eighties, lived here all her life.'

'Where does she live?'

'The little bungalows towards the church,' she pointed out of the window, 'Valley View' it's called, don't ask me what number mind, but she's got a bird bath on the grass right outside her living room window. She likes to watch the birds.'

'OK, thanks, that's great. Anyone called Wilkie live in the village?'

'Well, not exactly but I'm sure that was Marilyn Stone's name before she was married. She lives in 'Cheviot House'... over the green there.' She pointed towards a double fronted stone house, standing on its own over the village green.

'How old is Marilyn?'

'Well now, it's hard to say, I reckon about fifty. She's got two girls, one's at university, so yeah I'd say around the fifty mark.'

'Thank you, you've been really helpful.'

'Can I ask what this is all about?'

'It's nothing really, just a few questions about an old incident, that's all.'

'I knew she couldn't resist asking you what it was about,' said Peter as they left, 'not even a bloody sandwich in sight in there - nothing!'

'You're in rural countryside here and it's out of the holiday season, we're lucky it was open. There's not a Greggs for about thirty or so miles.'

'That's why I live in a bloody city, too damned inconvenient living in the countryside!'

'Who should we see first then?' asked Peter.

'How about this Betty woman, she would have hopefully been around when William Wilkie drowned? She might be able to give us the 'low down' on his death.'

The cottages stood in a row of typical 'aged persons' houses. They had window boxes that had obviously been beautiful in the summer but were now touched by the cold air of early autumn. As described by the barmaid, there was the bird bath standing in front of a window.

'Right, that's it, come on,' said Sarah, eager to get on. She looked towards Peter, who was shoving the last of her biscuits into his mouth.

'God, Peter that's gross.'

'Ah shut up man, I'm bloody famished.'

The old lady who answered the door had dyed blonde hair in a bob. She was dressed in black stretchy trousers and a big green Aran jumper - not quite what Sarah had envisaged this eighty odd year old woman would look like.

'Can I help you?' she said.

Sarah introduced them and the old woman was quick to let them into the small living room.

'Betty is it? You don't mind me calling you Betty, do you? Sorry, the lady in the pub didn't tell me your second name.'

'Yes, she phoned me to tell me you were coming.'

'*Jesus'* thought Sarah, the jungle drums certainly work fast in Elsdon.

'I can't imagine for one minute why you want to talk with me.'

'It's an old case that we're working on Betty, we just want to find out about a few things that happened in Elsdon over fifty years ago.'

'Yes pet, what's that then?'

'Can you remember anyone called William Wilkie?'

'Why sure I can, he lived at Crag Farm, less than a mile out of the village. Lovely lad he was, drowned you know!'

'Yes, we know that. Can you tell us about that Betty?'

'What, the accident?' Sarah nodded. 'Well, he went out on that lake of his, fishing supposedly and fell in - drowned! He hadn't been

married very long, his poor wife was inconsolable. Now what was she called again... Martha, that's right Martha.
She had been a teacher somewhere in Newcastle I think, and gave it up when she married Billy. We never learnt to swim in those days, reckon he couldn't swim…different era these days. Now they learn to swim as kids at school - none of that then.'

'Did you know Martha?'

'Not really, saw her out with Billy a few times, but didn't really know her though.'

'Did Billy own the farm or just rent it?'

'No pet, the Wilkie's owned the farm outright, been in their family for years. I know there was a bit of animosity when the farm was left to Martha, cause Billy had a younger brother you see, but he was never interested in the farm or his family for that matter. But by rights I suppose he thought it should have been his - the lass deserved it if you asked me. She nursed Billy's parents and apparently used to work on the farm as well, a real grafter she was. Billy's parents both went a bit 'doo lally tap', - they call it dementia these days. It was sad to see them so confused all the time, not knowing where they were. Then one day Billy and Martha went to Alnwick for the night, a treat for her birthday apparently, and the old buggers had been out 'mushrooming' - picked up the wrong type and that was it. They were stone cold when Billy and Martha got back, that lass was heartbroken I remember, she blamed herself for leaving them. It was only about another year until Billy drowned... aye, she had some tragedy that lass.'

'Do you know what happened to Martha, Betty?'

'I heard she went back to teaching. She was a kind lass mind, she bought Cheviot House in the village for Billy's brother, Harry. I think she felt guilty selling the family farm but she saw him alright in the end... Harry was never interested in farming anyway.'

'Is Harry still alive?'

'Na pet, died about three years ago. His daughter lives in the house now with her family.'

'Is that Marilyn?'

'Yes pet, that's her, lives there with her husband and two lovely girls, bonnie lasses they are.'

Betty continued to tell them other stories of village life in Elsdon, whilst Peter was shuffling, making it clear to Sarah to wrap it up.

'That's great Betty, thanks for all that, we'll leave you in peace now.'

'I should have offered you a cup of coffee, sure you don't want to stop for one?'

'No, honestly Betty, we'll get away now, we finish our shift at four, so we need to get going.'

As they walked to the car, Peter laughed 'you see, not everyone thinks old Martha was a cold hearted serial killer.'

'Peter, you don't think like me at all, do you? I was just thinking that was more info proving she bloody was. Let's just see what Harry's daughter has to say... but I bet I can guess.'

'I think I can guess what's in your head, but I think you might be jumping on the bandwagon a little bit.'

'We'll see!'

They walked over to Cheviot House. 'Smell all that lovely fresh air Peter, not like that stale air in Wallsend.'

'I can just smell cow shit or something really rank, you're probably just immune to the smell by now.'

A tall willowy woman with blonde hair answered the door of Cheviot House and looked a little startled at the two strangers standing on her doorstep. 'Hello,' she said, looking at them suspiciously.

'Hi, don't worry, we're not selling anything, we're DCs Miller and Burke from Northumbria Police. Are you Marilyn, formerly Marilyn Wilkie?'

'Yes,' she said, now looking very worried. 'Is something wrong?'

'No, no, we just want to talk to you about a very old case we're dealing with, may we come in?'

'Of course.' She led them in to a large square shaped sitting room, with views across the village green.

'I take it Harry Wilkie was your Dad, is that right?'

'Yes, he died a few years ago. I'm afraid you've got me absolutely baffled as to what this is about.'

'We're really here to speak to you about your aunt.' The woman wrinkled her brow in confusion, obviously trying to place who they were talking about. 'Your Uncle William Wilkie's wife - Martha?'

'Oh my God, yes, I never met her though, is she still alive? Sorry, I never really thought of her as my aunt.'

'No, I'm afraid she died a few months back but we're just trying to get to know a little about her earlier life with your uncle.'

To their amazement she started to laugh and sat down in the arm chair. 'Please sit down,' she said. 'You probably think I'm crazy laughing like this but I wish my Dad was still alive, he absolutely hated the woman. He always said that she'd come to the attention of the police some day.'

'Really, why's that then?' Peter asked.

'Well,' she said, taking a deep breath and giving a half smile. 'He always told the story of how she was responsible for his mother and father's death… said he was sure of it. Until his dying day he was bitter about Martha Curry, of course that was because when Uncle Billy died she inherited the farm. By rights it should have gone to Dad and stayed in the family but Martha inherited the lot.'

'Why did he think she was responsible for his parent's death?'

'Well, it's a bit of a long convoluted story. He said his parents were both healthy before Martha moved in but within months his dad started getting disorientated and confused… then low and behold his mother started to go the same way within a few weeks of his dad. Then the story goes that Billy and Martha went out for the night leaving them to fend for themselves. When they came back the next day they had both died. Now how right this is I don't know but they supposedly ate poisonous mushrooms... apparently they had gone out into the woods, collected them and eaten them thinking they were just normal mushrooms. My dad was absolutely convinced Martha had left them for his mum and dad to eat... and possibly that she was even trying to poison them before that - I'm just repeating what my dad said mind, how much of it is true I have no idea. Then, of course, within a year Uncle Billy was dead too!'

'So, Martha inherited everything?'

'She did, yes, but Dad said she bought him this house to shut him up, cause he was always making a fuss about everything that had happened.'

'Did he go to the police?'

'He always thought they wouldn't believe him. He wasn't that old at the time, I think he was only around nineteen or so and by all accounts a bit of a lad in those days too... and because Martha had been a teacher he thought they would believe her over him.'

'Did he know what happened to Martha after she left Elsdon, did she ever come back to the village?'

'I don't think my dad ever saw her again to be honest. We know she went back to teaching, but nothing else. This was obviously all before I was born, again all Dad's words but there were a few of Dad's cousins who were suspicious of Martha too.'

She smiled at the officers, then her eyes widened. 'Wait a minute, this has nothing to do with those old bodies they dug up on the other side of Rothbury, does it... I read about that in the gazette, was she one of the bodies?'

'I'm sorry, we can't really say too much at this stage, I hope you understand.'

Chapter 44

The Ford Mondeo was on its way back to the MIT's base in Wallsend with Sarah and Peter quietly contemplating what they'd uncovered at Elsdon. Peter now sceptical about the legitimacy of the rumours surrounding Martha's past and Sarah absolutely convinced that Martha was not quite what she portrayed herself to be.

'It's all a bit far fetched Sarah, a young lass of twelve trying to poison her dad and then mysteriously killing him with a bull. I think I'm right in saying it is actually just all a 'load of bull'. I'm not convinced that a twelve year old girl would even know how to poison someone... and of course also have access to the poison to do it.'

'Hey, my kids were both pretty savvy at twelve.'

'Yeah, but they had the use of the internet, it would have been much harder in those days, kids were more naive.'

'What! On a farm! You are joking aren't you? I'm sure she'd have known all about poisons - they'd have used it to control the vermin. It would probably have been easy to get back then too, they weren't quite as safety conscious as we are these days.'

They both fell silent as a deer ran across the road in front of the car, then Sarah continued…

'Don't you think Burt Foggo was convincing then? He was to me... you can tell he really believed in what he was saying.'

'I'm not doubting that but all that 'child of the Devil' crap, it was already probably planted in his mind in the first place - put there by her rubbish parents. Perhaps at that stage everywhere Martha went it all followed her around. She was definitely tarnished.'

'Na, there's just too much Peter, think about it logically… her deathbed confession, all the ramblings about gorse bushes, nettles, knives, water. I'm afraid it all adds up to me!'

'So wait a minute, I think I know where you're going with this - you're saying she killed her father, her in-laws, her first husband and the two unidentified bodies in her garden? She killed people… lots of people!'

'The baby as well, that's seven!... Peter... that's seven! That's what she was bloody confessing at the end, according to Rani Weiss. She kept saying 'seven', it's the seven people she's killed.'

Peter Burke started to laugh, 'you're updating the boss with this one, I can tell you. I'm not telling her that. I think you've been watching too much Miss Marple on the telly or that Midsummer Murders crap. It's all just pure speculation.'

'After fifty years Peter, that's all it's probably ever going to be.'

They arrived back at the station at 3.30pm, with half an hour to update the DS on what they'd found before the end of their shift.

'Go on then' said Peter, 'tell him your theory.'

Sarah updated DS Anderson. The old sergeant listened intently, with a few episodes of furrowed eyebrows and the odd grin, interspersed with a 'really?'

'Well now!' he said.

'You don't believe it in the slightest, do you Sarge?' Peter grinned.

'I'm not saying that, seems like there's been too much that's happened in that woman's life to be all coincidence, besides, today the search team have just found a knife wrapped in brown paper and an old tea towel, stuffed between the rafters in the roof of her cottage.'

'See!' said Sarah, looking at Peter, 'you thought I'd be ridiculed for even suggesting it, didn't you?'

The DS raised his eyebrows at Peter, 'Karen Foster's in her office, pop up and tell her what you've uncovered.'

The two officers bounded up the stairs, Sarah eager to update the SIO and both eager to finish work on time. 'Just don't mention your 'seven' theory Sarah, honestly man, it makes you sound like a bloody 'wannabe' sleuth from an old movie.'

'Ah sod off Peter.'

They found Karen Foster on the floor, picking up papers that had fallen out of a folder she was reading. There were books, files and manuals all over her desk.

'Afternoon ma'am, the DS has sent us up to give you a quick update on the results of our enquiries today.'

'You were speaking with Rani Weiss today, yes?'

'Yes ma'am, plus we did some enquiries in Elsdon and also with an old school friend of Martha's at a farm near Rothbury.'

'OK, go on then.'

'Well ma'am, it was all rather interesting.' Sarah read out the notes taken at Moon Castle about Martha's confession, and the visit to the special place on the moors.

'So you went to visit this Burt Foggo, I take it?'

'Yes ma'am we did, turns out he's been keeping a secret for way over sixty years. He said he helped Martha give birth to a baby at that very spot, the special place Martha wanted to visit.'

'So what happened to the baby?'

'They buried it.'

'Oh my God, how old were they for God's sake!'

'She was twelve, I'm not sure exactly how old he was, he was a bit older, but not much. But it wasn't Burt's child, he said that Martha's father used to abuse her... rape her.'

'Oh my God, really?'

'That's what he said, and that's not all, he went on to say that he suspected Martha had killed her father out of revenge.'

Sarah went on to tell her about the rumours of the poisoning and about the bull.

'It's all a bit far fetched ma'am,' said Peter.

'I think in that situation I'd have killed my father too, not sure I'd have had the gumption at twelve years old though.'

'Apparently she had an awful childhood, her father would strip her naked and lock her in a dog kennel at night. Burt said he rescued her on many occasions.'

'Remind me, are there any siblings still alive?'

'She has a sister called Julia. I think Trevor's been trying to contact her again today. She also had four or five brothers - but we believe they're all dead now. I don't think she actually had that much to do with her family anyway.'

'So, what did you find out at Elsdon?'

Peter decided it was now his turn to speak up, to give a more balanced view. 'We managed to speak with an elderly resident who'd lived in Elsdon all her life, she knew the first husband William Wilkie when he was young and also knew Martha. She told us that after William drowned she was absolutely devastated.'

'Yeah, but she also told us...,' said Sarah interrupting, 'that after Martha married William she moved into the family home. Not that long after both of William's elderly parents became ill - she nursed them both but they apparently died after eating poisonous mushrooms.'

The DCI began to laugh, Peter had known all along that someone like Karen Foster wouldn't believe the whole saga.

Sarah continued regardless - 'then of course William drowned in the lake on their land - he'd taken a boat out and had gone fishing, couldn't swim apparently.'

Sarah kept going, even after her anger rose at seeing Peter's' I told you so 'face. 'So, we managed to find William's niece who still lives in the village. One of the first things she said to us was that she wished her poor dad was still alive to see this day, so he could have told the story himself. Apparently, he believed that it was Martha who gave his parents the mushrooms!... The story was that William and Martha had gone out for the night, leaving the old couple at home and when they came back they found that they'd both eaten mushrooms, which they said they must have gone out and picked that day. They both died from poisoning.'

'The old woman we spoke to did say they both suffered from dementia though,' said Peter.

'Yes, dementia that didn't start until Martha moved in with them.'

'Remind me, how long did she live at the farm?'

'No longer than three years altogether, probably less.' said Sarah.

'How old were William's parents?'

'Just in their late sixties!'

The DCI walked towards the window, 'so we've got the father, the baby, the two in-laws, the first husband... that's five and the two bodies in her garden, that's seven.'

'Yes ma'am' said Sarah, giving Peter a deliberate stare, opening her eyes wide as if to say 'I told you'.

'That's what Rani Weiss mentioned she kept saying wasn't it, seven, she was on about the seven people she killed.'

'Ma'am, Burt Foggo said the baby was tiny, it probably wouldn't have survived anyway,' said Peter.

'At the very least she may have felt responsible though.'

'Well perhaps she just felt responsible for her in-laws' and husband's deaths too.'

'Can I remind you DC Burke that she has two bodies buried in her garden and a knife hidden in her loft? She didn't just feel responsible, the evidence is now definitely pointing towards the fact she really was responsible!'

'We really need to speak with her sister and this niece of hers. Make sure you track them down. I want Burt Foggo formally interviewed ASAP and Rani Weiss re-interviewed too. We'll have to see if the knife throws up any forensic evidence. I'll speak with Jamie Jones about the best way forward and ask about the possibility of excavating the baby's remains on the moors. I know it's from a long time ago but I also want to know what's on Mr and Mrs Wilkie's death certificates.'

DCs Miller and Burke were pleased they were going to finish on time tonight; Peter absolutely starving and Sarah desperate to get home to see her boys. 'You know Peter, you should have watched more Miss Marple when you were younger, it might have made you a better detective.'

'Sod off Sarah, I'm off to live in the present. My head is bloody mashed with all this old stuff - we'll never get any proper evidence, plus our main suspect is dead... it's all pointless!'

'You've still got to wrap the crime up though, Peter!'

Chapter 45

Jamie Jones sat sorting and cataloging photographs of a recent city murder victim, needed for court the next day when his mobile began ringing.

'Jamie Jones,' he answered.

'Jamie, it's Karen Foster, are you in the station?'

'Yes'

'Could you pop up a second for a quick chat, I need some information?'

'Yeah, sure, two minutes.'

He had already heard that one of his colleagues on another shift had recovered a knife from the scene of the bones and suspected that was why she wanted to talk to him. He knocked and went into her office.

'Jamie, I just need a bit of forensic advice.'

'OK.'

'You'll probably be aware we found a knife in the loft of old Martha Dickinson's house.'

'I had heard, yes.'

'Do you know the circumstances?'

'No, I've been working on another case.'

She took him around to her computer screen, 'just have a look at these photos, will you? I want to know what evidential value they'll still have.'

He had to step over a couple of cardboard boxes full of green buff folders to get near to her screen. The first photo showed the knife in situ and you could just make out the green and white checked fabric pushed into a hole in the brickwork near the rafters. The next photo showed the item removed, revealing it was wrapped in a brown stained tea towel. The next photos then revealed a brown paper parcel inside the tea towel with the knife encased inside.

'What I'm wanting to know,' she said, 'is whilst that's obviously blood on the tea towel, what's the chances of DNA after... we're presuming now, twenty-seven years?'

'I take it you're thinking it's her husband in the garden?'

'Yeah, it's all pointing that way.'

Jamie sat down on her chair flicking back to the original photograph and the site of the secretion. 'Well, let's see... hidden in a loft for that period of time I'd usually say you had absolutely no chance because of the fluctuating temperatures. Loft spaces are burning hot one minute and then can be freezing cold the next. This degrades the DNA, but... and it's a big 'but' mind, because of the fact it's been wrapped firstly in paper, then a cloth and shoved in that hole in the brickwork, you might have a chance - it's a small chance though. Lying in the cool stonework may have kept the temperature more stable, but I'm guessing at that.'

Jamie went back to the photograph of the knife itself, 'there's a small amount of blood still on the knife too, near the handle. See, it's probably been wiped and they've missed that bit - they probably used that tea towel to wipe it. You might still get fingerprints off it, you never know! Wasn't the old woman done for shoplifting?'

'It was only a community resolution not a charge but I suppose they might still have taken prints if she was arrested and taken to the station for processing. They could still be on file, let's have a look.'

Jamie shifted from her seat and she logged onto the local 'Computerised Information System'. 'Let's see, Martha Dickinson… ' She typed the name and a few came up, 'there, that's her... Rothbury.'

The screen was black with orange text and the record was obviously her. 'Right, let's see, ah there is an arrest screen.' The DCI entered the two digit code and the arrest screen popped up. 'Jeez, what had she stolen from Morrison's for that value... £380.23? I didn't think that would even be possible on one attempt.'

'Have a look at the property screen. Let's see, they should have listed what it was.'

She input the code… 'Groceries' she said, disappointedly. But in the text field below, the arresting officer had listed some of the items - champagne, whiskey, wine, salmon, beef joints, all high value goods.

'She's not exactly your 'run of the mill' old lady who forgets to pay for a few things, is she?'

'No,' Jamie agreed. 'Was she suffering from dementia?'

'Na, neighbours said she was as sharp as a tack, right to the very end.'

'Go back to the arrest screen and then the disposal,' said Jamie. She flicked through the screens. 'There it is!' Jamie pointed at the 'fingerprints taken' box showing a 'Y'. 'You've potentially got Martha's fingerprints on record, if they haven't been destroyed.'

They looked at each other and smiled.

'I'm afraid you don't get off that easily Jamie, I've got another question I want to ask you... if a newborn baby was buried over sixty years ago, would there still be evidence of that baby... would the skeleton have survived?'

'Now that's a question! Well, babies' bones aren't really properly formed when they're born, they're much softer than adult bones...'

'I thought that.'

'... so deterioration would be much quicker... to be honest I'd doubt there'd be much left after that amount of time. Plus, of course you've got foxes and other scavengers that might have disturbed the grave. Where was it buried?'

'Out on the moors beyond Rothbury!'

'Mmm, I guess it would be peaty soil up there, I think..., mind I'm no soil expert... but the acid in the peat helps preserve bodies. I'm sure you'll have seen the mummified bodies on TV being pulled out of peat bogs. It's the acid and the lack of oxygen that stops natural decay. I'd say after that length of time I'd be surprised if anything was left but due to the fact it's on the moors I'd say you've got a chance, a small chance! Your best bet is to give Emma Bould, the Archeologist, a call - she'd know much more about soil conditions than I do.'

'That's it Jamie, great! I'll let you get back to whatever you were doing.'

'Yeah, no problem, see ya.' He left the office, making his way back downstairs to his never ending backlog of paperwork.

Chapter 46

It had now been over two weeks since the release of the article in the local newspapers requesting help in the identity of the two bodies found in Aspley. Readers were asked to come forward with details of any loved ones or friends who had gone missing around twenty-seven years ago.

The Murder Investigation Team had received over two hundred responses to work through. It was DCs Trevor Stapleton and Susan Neary who had been tasked with following them all up.

'Are most of them local responses?' Trevor asked, as Susan was looking at them on the screen.

'Majority yes, but there's a few from down south, one from Ireland and a couple from the Midlands. What's ya bet they're all rubbish?'

'Let's see, shall we?'

'I'll print it off, there are a few duplications of names. I'll highlight half for you to contact and half for me, OK?'

'Yeah fine, whatever.'

The two officers chatted away on the phone for about an hour, jotting down their findings as they went.

'Right, what you got, any strong leads?'

'No info at all on the male... all mine were in regard to the female. I had three people mention a Fisacherley woman.'

'What's her full name?'

'Didi Fisacherley'

'Yeah, I had a Fisacherley too, but it wasn't Didi. Wait a minute,' he went back through his notes, 'mine's a Deirdre Coleen Fisacherley. It was that Irish enquiry you mentioned earlier. Some woman said she'd been trying to locate her mother for years, said she worked in Northumberland and then just went missing. She'd managed to locate one of her old colleagues years ago who said she'd just upped and left her job with no explanation. Is Didi short for Deirdre?'

'Not sure but it's got to be her, Fisacherley's an unusual enough surname. Did she say where she worked?'

'In a pub. She apparently worked in a few local pubs but the woman she spoke with had worked with her in the Shoulder of Mutton at Rothbury.'

'Yeah, sounds like the same woman. What about a description?'

'Both described her as a small woman, late thirties, long curly red hair, freckles, the life and soul of the party apparently.'

They both sat discussing the results of their enquiries, making sure that Didi Fisacherley was their strongest lead and ruling out some of the others. 'See if there's anything on CIS for her, will you?' Trevor asked, 'you never know she might have come to our attention at some point. I know it's twenty seven years ago but some of the files were uploaded from the old paper records.'

Susan tried inputting both Didi and Deirdre Fisacherley and numerous other different spellings. 'Na, nothing, not even a missing person report.'

'Check PNC, see if there's anything on there. I know it's unlikely, but...' Susan logged onto the Police National Computer. 'There's a Deirdre Fisacherley on here but the record is only from a year ago, besides completely wrong age group - this one's far too young.'

'I'll phone the daughter back,' said Trevor. 'I didn't ask her if she ever actually reported her mother as a missing person and I'll see if I can get a better description or even a photograph.'

'Hello Mrs Bowen, it's PC Stapleton again. I'd just like to ask you a few further questions?'

'Oh Jesus - you think it's her don't you?'

'It's far too early to say but we've had a couple of other people mention your mother's name. I just have a few extra questions for you.'

'Really? OK, go on.'

'Did you ever report your mother as missing to the police?'

'No, no... she left us kids when we were in our early teens. She'd write a few letters but they were few and far between. Time moved on and I didn't hear from her for well over twenty years. Then I watched one of those programmes about tracing long lost relatives and it just sparked something in me, so I contacted her last address in Northumberland. I went completely 'around the houses' until eventually I managed to speak with an old friend of hers who worked with her in a local pub - it was 'The Shoulder of Mutton.' It's imprinted on my brain. This friend said that one night my mammy just didn't turn up for work. They checked the flat above the pub where she was living and she wasn't there, no explanation - nothing. Then a woman turned up, said she was a friend of my mammy's, she collected her belongings and she told Bob, who owned the pub that my mammy wasn't well and was staying with her for a while before moving back to Ireland.'

'Did anyone mention the name of this friend?'

'No, she never said.'

'They never saw her again, apparently my mother had done a 'moonlight flit' before, and let's face it, she did exactly the same to us kids. I don't think her friends at the pub were totally happy about it but they eventually just accepted that she wasn't coming back.'

'Do you have any photographs of your mother?'

'Yeah, but they're really old, she was probably only in her early thirties at the time.'

'That's fine, if I give you an email address would you be able to send them?'

'Yeah sure, they're in my photographs on my tablet. I'll do it now.'

Within a few minutes of passing over the email address Trevor was looking at Deidre Coleen Fisacherley, the tiny framed young woman. The photo was an old black and white one but you could still see her freckled complexion.

'This might be our mysterious lady buried in the garden,' he said, pushing the photo in front of his colleague.

Susan's two responders to the newspaper article turned out to be colleagues of Didi. One had confirmed she was the lady who had spoken to Didi's daughter, the other was another barmaid from the pub who moved into her old flat after she'd left.

At lunchtime they updated the sergeant with the results of their enquiries.

'The two women who knew her... did they know if she had any connection with James Dickinson?' Sgt Anderson asked.

'They both knew who James Dickinson was but didn't know that much about him, said he was the 'strong and silent' type and knew nothing about any connection between them. But they did say Didi used to flirt with all the male customers, so they might not have picked up that there was anything between them.'

'So her flat was emptied by this friend of hers?'

'By all accounts, this woman just took Didi's clothes out of the flat. She didn't own that much as it was fully furnished but she left behind all her bed linen, kitchen stuff, ornaments and the like, which the new barmaid who took over the pub flat always felt guilty about.'

'Well, it's going to be impossible after all this time trying to find out who the mysterious friend was. But there's quite a lot of info there. I'll update the SIO and show her the photograph - good work guys.'

Chapter 47

The Search Team officers had been issued with warrants and tasked with looking for a specific spade, and each given a detailed description of what to look for. The blade of the spade was curved not straight, it was fourteen inches across with some damage to it four inches from the right hand edge - this being a 'V' shaped knick on the blade bottom. They were instructed to check all outbuildings in Aspley and specifically a cabin belonging to a neighbour of Martha's, where she was known to frequent. No one had mentioned this cabin during the first search and it had been missed in the initial search - the cabin being hidden in woodland, a short walk out of the hamlet.

Due to another murder in the city centre, only two officers were assigned to the job - Matt Young and Steve Hassan. They arrived at 8.45am, parking up their unmarked blue transit van. Dressed in dark blue boiler suits, the officers started their search with Martha's tiny shed. It had already been inspected once but now they were looking for something more specific. The shed was only six foot high by three foot wide with very little depth, it was more like a cupboard than a shed but she did have a couple of spades still in there. It contained an old rolled up tarpaulin, some wood, a few cracked garden ornaments and some small garden tools, such as trowels, wire brushes and a little rake.

'I've already had everything out of here in the last search!' said Matt, 'just get the two spades out.'

Steve reached in and pulled one out, 'it's curved.'

'Yeah, but no damage. It looks quite new as well.'

'The other one's older' said Steve, pulling at the well-used wooden handle, 'na, straight as owt.'

'Seems like a bit of a waste of time to me, apparently those bones were there for twenty-seven years according to the DS.'

'I'm quite interested in going down to that cabin in the woods mind. The owner has left the key at 'Number Three'. She says she hasn't been in it for years.'

Arthur, at 'Number Three' opened his door to the two search officers. They introduced themselves, handed over the necessary paperwork for Rani Weiss and asked him for the key.

'Yeah, I'll just get it for you, just a second. I'll have to close the door while I get it, as the dog will be off like a shot.'

Arthur had already been down to the cabin earlier to check there was nothing of interest in there. It was obvious to him that Rani hadn't been there for ages as the chairs and table all had a thick layer of dust on them. Joe Weiss' desk and filing cabinet were scattered with old crinkled bits of paper and the filing cabinet itself had been forced open, but Arthur knew all about that! He handed the key over to the officers amid deafening barking coming from behind him. 'Sorry' he said, 'he's very territorial.'

'Whereabouts is this cabin then?'

'If you go down that track about half a mile or so you'll see a bit of a gap in the rhododendrons on the right and there's a little wooden bridge constructed to get you over a ditch. I don't think anyone goes down there anymore - the bushes might be a bit overgrown, so if you can't find it come back and I'll show you.'

'Great, thanks for that, I'm sure we'll be OK.'

The two officers left Aspley, making their way down the muddy dirt track and leaving behind a rather nervous Arthur in their wake, who was now wondering what on earth they could still be looking for. He hadn't heard that they'd found anything in Martha's cottage but he guessed someone must have mentioned the cabin. He assumed they were just making sure there wasn't any evidence in there.

The gap in the hedgerow was overgrown but the officers noticed the wooden boards hidden under the leaves of the rhododendron bushes, just as Arthur had described.

'What's your first thoughts here, Matt?' Steve asked, standing back looking at the foliage.

'Yeah, obviously someone has been here very recently,' he said. Both officers noticed the vegetation hadn't quite settled back into its normal position.

When they arrived at the wooden log cabin, which was nestled amongst the trees, they found the door wasn't actually locked. On opening the door and on closer inspection they could see footprints in the dust on the floor.

'Look, the filing cabinet's been forced.'

'That doesn't look recent though, look at the state of the papers that have been dragged out. What's on them?'

Both officers started reading some of the old files. 'This one's entitled - 'characteristics'.'

'That's cause the bloke who owned it was a psychologist, he obviously worked down here, there's even a typewriter - look!'

'Bloody hell, I wouldn't like to type on that old thing.'

'Hey look at this, there's still loads of alcohol in this cupboard. The local kids obviously haven't found it yet.'

'I don't think there's any kids live here, I certainly haven't seen any evidence of them anyway.'

'Do you think that old bloke or the owner has come down when they've heard we were going to do the search?'

'I don't know, I suppose it could have been anybody if the door was unlocked. Sally Hargreaves, who's interviewed quite a lot of the neighbours thinks a few of them are a wee bit twitchy. She thinks they know more than they're letting on. It's a bit of an odd place Aspley, don't you think?'

They searched the full cabin and also under the surrounding decking but there was no sign of a spade and nothing else of interest. 'One thing was for sure' said Matt, 'the owner definitely needs some advice about keeping the place safe. There's too much in here to leave it unlocked.' Matt locked the door and tried the handle, making sure it was secure.

'OK, it's locked now, come on we'll go back up to Aspley and try some of the neighbouring houses.'

Ronnie had already been alerted by Arthur last night that officers were returning in the morning to search the cabin, but hadn't thought for one minute that they'd be back knocking on his door.

The two officers identified themselves, showing their badges and handing him a piece of paper entitled 'Warrant to Search Premises'. 'We're after having a look in any old outhouses or sheds you've got please.'

'What? I don't suppose there's anything of interest in my shed. Are you looking for something specific?' Ronnie was thinking that they might be looking for the old skillet Martha had used to bash James over the head with, but was also well aware that Joe got rid of that years ago.

'Just a general search sir, nothing to worry about, only sheds and outbuildings.' They both noticed that he looked overly concerned about the impending search and wondered what they might find in his shed. Years of doing the job had made them acutely aware of people who were overly nervous about searches, even if they were just hiding the odd pornographic magazine.

'I'll just go and get the key. If you can go around the side of the house, there's a gate that takes you into the back garden, I'll not be a minute. I'm not a hundred percent sure where I put the blooming thing.' Ronnie flew back into the house and into the master bedroom and poked Clara, who was fast asleep after a late shift at the hospital.

'What the hell!' she exclaimed, shocked and annoyed at being woken.

'The police are here, they want to search the shed.'

'What the hell are you panicking for Ronnie, they're not going to find anything, are they? Bugger off!'

With that he left the bedroom thinking she was probably right anyway. There was nothing in there that could possibly incriminate him.

The two officers were now outside the shed waiting for him. 'Here we are' he said, showing them the key. He unlocked the door of the green wooden shed and in they both went, he watched from the doorway as they rummaged through all his tools.

'Hey,' said one of them excitedly, nearly stopping Ronnie's heart, 'what's this for?' In the cardboard box was an old steering wheel for the car he was rebuilding.

'That's a steering wheel for a TR4a.'

'Really? Are you doing one up?'

'Yeah, it's in the garage.'

'I love vintage cars, I'm busy doing up an old Triumph Stag, just love the old Triumphs. Can I see it?'

'Yeah sure.' Ronnie was eager to move them far away from the shed.

They finished their search and Ronnie locked the shed after them, the three walking purposefully across the perfectly mown lawn, back through the gate and around to the double garage at the front.

'I'm dying to see this!' said Matt.

Ronnie pulled up the door, revealing the green bodywork of the car. 'Wow! It's beautiful, a lovely looking car. You're nearly finished restoring it. Hey, it doesn't need much more and you'll be out on the road with it.'

'Yeah, I just need a gearbox for it, which I'm struggling to find.' Ronnie's eyes were now following the other officer who was walking around the garage looking on benches. He knelt down in the corner of the garage, looking at the spade Ronnie had just been using in the front garden.

'Matt, come here a sec.' He beckoned the other officer over to look at his find. The two officers were both very interested in his spade and Ronnie's heart was starting to beat faster.

'Oh my God, you're not thinking that was used to bash someone's brains out are you?'

'No sir... is it yours?'

'Of course it's mine, I've used it for years.'

'Can you remember where you got it from?'

'I think that I inherited that one from my parents when they died. I took quite a bit of stuff as we were newly married at the time and didn't have much.'

'How long ago was that?'

'My parents died just after I joined the army, that'll be thirty odd years ago now.'

'We'll have to seize it I'm afraid.'

'What the hell for? This is ridiculous, even if it had been involved in a murder all those years ago surely there'd be no DNA or anything on it anyway? I've been using it for years.'

The officers, totally ignoring Ronnie, began chatting between themselves.

'Is Jamie Jones on today? We probably need some advice as to whether we just seize it or get it photographed in situ'

'I'm not sure, give him a bell.'

Ronnie watched as the older officer walked away to make a phone call. He tried to listen but could only catch the odd word.

When the call was over he walked back to a now worried Ronnie and his colleague. 'Says it's best that it's photographed in situ first.

Apparently there's a CSI at a job in Alnwick - he's getting him to come across to photograph and seize it. Shouldn't be too long.'

Ronnie asked again what they wanted it for but the two officers weren't forthcoming. They explained that they were just waiting for forensics to come to photograph it and take it away and he could go back into the house if he wanted. Someone would be out to talk to him in due course.

Ronnie went inside and straight to see his sleeping wife again. Speaking in a whisper he gave her a shake, 'Clara, wake up, wake up, they're going to take my dad's old spade away for forensic testing.'

'What the hell are you going on about now?'

'They're taking my garden spade for evidence.'

'Ronnie, I keep telling you after all this time... what are they going to prove. Martha stoved James' head in with a bloody skillet anyway, not our bloody spade.'

'Sssh, they're still outside. Well, they obviously want it for something, don't they?'

On the drive, the officers waited for Dan, the 'Crime Scene Investigator' to show. Steve lowered his voice, 'did you notice he mentioned the spade being used to bash someone's brains out! Lucky guess?... or did he know exactly what happened?'

'I know, I was thinking exactly the same. Someone could have let it slip about the trauma to the skull I suppose.'

'Everyone was told to keep quiet about possible injuries, so I very much doubt it. I tell you, that guy we got the key off was dodgy too. He's been into that cabin to check or he's had someone else do it.'

Dan eventually arrived and photographed the spade in the garage. He then bagged and seized it, posting a receipt through Ronnie's door.

'Do you think that's it?'

'Yeah, looks like it to me,' said Dan, 'I helped with the excavation of the skeletons and it sure looks like a match with the one used to dig the grave. But it'll probably get taken to the lab, they'll be able to say for definite.'

Back at the station Jamie Jones and Dan compared the photographs of the cast with the ones of the spade.

'Yeah, that's definitely it, Dan!'

Chapter 48

Chief Inspector Karen Foster had gathered all interested parties together again to discuss the Aspley bones case. The aim of the meeting was to ensure she knew every detail of the progress the officers were making, to see where she needed to focus on in the investigation. This case was different to most murders the team had dealt with in the past as usually they had a fresh body and often a suspect. But in this instance the only concrete evidence they had was the actual bones themselves, a knife and an old spade - everything else was just rumours and their main suspect was now dead.

Present at the meeting were the Murder Investigation Team officers, Exhibits Officer, Crime Scene Manager and Karen Foster's bag man, Nigel Lowther.

'Right, we'll start if that's OK folks? Well, it's been a very interesting first few weeks, I feel like I've had a bit of a 'baptism of fire' in my new job and I'm not out of that fire quite yet. I just wanted to give you all a quick timeline of events and then we'll go from there. Firstly, we have the two bodies in Martha's garden. I think we can safely say now that this will be James Dickinson and Deirdre Fisacherley but DNA was inconclusive, they've got profiles but no match. They're going for familial DNA testing on the female as we've located a daughter who's willing to participate by giving us her DNA for comparison. With regard to the male, we're solely searching for dental records at this stage.'

Karen Foster looked around the table to make sure all were engaged and following the conversation. 'Then, enquiries revealed Martha's garbled deathbed confession and her request to visit a specific location up on the moors, where she was known to lay flowers. On questioning Rani Weiss further about that visit, she revealed they had met a childhood friend of Martha's... a Burt Foggo.'…

'Now... and this is where it gets interesting, Mr Foggo told us that he had been present when a young Martha gave birth to a child out on those moors, at the exact spot of her visit. He also outlined the subsequent burial of that baby at that very same location. Mr Foggo had also been sitting on a suspicion…a suspicion that he'd kept quiet about for over sixty years - that Martha was responsible for the death of her father, who he believed she killed out of revenge for years of abuse and for raping her as a child.'…

'It doesn't end there... this information led us to question the death of Martha's first husband, a William Wilkie from Elsdon, who died in his twenties in a drowning accident. Then, further questioning revealed that Martha's mother and father-in-laws also died in suspicious circumstances... poisoned after eating mushrooms. Am I going too fast ladies and gentlemen? Now, we can either think this woman is 'the' unluckiest woman in the world or in fact a cold blooded serial killer.' She watched the team as a few wry smiles unfolded.

'Right! OK, speak out if you believe she was just one unlucky, maligned human being?' No one spoke.

'Speak out or raise your hand if you think we have uncovered Northumberland's most prolific serial killer.' For a few seconds no one raised their hands or spoke, they just looked at each other. Then DC Sarah Miller stuck her hand in the air, 'I do', she said. Slowly, all but one then followed her in agreement - all but DC Peter Burke.

'I'm sorry ma'am' he said, 'I'm not convinced yet. I've been on cases before where rumours have turned out to be just that - rumours. I know it's looking that way but I feel we need more hard facts.'

'Well Peter, we do have some forensics back that might dispel your fears but I digress for now. I want to ask a few questions before we come onto the forensic results.'

'Have we managed to track down Martha's sister or niece yet?'

'No ma'am, the sister Julia was initially spoken to at the beginning of the enquiry but we haven't been able to contact her since and the niece is out of the country. We've still got someone working on it.'

'OK, I guess Rani Weiss' statement will have to do for now. It would have been good to speak with the niece but we'll have to make do. Although the confession she made contained the ramblings of a dying woman on morphine, it did hold some key elements that simply can't be ignored. Although 'drug induced', she did utter the words she had killed people... a confession in my book.'

'It could have been just part of the poem she was reciting ma'am.' Peter interjected.

'... and she mentioned a knife... all be it in relation to buttering bread apparently. She mentioned the nettles - as per Burt Foggo's statement, she mentioned water and funnily enough, mushrooms. It would help if we could speak with that bloody niece of hers though, she might have confessed more to her, we just don't know.'

Sarah spoke, 'I phoned Rani Weiss yesterday and she remembered a little more. She said she was sure Martha was going on about a skillet to hit someone over the head with. To be honest, I think Rani has been holding on to that bit of info in case she incriminated Martha further, but in learning about Martha's first husband, perhaps she realised she should mention it?'

'What exactly is a skillet, is it just a frying pan?'

'Yes ma'am, but the old fashioned ones were exceptionally heavy.'

'Any pans recovered from the house, or from the sale rooms?'

'No, some of the smaller items actually went to a car boot sale and a lot of stuff went into a skip.'

‘Well, it probably wouldn’t be any good to us anyway but make efforts to trace where it could have gone.’

‘Let’s move on to forensics. Jamie, do you want to give us an update?’

‘Yes, fine, I’ll start with the knife. As you mentioned, it dispels Martha’s innocence... the fingerprints had actually survived the conditions in the loft and partial prints were recovered from the blood you could see near the handle. Although partial they have been matched with Martha’s prints and now prove she held the knife after the blood was on there. We got a partial DNA profile from the blood on the knife matching with the profile of the female. With regard to the two bodies, DNA has been obtained from both sets of teeth but there’s no match for either on the DNA database. As you’ve mentioned, the daughter of who we now believe to be Deirdre Fisacherley has agreed to give her DNA and we’re waiting for that result. No one has come forward yet in relation to the male but the lab can look at other DNA databases available, if we want to take it forward. The profiles of the blood we found at the murder scene is a match to that of both victims.’

Jamie looked at the SIO and raised his eyebrows. ‘Of course one of the most interesting exhibits was the spade found in a neighbour’s garden. This is a definite match with the spade used to dig the grave.’ The confirmation had only come through this morning, so he knew Karen Foster would be very heartened by this bit of news.

‘That’s amazing after all that time.’

‘Yeah, it’s been really advantageous as to just how long people hold onto old tools - they were made to last in those days.’

‘Sarah, Peter, did you interview this neighbour?’

‘Yes ma’am, his name is Ronnie...,’ she shuffled through her papers, ‘Ronnie Neill, ex military and currently working in security. He would have only been in his twenties when the incident happened but he knew Martha well, and knew James Dickinson too, but did stress he didn’t really know James very well. He told us that he helped with the construction of the fountain in Martha's garden though.'

Karen Foster looked at Jamie, 'the spade marks, could they be from digging when he put the fountain in?'

Jamie Jones smiled and shook his head, 'absolutely not, the marks were formed around the sides of the grave itself. No, the spade was definitely used to dig that grave. Proving who actually used the spade to dig the grave is a different matter.'

'What's he like, this Ronnie Neill, Sarah?'

'He was a bit nervous I thought and one of the search officers I spoke to said he was decidedly twitchy when he spoke to him and... when they found the spade, he made comment that he couldn't understand why they'd want it, as he knew, and I quote 'it wouldn't have been used to bash anyone's brains out'.'

'Anyone tell him about injuries to the skeleton?' All shook their head. 'Who else spoke to him?'

'I did,' said Jamie, 'but certainly didn't mention anything about the trauma to the skull to him. When I was at his house updating the new owner on how long we'd be there, I mentioned the removal of two bodies. He literally went green at that. I'm no psychologist but his reaction wasn't what I'd have expected from an ex-marine - he had to have a drink of water. I thought at the time he was a bit odd but put it down to the fact of living somewhere near where bodies were buried. I guess it freaks some people out. I know the Rothbury beat officer spoke to him too but that was before we knew there were two bodies, so she couldn't have mentioned the trauma either.'

Sarah continued, 'to be honest ma'am, I've spoken with all the neighbours now except the couple who've gone to Spain and there's just something about a few of them. There are only the five households who lived there when James Dickinson did, the old couple at 'Number Three', the old guy at 'Number Five', Ronnie Neill and his wife Clara, the couple in Spain and ex PC Sarah Bruce, who lived next door but knew very little about her neighbours. Rani Weiss lived there but she was just a child and has no recollection of James Dickinson. But... I do think some of them knew that James was buried in that garden, I just have a feeling!'

'Knew about the murder?'

'Yes, it just seemed strange that I managed to get quite a bit of information about James from neighbours who didn't even live in Aspley at the time, but the ones that did gave me nothing, clammed up about him. Even vague descriptions of what he looked like... it was just odd, even Sarah Bruce the ex cop struggled to recollect anything from that time. And you've got the couple who fled to Spain when the bones were first discovered and haven't answered their mobile yet. Plus, Gerald Bainbridge, the old guy who reckons he's got dementia and can't remember anything - but he can get himself onto buses, go out for meals and do his shopping. Then Arthur on the corner, he can't remember much about James either and said his wife was too ill to speak with us - she also suffers from dementia - neighbours have confirmed she's pretty bad. And Ronnie of course, she was alright - his wife, but he seemed very nervous.'

Karen Foster pursed her lips, thinking… 'well, he's obviously going to have to be re-interviewed about the spade. Bring him in and caution him. I want him told that we suspect Martha of being responsible for seven murders... scare him a bit... tell him we know it was his spade that dug the grave - see if he folds. Which one of you hasn't he met yet?... Dave? 'She looked in the direction of the Detective Sergeant, 'I'd like you to do it and Sarah, I think you should do it too.'

The two officers nodded their agreement.

'Right, thank you everyone! So ladies and gentlemen, I think we now have our correct seven! The 'seven' Martha kept mentioning in her confession: one - her father, two - her baby, three, four - her mother and father-in-laws, five - her first husband, six and seven - her second husband and his lover. Now, I will be looking into whether we can go ahead with marking our two Aspley murders as a 'detected' and I'll need advice about the other cases that have come to light and whether it's worth pursuing investigations. Plus, I need to speak with the Archeologist about exhuming the baby to see if there's any evidential value in it. I'm not one hundred percent sure of the Home Office criteria for detections in a historical case like this but that's my plan anyway. I want feedback from the interview with Ronnie Neill as soon as it's done.'

Chapter 49

Karen Foster drove into work that morning feeling a sense of trepidation. She'd never dealt with a historic case before and had very little dealings with murders during her fifteen years in the Force. But she was enjoying her new role. She said her 'good mornings' as she made her way up the stairs to her office and plonked herself down on her chair. DS Anderson had obviously been waiting for her as her backside hadn't even hit the chair when he walked through the door. 'You'd better read this ma'am,' as he pushed a newspaper in front of her.

'What is it?'

'The Alnwick Gazette... it's the front page...

Northumberland Murders

Police yesterday confirmed that the skeletal remains of a male and female found in a garden in the tiny hamlet of Aspley, near Rothbury, had indeed been murdered. They stated that the murder probably took place about twenty-seven years ago. The bodies were hidden in a private walled garden belonging to the former headmistress of Rothbury Infants' School. Mrs Martha Dickinson, (formerly Curry) was headmistress at the local school for over twenty-eight years and she moved to the renovated stable cottage around the same time as taking on the role.

A police spokesman declined to give details of the possible identity of the bodies but indicated that they were now following strong leads and working with family members to ascertain their identity.
The two bodies were said to be buried under a large ornamental water fountain constructed by Mrs Dickinson in her small private walled garden in Aspley,

seven miles from Rothbury. Residents of Aspley have confirmed that the house and garden were recently being renovated by the new owners and the removal of a large fountain had unearthed the graves. They confirmed that Mrs Dickinson owned the property until she died four months ago.

The Gazette can now reveal that Mrs Dickinson had also been involved in a suspicious incident as a child, which resulted in the death of a young girl. Martha Dickinson, then known as Martha Curry, earned a scholarship at the Duchess' Grammar School in Alnwick and befriended the daughter of local politician, Reginald Cresswell. The Cresswell family took pity on Martha, who was the daughter of an impoverished tenant farmer in the Coquet Valley, providing financial help to ensure her continuance at the school and had even taken her on a family holiday to St Andrews in Scotland.

In the Autumn of 1951, the Cresswell's daughter, Regina, died after drowning in her bath in the presence of her school friend, Martha Curry. It was revealed by the niece of the Cresswells' 'live in maid', Mrs Lillian Lyle from Alnwick, that her aunt, Kate Fairmoor, had been present in the house at the time of the death and held Martha solely responsible for Regina's death. Mrs Lyle's aunt had told her that after the death she had contacted the family doctor about bruising on the deceased's face, and that both believed that the injuries to the child's face had been caused by holding her under the water. The case was not pursued due to the fact that Regina Cresswell had previously suffered from fits, what we now know to be epilepsy. The Cresswell family kept quiet about the incident and did not want police involvement but were said to be totally devastated after the death of their only child. Mrs Lyle revealed that her aunt had been haunted by the death of Regina, known as Reggie to friends and family and was absolutely convinced of Martha Curry's involvement.

Kate Fairmoor also told her niece that she had previously warned the Cresswells' about the young girl when Martha was first introduced as Regina's friend. Mrs Fairmoor came from the Rothbury area and knew of the child's reputation and told her niece that Martha's own parents referred to her as the 'Devil's Child'. There were also allegations that she had attempted to poison her father, Ernie Curry, who later died after being trampled by the family bull. Many locals rebuffed the rumours believing the Currys' to be fantasists but the Cresswells' maid always described Martha as a very devious and dangerous child. When Mrs Lyle read the recent article requesting anyone to come forward about information regarding the identity of the two bodies, she realised that the house owner was in fact the same Martha her aunt used to talk about.

Karen Foster sat reading the article, while Dave Anderson looked on patiently.

'Are they allowed to print this sort of stuff... and where did they get all the information from, they haven't even held back on publishing the names?'

'I guess you can print what you like when someone's dead!'

'But if she did kill this Regina, that makes eight not seven... ah the baby, I bet she didn't kill the baby, hence the pilgrimage and the flowers. I must admit I was always a bit 'iffy' about the baby. If it was as small as Burt Foggo said, it wouldn't have survived anyway. It's making a bit more sense now.'

'What sort of motive would a thirteen year old have to kill their friend though?'

'Pure jealousy I would presume. Martha would have had nothing and I guess her little posh friend would have had everything she wanted. I think you can see her motives all the way along the line…'bastard' of a father who raped her, her in-laws... I suppose we don't know how they treated her but they were wealthy... I guess motive enough. Then get rid of your husband and you're quids in, you get the lot - the money, the farm and your freedom back. She obviously loved teaching and had given it up to marry William. Her second husband used to beat her and that's definitely going to be Deirdre Fisacherley in that grave with him. Martha probably caught them at it - again, there's your motive.'

'You believe the article then?'

'I don't like it, it's gossip really but yeah, I do believe it. Get onto the Gazette will you and get this…' she scrambled for the name 'Lillian Lyle's address and send someone to interview her. I'm really surprised they printed her name. When are you bringing Ronnie Neill in?'

'This afternoon.'

'I wonder if he's read it yet. Show him it in the interview Dave, see what he says. You can just see future headlines when those who knew Martha read the Gazette and come forward about other suspicious incidents, which they will I'm sure. It's definitely going to have 'serial killer' in it.'

'What about the baby, ma'am? Are we still going to do the dig?'

'To be honest, I see little point after all this time, especially if the evidence is pointing towards the fact that it died at birth. Burt Foggo said in his statement that he didn't think it was anywhere near fully grown, so it's chances of survival would have been very slim, even in this day and age, never mind sixty plus years ago. Emma Bould said it was possible there'd be remains but only if the conditions were absolutely perfect, but it was always unlikely. No, I think we should let the poor mite rest in peace.'

Chapter 50

Ronnie Neill spent the worst afternoon of his entire life at Wallsend Police Station being interviewed by two detectives - and he'd previously had some really bad days! He had declined legal advice, thinking it made him look more guilty but half way through the interview he was starting to regret his decision.

He felt sick to his stomach when the two detectives outlining the case revealed that Martha was shockingly being investigated for seven murders.

'Martha? You think Martha Dickinson killed seven people, get away, are you joking?' He laughed but bile was coming up into his mouth and he had to keep sipping on the warm water in the plastic cup on the table in front of him. His thoughts were running at a super fast pace - *why were these people saying something so completely ludicrous?*

The Detective Sergeant eased forward, putting his elbows on the interview table, staring Ronnie straight in the face. 'We also suspect, Mr Neill, that she must have had some help.'

'For God's sake, you don't think I bloody helped her, do you, cause I bloody didn't? What on earth makes you think I did?'

'We know Mr Neill that the garden spade seized from your garage was used to dig that grave in Martha's back garden.' He looked at the officers in shock. He believed that he'd 'covered all bases' with regard to forensics. He thought he had researched and considered every possible forensic technique going that could possibly link him to that day, but he had only thought of the spade with regards to DNA - and then discounted it.

He half laughed, 'Na, you're barking up the wrong tree. I helped put Martha's garden fountain in, probably with that very spade. Anyway, how the hell have you come to the conclusion it was my spade?'

'It leaves a very distinctive pattern Mr Neill.'

'Yeah but I've already told you, I was digging in her garden.'

'Yes, but forensics can reveal the actual footprint of the grave and from this they can see the type and patterns of the tool used to do it.'

Ronnie suddenly felt an overwhelming urge to tell the truth, a truth he'd held onto for twenty-seven years. But it wasn't just his neck on the line he thought, it was Arthur's and Ella's, old Gerald's, Nina and Bill and most of all, Clara. They were all present that night, they had all helped in some way, either to bury the body or destroy evidence and this wasn't now just a domestic abuse situation gone tragically wrong like they thought at the time, it was seven murders... seven bloody murders. His brain was racing, trying to grasp onto reality.

'Can I ask who she was supposed to have murdered? I still think you must have got it wrong. I knew Martha and find it bloody unbelievable?'

The Detective Sergeant placed the newspaper on the table in front of him. He read the article, feeling sick and confused at the thought of Martha killing a young girl, a friend at that, 'This has got to be rubbish, it's all just gossip,' he said.

'Let's just concentrate on your involvement in all this, shall we Mr Neill?' said the woman officer.

'I'm telling you I didn't have any involvement!' His army training was now starting to kick in. *Come on,* he was saying to himself, *pull yourself together.*

'It was your spade Mr Neill, wasn't it?'

'But I didn't dig any bloody grave.' Ronnie wondered if they could see the look on his face that Clara said was there when he was lying. These guys were trained to spot liars but he was trained not to break under pressure. His days in the army were well in his past now but he knew he had to stand his ground and stick to the story.

'Martha used to steal everything, I bet she took my spade. It was a regular occurrence to get your tools or the odd garden ornament stolen if it was left in the front garden. We used to go to Joe Weiss who lived next door and he would go into Martha's and get it back for us. Everyone knew she had a bit of a problem, we just accepted it.'

'So if you didn't help Martha bury those bodies who did?'

'We'll all I can say is it wasn't me… she might have done it on her own, I don't know.'

'So, that tiny woman dug a huge grave in her garden with your spade, then dragged two bodies into that grave, one a nearly six foot, heavy set man. Really?'

'Well, if that's what you're saying happened she must have done. I repeat - I certainly didn't help her.'

'Do you know who did?'

'No, of course not.'

The interview went on, going back over the same points over and over again…could he remember seeing anything unusual, did he know for certain she took the spade, did he see anything when erecting the fountain, did he think it suspicious she wanted such a big fountain in such a small space? The questions just kept coming and coming and he was starting to become very weary.

At the end of the interview the Detective Sergeant sat back in his seat. 'Can I tell you what I think, Mr Neill?' Ronnie sat with bated breath, waiting. 'I think there's a few of you in Aspley who know exactly what happened and how those bodies ended up in that garden.'

'Rubbish!' Ronnie felt he could answer that one truthfully. 'I don't believe anyone from Aspley knew. I'm sure someone would have spoken up after all these years. One thing I can say is... I for one did not know there were two bodies buried in that garden... I swear. I wouldn't have risked everything to cover up a bloody double murder. Why the hell would I?'

'I don't know Mr Neill, you tell me. Loyalty? ... Money... Sympathy?... Anger?'

Silence.

'Interview concluded at sixteen twenty-seven hours?' The officers started putting paperwork back into green folders. 'You can go Mr Neill, we'll be in touch.'

'Thank you,' he said, shakily standing up. He couldn't wait to get out of that stinking, claustrophobic room and get back to Clara, who was waiting to pick him up.

After the interview, DC Sarah Miller went straight upstairs to update the DCI with the result. 'Said he knew nothing!'

'And the spade?'

'Said that Martha used to steal things... things that people left lying around, so he said she probably borrowed his spade at some point.'

'Any of the other neighbours mention that?'

'Yeah, a couple said she had a problem and did take garden ornaments and the like. We can't prove anything ma'am, not if he sticks to his story.'

'So you think he's lying?'

'Well, I think he definitely knows more than he's letting on.'

'What about bringing some of the other neighbours in?'

'Well, I haven't managed to speak with the couple in Spain yet but they're all adamant they don't know anything about it. The only real evidence we had that incriminated any of the neighbours was that spade. If they all stick to their story we have nothing.'

'I guess that's as much as we can do for now, we'll have a think.'

'I guess so ma'am.'

Ronnie sat on a wall near Wallsend Police Station waiting for Clara to turn up. The relief he felt when he saw her pull around the corner was immense. He casually got into the car in case anyone was watching. She looked at him, 'well?'

'Just drive!'

She kept quiet until they were on the dual carriageway. 'Come on then, what happened?'

'Our neighbour, little 'prim and proper' Martha Dickinson committed seven murders!'

'Get lost Ronnie! What on earth are you saying that for? They wouldn't have told you that anyway.'

'They bloody well did, they said she was suspected of being involved in seven murders... exactly that! They showed me an article in today's Gazette, saying she had killed her little school friend and also her own father.'

'Oh my God! I wonder who else she killed? If there was supposed to be seven... that's hilarious.' Ronnie looked at her in horror as his wife started laughing. 'I can't believe little old Martha was a serial killer, it's preposterous.'

'I just can't get why you're bloody laughing Clara, it's just so not funny.'

Chapter 51

Driving back into the confines of Aspley was a bitter-sweet exercise for Ronnie. He was pleased to be going home but tensed up at the thought of driving past Martha's old cottage again. 'She couldn't have done what they're saying Clara, she just couldn't have... we knew her for God's sake.'

'I guess you never really know anyone Ronnie, just remember that the next time you're pressing my buttons.'

Sometimes his wife could be a real 'ass-hole' he thought to himself.

The car made its way down the tree lined lane, rattling and bouncing as it hit several deep potholes. They were both alerted by flashing blue lights ahead, coming from the car park outside the cottages and they made the same assumption - it was a police car. As they got nearer they saw it was an ambulance and two men wearing green were coming out of 'Number 3'. As they got closer they saw Rani's car was also parked up nearby.

'Bloody hell, this doesn't look good Ronnie - it must be either Arthur or Ella who they've come to see.'

'Park up, we'll see if we can help.'

'I'm not sure Ronnie, they might not want us interfering.'

'I'm going anyway, just pull over,' Ronnie said, as he opened the car door, 'you go and see to Maisie and I'll be around later.'

'Well, give me a bell if you think I can help with anything and don't stay if you're not wanted, do you hear?'

'Yes, yes, OK.'

Ronnie tapped quietly on the cottage door and waited. The door was opened by a teary eyed Rani.

'What's happened, is Arthur OK? Is Ella poorly or something, what's happening?'

'You'd better come in Ronnie.'

Ronnie followed Rani along the dark hallway and into the living room. Arthur was sitting on the sofa holding Ella's hand, whilst Merlin the dog was curled up next to Ella, with his head resting on her knee. The room was quiet and the dog surprisingly just slightly raised his eyes when Ronnie entered, not doing his usual 'lick attack' when someone new came into his vision. On glancing at Ella, he saw the thick white hair styled beautifully, curtesy of her adoring husband. The plump and happy face was shining but on looking for the twinkle in her eyes he saw it had irrevocably gone. Ella was clearly dead.

'She just slipped away Ronnie,' Arthur said, 'my beautiful, kind hearted Ella has gone. I've been with her for over fifty-five years and she's gone, just like that, no notice, no goodbyes, nothing! I told her to have a little nap and Merlin snuggled up with her. Ten minutes later I tried to rouse her and she just wouldn't wake up. I dialled 999 and phoned Rani but I knew she'd gone. I could see Merlin knew it too - he hasn't moved from her side, even when the paramedics checked her over he just lay there not moving.'

'I'm so, so sorry Arthur... is there anything I can do?'

'Na, nothing you can do lad, can't bring her back, just stay a while. I'll need to speak with our Fiona and Jack at some stage to let them know. I'm not sure I can actually say the words Ronnie!'

'You don't need to Arthur, I'll do it for you if you like.'

'No, please I'll do it,' said Rani, who had tears now rolling down her cheeks, 'I think it would be better coming from me. I'll just need a few minutes to compose myself.' The young woman made her way around the back of the sofa and bent over putting her arms around Arthur's neck. 'I just want you to know Arthur that you gave Ella the most wonderful life. She was always happy and she loved you so, so much and nobody could have done more for her than you... nobody Arthur!' Ronnie was overcome as he watched Arthur start to sob, holding onto the girl's arms.

'Ella loved you too pet, didn't she?' he said, between the sobs.

'She was like my grandma Arthur, no... she was my grandma and I adored her too and I'm going to miss her so much.'

'Me too pet, me too. In fact I don't know what I'm going to do without her.'

'You'll be OK Arthur, I know she's going to leave a massive hole in your life but don't forget I'm not far away and I've got seventeen bedrooms if you ever feel like a bit of company.'

'Thanks pet, you've got a big heart, just like your dad.'

'I'm staying with you tonight, no arguments! Right!' she said, wiping her face with her hands and taking in a deep breath. 'Right, I'm going to phone Fifi and Jack now.' She left, heading out into the walled garden with her mobile to make the call.

'How did you get on at the police station lad?'

'I think that's the least of your worries at the moment Arthur, we'll discuss it some other time. I'm fine and I'm here, aren't I? So it's all OK.' After the day Ronnie had had he couldn't believe what he was actually saying but Ella's death just trumped everything - she had played a special part in his life too.

Rani eventually came in from the garden, 'Fifi and Jack are coming straight down in the morning. They're leaving Oban around six o'clock so should be here around lunchtime tomorrow.'

'What about Bob Scott, we'll have to keep him away, you know what he's like?'

'Your Fiona isn't phased by her ex anymore Arthur, besides Martin's coming with them. He'll make sure they're both safe. Martin can handle himself and Jack's as strong as an ox now - bet he could handle himself now too. Besides, time has moved on and I'm sure Bob Scott has too!'

'But it ended so badly, I'm not so sure Bob has moved on.'

'Well, your Fiona wants to come back to be with you, so if there's any concerns they could stay with me - he'd never get through the security at mine.'

'I'll think about it pet. Will she want to see her mam?'

'I don't know Arthur, I didn't ask. I've phoned Ella's GP for you and he's coming out. He'll tell us our options from there. When did Ella last see him, can you remember?'

'Just last week.' Arthur stroked Merlin's head, 'not sure we're going to get this chap away from my Ella that easily... he knows doesn't he?'

'I think he does Arthur, I think he does!'

Ronnie sat in the armchair watching proceedings, now emotionally and physically drained from the events of the day.

That night, after telling Clara the news, Ronnie spent the night 'tossing and turning' in bed. He'd tried whiskey and paracetamols but to no avail, sleep was beyond him and his brain continued to go over the events of that day. In the morning he decided to go straight around to see if he could help at 'Number Three'.

Arthur was at the window, filling the kettle and came immediately to the door to greet him. 'Come in lad, I've got something to tell you.' Ronnie followed, seeing Rani sitting in the armchair, Ella now gone from the room and Merlin in his basket but still very subdued.

'I've told Rani everything!'

'Sorry Arthur, I'm not sure what you're talking about.'

'Na, you don't have to pretend lad, she knows the lot…the abuse, the body, digging the grave... everything!'

Ronnie looked towards Rani who was now looking at him intently, 'you do realise her mother's a bloody police inspector or something, don't you?'

Rani reacted, 'actually, I believe she's a superintendent now but don't worry, my mother is the last person on God's earth I would speak to. Besides, my dad was heavily involved in it all too, wasn't he? I'd hate it all to besmirch his memory.'

Ronnie wasn't sure about this. Could this young girl be trusted with such a big secret? 'I'm sorry,' said Arthur, 'with everything going on I just had to tell her. I guess I haven't that much to lose anymore now Ella's gone.'

'Yeah, but I have!'

'If anyone finds out anything I'd just say it was me who buried that body, you've got nothing to worry about anymore lad.'

Ronnie turned to Rani, 'I take it you knew nothing about this?' Rani just shook her head.

'Do you think your dad knew there were two bodies in that grave?'

'Absolutely not, I'm sure Dad would have been just as horrified as you. With Dad you could always make one mistake and he'd help you out and encourage you to learn from it, but two... he wouldn't have helped Martha cover up a second murder. I know Dad, he'd have seen all the domestic abuse and he'd have understood that she had to protect herself, that's why he'll have helped her.'

'I take it you've seen the Gazette?'

'Yeah, apparently responsible for the death of her young friend and apparently her own dad. I still can't believe it.'

'Well, there's a bit more than that Rani and I know you'll find this hard to believe... the police are investigating Martha for seven murders.' The girl went silent, bringing her hand to rest on her forehead, not quite knowing what to say, 'surely not?'

'I'm telling you it's true, they think she killed seven people.'

'Oh my God! That's actually what she was saying before she died... she kept repeating 'seven'... 'there were seven Rani.' She was confessing to how many people she'd murdered. I thought it was only gibberish, just the drugs talking. God, is that why she dragged us up to the stones on the moors? Are there people buried up there? I wonder if she told Africa anything before I got there? I know towards the end, Africa said she was freaking her out with all the things she was saying.' She continued...

'The police told me she had another husband before she married James. I guess one of the seven could be him, do you think?'

'Possibly, so the two in the garden, the first husband, that young girl...'

'Her dad...'

'Yeah, her dad... I wonder who they think the others were then?'

Arthur was sitting back on the sofa only half listening to proceedings. 'She once told me her in-laws were 'horrible, abusive people', they were her exact words. I didn't question her further, I thought she was talking about James 'parents which would fit - but perhaps she was talking about her first husband's parents? It seems like if someone was mean to her she just got rid of them.'

They all sat pondering until Rani spoke, 'killing them is rather extreme though, isn't it? We never really knew her, did we?'

'What did the police arrest you for Ronnie?' Rani asked.

'They didn't arrest me, they just questioned me. They seized my dad's old spade from my garage and told me it was the one that dug the grave.'

'What, after all that time, they knew that, how?'

'Yep, because it had damage on the blade - it left a distinctive mark when I used it but they can't say for certain who used it though. They tried so hard to get me to confess.'

'Bloody hell!'

'I know... I said Martha used to take stuff all the time, so she could easily have borrowed it.'

'Thank God for Martha's kleptomania, aye?'

'Yep, it was definitely my salvation, I can tell you.'

Epilogue

Eight weeks after the discovery of the two murder victims in the walled garden in Aspley, Karen Foster sat within her now familiar office, reflecting on her working life. She was pleased with her first few months' work as a new DCI and her murder detection rate but she couldn't help feeling slightly underwhelmed by her success. She felt strongly that the three detections now under her belt for the murder in Newcastle and the two Aspley murders should have actually been eight, not three. '*Now eight in the first couple of months would have been a real achievement*,' she thought.

In her first week in the job she'd been confronted with the Aspley case and also a 'cut and shut' fatal stabbing in Newcastle. In the latter, the offender had quickly been forensically identified, processed and locked up. It had been a very easy first detection for her but the other two detections from Martha's garden were more complex. The forensic evidence clearly pointed towards Martha as the killer, with her fingerprints being found in the victim's blood and indeed the only prints on the knife but the case had opened a 'Pandora's box'.

The samples they'd taken for identification purposes came back from the lab and provided good conclusive evidence. The male bones recovered were now known to be those of Martha's first husband, James Dickinson. His identity was proven by running his DNA through a familial DNA database and getting matches with several second cousins on both his maternal and paternal side.

Deirdre Colleen Fisacherley's daughter had come forward as she had promised, providing police with a DNA sample and that proved beyond reasonable doubt that she was not the other set of remains. Everyone had been convinced it was Deirdre Fisacherley in that grave and the results had left them reeling, so much so they double checked by testing another of Deirdre's children just to be sure - and again there was no match. When it was proven it wasn't Deirdre they ran the DNA profile of the now unknown female on the database hoping to identify a family member but only very distant relatives were a match. The closest the database could provide was a fourth cousin and investigation into this line proved fruitless. So, they were left considering their next move to identify her, if indeed there were any options left.

The DCI now had an unidentified murder victim on her hands. She had been pleased with the detection but hopping mad it wasn't the barmaid from Rothbury - that would have just tied up the loose ends nicely. She was also left with five further 'potential murders' but she had nothing but hearsay as to their credibility and many considered it was all just pure gossip. But Karen Foster always worked with the 'rule of probability'. To her it was very likely that a woman who'd been found to have committed two murders could have more than likely been responsible for more. On asking for advice from fellow senior officers and a friend in the CPS, Karen Foster had been told that a 'garbled' death bed confession was not enough to assume guilt. She had felt strongly that the whole issue was being clouded by the fact Martha was a woman and also that outwardly she'd led a very respectable life.

The enquiries her team had conducted were almost exhausted; they had spoken with Elsdon residents, family members of the deceased, friends and neighbours of Martha's - all proved unproductive. They'd managed to speak by phone with the neighbours who had fled to Spain but they said they didn't know James Dickinson and didn't really know Martha all that well. Karen Foster was absolutely convinced, as were many of her team, that some of the neighbours knew much more than they were letting on but for some reason they stayed loyal to Martha.

She'd even given assurances that nothing would happen if they confessed to having helped her conceal the crimes but no one would break.

The Regina Cresswell case had been the best one to pursue, although it was a long time ago that the attending doctor had allegedly had his suspicions about the cause of death. However, the death certificate was viewed and bizarrely it stated 'drowning after episode' but on speaking to an Archeologist about exhumation of the child's body he stated that if the story of her death was as described there'd be no evidence to find. So, the Regina Cresswell case wasn't going to be recorded as a murder, much to her annoyance. Neither was the death of William Wilkie, whose death certificate stated accidental drowning. The cause of death for William's parents, Peter and Ethel Wilkie, remained as having been accidentally poisoned after eating deadly fungi, whilst Ernest Curry's death from crush injuries sustained in a farm accident remained unchanged.

The Murder Investigation Team had worked diligently on the case and no concrete evidence of foul play had come to light. It was all just general gossip, comments like - 'they never trusted her', or 'you do know they called her the Devil's child, don't you?' or 'well, they said she killed her own father'. But there were those who would hear no wrong about Martha, such as some of the children she'd taught, fellow choir members, the St Mary's vicar and the domestic abuse victims from when she worked in a woman's refuge. Loads of people said she'd changed their life - she'd championed underdogs and empowered the vulnerable. But Karen Foster was sure Burt Foggo's statement showed the characteristics of a psychopath. He'd certainly described an extremely manipulative child who demonstrated little empathy and no remorse.

For now the case was to be closed but the DCI had one last 'throw of the dice' in mind. If Martha's sister Julia or niece Africa re-entered the country, she had an 'all ports' alert logged and she'd be notified of their re-entry into the UK. She was absolutely convinced Martha had revealed more to her niece on her deathbed than she had to Rani Weiss, plus the sister became uncontactable not long after being initially spoken to by the team.

But for now that was it, she'd have to leave it in the hands of journalists and the historians to write about Northumberland's child of the Devil, now believed to be one of the most prolific female serial killers in Great Britain.

Thank you so much for reading Gorfen Letch, if you have enjoyed it please could you give it a quick review on Amazon or Goodreads - it's what keeps indie writers going. Thank you

---

Printed in Great Britain
by Amazon

65376878R00159